SHAMBHALA

SHAMBHALA

BRIAN E. MILLER

Library of Congress: 2012941410

ISBN: 978-0615647395

Cover and Interior Design: AuthorSupport.com

Author Website: www.BrianEMillerBooks.com

*"Alone and without his nest
shall the eagle fly across the sun."*
~ KHALIL GIBRAN

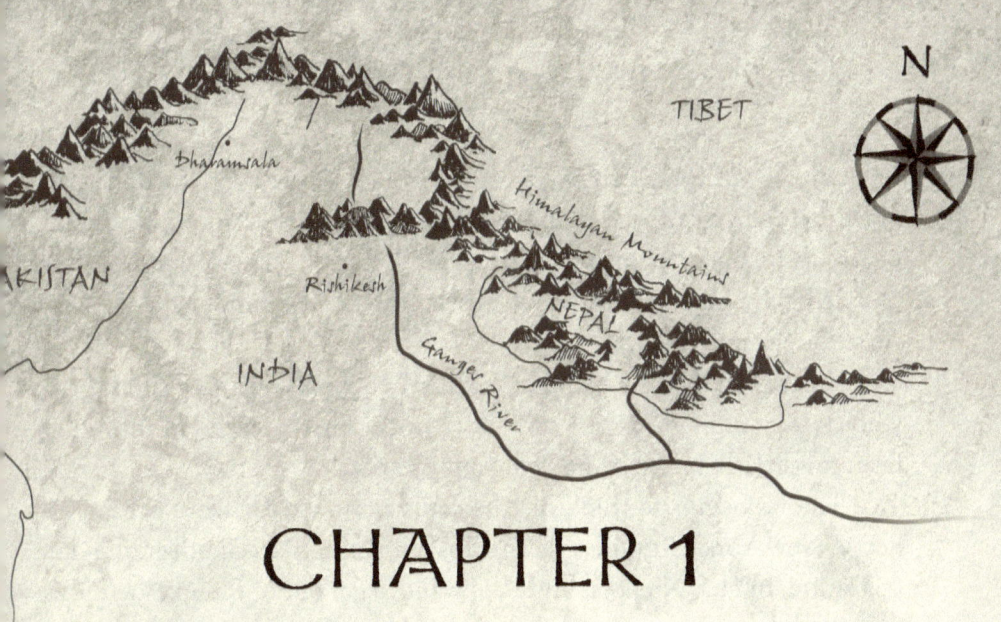

CHAPTER 1

S TRANGE HOW THE *cold freeze of death seems to warm a man in his final hour, slowing the heart, glazing the eyes, drifting the mind back to where this all began. Where did I go wrong?*

Rishikesh.

Rushing down from the high glaciers, frigid waters push eternally through channels carved in mountainous rock. Funneling through this small riverside mecca—and beyond—they form the most revered waterway in all of India, the Holy River Ganga, the Great Mother.

Cool morning winds roll off distant hills and down dusty roads dotted on either side with street vendors and shop owners preparing curries and countless other offerings. They will be hawked, haggled over, and sold, perhaps, for a few *rupees*. Spiritual wares, as well—yoga sessions, meditation instruction, and religious discourses—will find buyers, mostly eager Westerners.

Some would argue that the greatest gifts of Rishikesh lie beyond the hawking of street vendors, the colorful cafes, and the flood of Western tourists drawn to the ubiquitous yoga classes. This yoga mecca's more subtle offering is found in the surrounding hills: the soul-absorbing peace of natural piety, found through contemplation of the leaves of a tree, the torrent of a waterfall, the song of a bird, the web of a spider . . .

A small gathering exits a morning yoga class, emerging into the pale glow that radiates off the cold concrete of a building. Paul stands in tranquility as he breathes in sun-warmed air. Pushing aside a strand of dark blonde hair behind his ear, he looks over at Nicholas, who makes his way from the outside toilet.

"Great class. I really like that teacher," Nicholas says to a silent Paul, who stands smiling into the sun. Slowly opening his eyes and tilting his head toward Nicholas, he nods in confirmation.

Nicholas begins to think that he could permanently leave behind his hectic New York City lifestyle for this simple pattern of adventure and relaxation. In fact, Nicholas and Paul want to get out of Rishikesh, to trek deep into nature for some real peace and quiet. Today's journey will take them to a waterfall.

Paul steps out into the narrow street, still quiet in the calm of morning, and Nicholas follows. An auburn cow nibbles along the pavement, following a path of dinner scraps scattered on the side of the street. Smells of cooking fires and spices permeate the air. A rainbow of Indian saris glides along, each adorning a local woman carrying a small wicker basket. "Namaste," they greet in passing. Hands in prayer position, Paul and Nicholas return the salutation.

Nicholas's broad build and tightly shaven hair opposes Paul's tall, slim body and chin length hair that sits perfectly upon his head, with a slight swoop at its ends.

"What do you say? Breakfast at the café?" Nicholas suggests to Paul, patting his belly.

"Yeah, let's load up before we head into the jungle," Paul agrees.

They pass a vendor popping corn on a metal-spoked two-wheeled cart. Another vendor offers small statues of *devas*, along with Indian prints adorned with sacred mantras. Nicholas' fingers sift through the prints' textures as he passes by.

The café is a bamboo structure overlooking the river. They sit at a low table, Indian style, atop sky blue cushions. An Indian boy approaches with pad and pencil. They order two glasses of *chai*—and two big breakfasts.

Leaning back against a bamboo pole, Paul looks out across the river. Men bathe and pray on the opposite shore, pouring metal pots of water onto their foreheads as women soak clothes for washing. Bringing his attention back into the café, he catches the eye of a young beauty just settling at the table behind Nicholas. His blue eyes fix on her greenish brown orbs. They exchange smiles.

"Looking forward to getting out of the city for a bit," Nicholas says, breaking Paul's gaze.

"Yeah, I love it here, but we need our nature fix, man," Paul adds, easing back into conversation with Nicholas.

The waiter places their breakfasts down. Promptly cutting up his mushroom-and-cheese omelet, Nicholas mixes a forkful with some home-style, pan-fried potatoes and shovels down a mouthful. Paul again catches the eye of the winsome one, her blond hair falling straight, with a hint of braid complimenting her flower-girl air.

"Where are you from?" Paul asks.

An awkward silence.

Nicholas turns towards her, swallows another huge mouthful of eggs and potatoes, and blurts out, "Hey! Nicholas here." He extends his hand.

Taken aback, but smiling at the humor of Nicolas's intrusion, she merely touches his hand to complete the shake. "Where you from?" she asks, a hint of laughter in her voice.

"The States. New York," Paul says entering back into the conversation. "I'm Paul," he says, gracelessly slipping in his introduction.

"I'm Eva—from Ireland," she responds, wearing a bashful smile. "What brings you to Rishikesh?"

"This guy's doing some travel in India for a month, and I'm just here for a couple of weeks—hanging out," Nicholas answers.

"We're heading to the waterfall. You been?" Paul asks.

"No, I haven't. Which one?"

Hesitant to answer, Paul looks at Nicholas and says, "It's about twenty minutes down the road. I don't know. That's what I've been told."

"Twenty minutes Indian Standard Time, which is, like, at least an hour," Nicholas interjects with a laugh, turning sideways to relax with his back toward the river.

"Feel free to come along with us if you like," Paul invites, crossing his fingers under the table.

"I would love to, but I am taking a yoga class in two hours. If you guys are around later, some friends and I are hanging out at the Swiss Cottage. They have really good food, and we usually hang out there for a while afterward. It's cool. You should drop by."

"That's not far from Nishant, where we're staying. We'll swing by if we get back early enough," Paul says, keeping externally cool, yet internally ablaze with excitement.

With the two breakfasts inhaled, Nicholas lip-syncs, "Bill please," air-writing a check with his hand.

The owner nods.

"Well, Eva," Paul ventures, "Maybe we'll see you tonight."

"Yes, for sure, come down," she says, smiling as the two men exit the café's back room, saying their goodbyes.

Out on the dirt road, Paul feels like a giddy schoolboy. A silly smile overcomes him, "Did you see that princess?"

"She was beautiful! Hopefully she has a friend," Nicholas says as he chuckles, noting the connection Paul and Eva had made.

The morning chill has now dissipated. Paul stretches with joy, facing the sun and letting out a sigh of delight. They fall in with a crowd passing through a veritable tunnel of street vendors, the air alive with melodies of New Age chants, classic Indian music, and random instruments demonstrated by vendors. After a while the dissonance begins to fade—further and further as they escape further—first through a residential area, and still further, where the village begins to melt into forest and the country road to follow the curves of the river.

An Indian woman with almond eyes and a gold-stud nose ring squats, washing some steel dishes. She pulls her sari aside to keep it dry.

"May I fill?" Paul asks, holding his water bottle and pointing to the spigot that sits upon a round, blue-and-white concrete pillar.

The woman nods and smiles, finishes up her dishes, and makes her way a few feet to her home. Paul squats and fills his water bottle as Nicholas hands him his as well. Finishing up, he hands the bottles back to Nicholas to stash in the backpack. He washes his face and, with one swift movement, wets back his hair.

Onward they explore, bellies full, water abundant, spirits high. As the village fades further, only the sound of a distant temple bell resonates, announcing the vision of a few homeless Babas, draped in orange garb and sitting on the side of the street while shaking cups for *rupees*.

"Hare Om!" a copper-faced beggar greets them with a smile that pushes his aged wrinkles toward his eyes.

Not knowing if he is a genuine Baba or just a poser fishing for *rupees*, they toss him a *rupee* and move along. Paul notices a man wearing a white outfit slightly yellowed by time, white dusty sandals, and a white turban that swoops around his head, contrasting with his chocolate-brown skin. From a strap on his neck, a large red drum with silver garland and gold circles hangs to his waist. Propping himself up with a cane in one hand, with the other he taps out a haphazard beat with a wooden mallet. Drawing closer, Paul notices the man's right eye is solid white from an apparent accident. The few teeth he does have sit in his mouth, settled deep in his gums, his oral cavity surrounded by a graying goatee and mustache. The beating grows louder as they near him and notice that something of his character is amiss. Perhaps he is possessed, perhaps insane, perhaps both . . .

The man chants as he taps, "To go alone we seek for truth, darkness abounds thee who goes alone, darkness abounds thee, beware the sleeping tree that beckons thee!"

His gaze finds Paul, and the drum beats louder as they pass. The old man continues to chant as he beats out his rhythm, "He who seeks his home is he who goes alone!"

Paul gazes back to the old, decrepit man, who still stares at him. The old man's head bobbles like a puppet's, as if it might snap off at any moment.

"Quite the poet, huh?" Nicholas says nervously, breaking the serious spell.

"Ha!" Paul laughs audibly as they round a bend and the road opens to a vista more desolate than before.

Still haunted by the spell, Paul eases his confused, furrowed brow, "His English was impeccable. Strange."

"This country truly has some of the oddest things I have ever seen," Nicholas adds. They both laugh.

They come to an opening in the shrubbery on the roadside. It leads down to the sand and rocks lining the river.

"Let's walk along the river a bit, then we can cut back up to the other side a little further down," Paul suggests.

"Yeah? Let's do it!" says Nicholas, up for anything and just happy to be in India.

They resolve to take a dip in the glacier-cold waters to cool off and cleanse their spirits in the Holy Mother Ganga. The river is said to hold great energy, has been prayed to daily and nightly for thousands of years. Reaching its shore, they stop and take in its beauty, calm in some spots, with pockets of rapids that could easily pull one under or whisk one away into a maze of rocks downstream.

Filled with joy and excitement, they feel their hearts grow giddy. They climb huge boulders eroded by monsoon waters, leaping from boulder to boulder, startling lizards, exotic birds, and butterflies. There are pocket stones here of all sizes, shapes, and colors—stones of such beauty that Paul and Nicholas wish they had endless pockets to bring them home and share with others.

Feeling reverence for the beauty of it all, they explore further. When they find an open, shaded and sandy area, Nicholas removes his pack and sits down to rest. Removing his shoes, he thinks of how this spot would be perfect for yoga. He lies back on the sand and gazes up at clear blue.

Paul continues to poke around a bit, finding his way up a hill made of loose rocks that have settled on the slope. Noticing a little bird, silky black with a perfect white stripe on the top of its head and a dark-orange tail, Paul approaches slowly to get a better look. The bird pops its tail up and down, almost taunting Paul with its beauty. Carefully climbing the rocks, Paul reaches the top, and the bird flies off, swooping down and then settling on a boulder in the middle of the shallows of the river far below. Looking around, Paul feels as though the bird has led him up here. He observes the unique little world on the small, rocky, hilltop plateau.

Removing his shirt and wrapping it around his head like a turban, he sees a makeshift opening in the rock wall. The hollow opens under the shade of a tree. *It seems as though someone may live here*, he thinks. He sees the mouth of a small cave plastered over with brick and concrete and painted a bright orange. A small picture of Lord Shiva sits next to a carved *lingam*, a rounded, phallic stone Paul remembers having read about. It symbolizes many things, including abundance, fertility, and divine union of male and female. The rounded stone sits carved in a *yoni*, representing the female. The two conjoined forms venerate Shiva and Shakti, the divine male and female, their union symbolizing infinite endlessness.

Realizing this is a place of worship, Paul notices something written in Hindi, and above it, in broken English: "Who are you? I am that person when you have forgotten me you look to your peeping in self soul/spirit you will find there all that. Can you please give me all your troubled pain? I give to you pleasureful of human life."

Paul pokes his head in to check for any unsuspecting creatures. Spiders the size of fists are not uncommon here, but he decides to enter, finding an area that would hold two people sitting. The cave is about three and a half feet high and looks out over the rushing rapids of the river. A burlap bag on the floor, for sitting, and a light cotton shawl, folded up, create the perfect meditation spot.

This place is amazing! he thinks as he ponders a life of such simplicity. *Who*, he wonders, *lives here?*

He fantasizes about dwelling there, of building small fires at night and watching the monsoon rains as he sits snug in the safety of his rock fortress.

Giving it all away, would I find the answers I seek? The answers we all seek, those of happiness and truth?

Suddenly, Nicholas pokes his head in, then crawls in.

"Dude, this is awesome. Did you just manifest this?" Nicholas asks, half joking.

"I think I did," Paul confirms.

"The energy of this place is intense. You think someone lives here?" Nicholas asks.

"I think they do, check out the clothesline. They're probably down in the village right now. This cloth was here," Paul answers wearing the shawl over his shoulders. "And look! A mirror!" he adds, pointing out a small, jagged piece of mirror cemented in the wall in front of them.

Sitting in silence for a few moments, Paul closes his eyes to meditate, and Nicholas follows his lead. Quickly, they transcend deeper than they ever have in meditation, abiding in the bliss of their silent minds. After a few minutes, a soft and shallow exhale slowly lifts Paul's eyelids open, bringing his mind back to the cave. Nicholas opens his eyes as well, feeling the elevation of energy that has consumed them.

Softly ducking out of the cave, still in reverent silence, Paul silently points out the inscription on the mouth of the entrance. Tearing a piece of notebook paper from Nicholas's backpack, he jots down the phrase and completes it by drawing the Om symbol painted on top of the inscription. Folding the paper, he places it in his pocket to contemplate later. They sit for a while outside, staring out over the river and enjoying the bliss of silent awareness.

"Let's go cleanse ourselves in the river," Paul suggests to Nicholas, who stares with wide, euphoric eyes off into the bright, late-morning sun shimmering in white dancing diamonds across the water.

"Let's wash away our sins," Nicholas jokes.

Making their way cautiously down the rock hill that spills out onto the narrow strip of sand and jutting rocks, they disrobe and sink into the icy shallows. They dunk their heads and pop up, feeling alert and revived. They climb onto tan boulders that bulge out of the river, the sun warming them as they watch clouds float across the sky's vast blue.

After a while, dry and warm, they decide to move on toward the waterfall. The sun goes down early here, and they want to enjoy the trek up without rushing.

Coming back up the rock cliff fully clothed, they follow a path that runs up behind the cave and zig zags up to the street. The sun washes over distant hills as they walk. A small monkey makes its way down the side of the street, followed by two more. With soft, pinkish-red faces, and bellies and groins to match, they move casually along, their hair the dusty shade of the paths and surrounding hills. Suddenly there comes a sound from within the woods, and within seconds droves of monkeys pour onto the street. Some meander on all fours as others rustle and swish through trees, all migrating together toward town, where they hope to find food: leftovers from restaurants and treats, some given and some stolen from unsuspecting tourists.

The monkeys are of all shapes and sizes, each with a distinct character, like humans. Some are laid back, meditatively strolling along, others are in a frantic rush. Some are playful and kind, some aggressive, some inquisitive—but all are heading down the winding road to their food mecca, where they will disperse and act like beggars from the woods.

Paul and Nicholas are in awe and wear smiles from ear to ear. Within twenty minutes, the flood of monkeys has passed, with the exception of a few stragglers still ambling by. Nicholas rummages back through the images on his digital camera, reviewing the nearly one hundred shots he has just snapped. Paul sits atop a stone watching the monkeys disappear. Then, a smaller, younger monkey begins to cross his path on the other side of the road. Turning to look at the animal, he notices it is doing the same to him. The two lock eyes as if they have known each other for some time. A smile washes over Paul's face, and it seems the monkey is smiling back. This monkey is different than the others. He exudes the confidence of youth and an intelligent gaze of knowing. The two sit silently staring, when, suddenly out of the woods, crashes a larger, older monkey quick to scold the young one to move on, with a screech that jolts the young monkey, who reluctantly keeps moving. As the young monkey walks off behind the larger one, Paul watches in wonder. The young monkey turns around as he ambles further down the road, as if he, too, is perplexed by the connection they have just enjoyed.

Nicholas comes running over like a small child, almost tripping on himself, breaking the silent bond. "Dude, that was awesome!"

Paul smiles in affirmation, still watching as the young monkey vanishes out of sight.

"It's amazing how much they are like us," Paul says in wonder.

"Right! And with all of our seeming intelligence, we're not far from being them," Nicholas adds.

Once again a rustling in the trees draws their attention upward, where a different species of monkey is having its lunch. A large monkey with snow-white fur and a face like a piece of coal sits on the thick branch of a tree, ripping off leafy pieces and biting off mouthfuls. Paul notices that he has dropped a piece of branch and goes over to investigate. Picking up the branch that holds leaves with small, green bean pods, he walks back across the street to Nicholas, opening a pod, taking out a small, green bean, and placing it in his mouth.

"Is it good?"

"It's nice, a bit bitter, but probably full of nutrition. Here, try one."

Nicholas takes a small bushel from the branch, and the men sit and eat while they watch the monkey, who gobbles the whole branch: pods, leaves, and all.

"I bet if we followed the monkeys around we would learn how to survive in the woods," Paul says, fantasizing.

"Mmm, I bet if you cooked these they would be delicious."

"Right, a little butter and salt. Maybe the monkeys could learn a thing or two from us, as well." As they eat the beans, the men laugh and talk about how spoiled humans are. After eating a bellyful, they decide to move on to the waterfall.

The road is long, silent, and winding, with an occasional bus or large work truck that barrels down blaring a horn and leaving behind thick clouds of black diesel smoke. Hills rise on either side. Looking out toward the far hill, they are transfixed by the colors: greens and soft yellows dancing in a light haze. Exotic-looking trees hang in curious poses, sculpted by winds that blow year round. Some trees grow straight up and drop roots down from the sky, others twist in poses, as if doing yoga, looping in puzzling directions.

Coming to three small huts that seem to be in the middle of nowhere, they greet the shop owners, who patiently wait on this quiet crossroads. Ready to serve, the men sit beside pieces of tree that hold up tarps shading one owner from the hot sun as he places his metal pot on a burner, cooking up some *chai*. Looking up, he greets the men with a smile as his son calls out, "Hello!"

Paul and Nicholas return the greeting. Besides *chai*, the small hut offers *pakoras*, various biscuits, candies, chips, and bottled water for tourists afraid to drink the local water. The smell of *aloo pakoras*—niblets of fried potato and spices—flows out onto the street.

"We should have dinner here on the way back," Paul comments, breathing in the aromas.

"I'm down for that," Nicholas confirms, always up for the local food, which is usually better than in the touristy areas where they cater to Western palates.

Rounding a twisted corner of the road, the men behold a pale beam of sun. The beam finds its way through a tree and dances in ripples of light, shimmering across crystal-clear water. They realize the water must be coming from the falls upstream.

"This is it," Nicholas says.

As they hike up the trail, the world fades further into the silence of the jungle, a silence broken only by the sound of a rock moving underfoot, the melody of flowing water, and faint calls of birds and cicadas in the distance. Passing rapids they watch the currents swirling around rocks. All seems to be in perfect order—every fallen branch, every floating leaf embodies perfection.

After an hour of hiking, they come to a deep and broad pool. Nicholas removes his pack, cooling the sweat on his back. They sip from their bottles and cool off in the shade.

"I'm gonna take a dip," Paul says.

"Good idea."

Stripping down to their boxer shorts, they jump into the cold water, instantly feeling invigorated as they dunk under and then wade.

"This is great!" Paul comments. "The best part of Rishikesh is here in the woods."

"Right! The tourists don't know what they're missing," Nicholas adds as he lets out a loud whoop that echoes throughout the jungle.

Getting out of the pool, they bask in the warm sun.

"I can see the mouth of the falls. I think this trail will take us straight there," Nicholas says, standing on a rock that gives him a sight line to the cascade, not too far off.

"I'm gonna go like this. Our clothes are safe here," Paul says, wearing only his boxer shorts.

Nicholas picks up his pack, "I'm gonna take the pack. It has my passport in it."

Paul agrees as he folds up his clothes to put aside until he returns. The paper from earlier falls from his shorts pocket. Picking it up, he folds it and tucks it into the elastic waistband of his boxers, to read and contemplate at the mouth of the falls. Feeling a sense of adventure, wearing only his boxer shorts and a childlike enthusiasm, Paul takes off running. As he rounds a bend in the trail he yells out, "Meet you there! Just follow it up!"

Running barefoot through the wooded path, heart rushing, imagination flooding with wonder, Paul feels the wind whoosh in his ears as his hair trails behind him trying to catch up. At a break in the path, he veers off out of instinct and keeps running through thick brush and sand, finally stopping at a felled tree in the middle of the path. It protrudes out of tall, thick brush. Catching his breath, he can feel his heart beating in his chest, pulsating in his ears. He can't remember the last time he felt so alive and innocent. Admiring the strong tree that blocks the path, he runs his hand along its smooth, brownish-yellow trunk.

I better wait here for Nicholas, he thinks as he jumps up on the vertical trunk to get a better view of where Nicholas might be walking from.

Nicholas, though, is too far back to see.

Paul walks along the trunk, feeling the smooth, strong tree with the soles of his feet, walking out over the thick brush that grows upward from the ground. Looking out, he still can't see Nicholas, but peering out toward the main trail that runs up to the falls, he sees a large insect zipping out of nowhere, barreling toward him and buzzing like a kamikaze plane destined to smack straight into his head. With a lightning reflex, Paul smacks his face to ward off the insect, loosing his footing and slipping backward. Butterflies rush his belly as he falls into the thick brush below, smacking the backside of his head on a rock.

All the world dissolves into black as he falls unconscious.

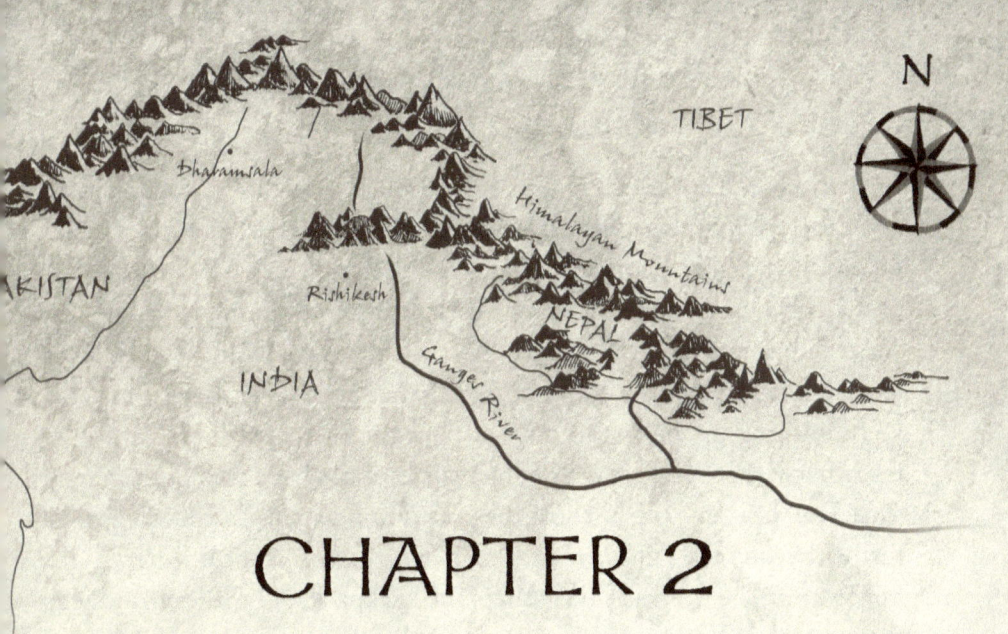

CHAPTER 2

FINDING HIS WAY to the mouth of the falls, Nicholas looks around in awe as a smile wells up from his belly. The smile finds its way to his mouth, widening his eyes to take it all in. Water falls gracefully as smooth salt pouring down, melting into the gorge below as it flows through the carved-rock valley, descending into the thick jungle. Figuring Paul must have gone off to meditate or explore on his own, Nicholas sits down on a rock that juts out on the side of the enclosed waterfall. Encased in smooth, chiseled walls of cold, dark mustard stone, shielding the area from the sun, Nicholas watches as water courses through the small reservoir, caressing each rock, finding every crevice, like an artist patiently and persistently carving an endless masterpiece.

Close by, in unconscious silence, Paul lies in the thick underbrush that consumes him a few feet from the river. Blood trickles from his head, slowly joining the rippling stream. The river of his body flows into the river of the jungle, and like all rivers, is in constant flux to find its way back to the ocean from where it came.

"Yo!" Nicholas echoes out into the jungle in an unanswered attempt to find Paul. He has been sitting patiently, waiting for about twenty minutes, growing curious about where Paul has run off.

"Paul!" he cries out again—unanswered.

He makes his way closer to the waterfall and decides to wash himself and cool off. Three streams pour down, joining together to form a heavy, falling shower that blasts into the clear water below. A breeze blows out of the carved rock walls, exhaling a cool breath into the warm jungle. The water falls heavy upon Nicholas's head as he laughs with joy and again lets out a loud, echoing "Wooooo, yeah!" that bellows from deep inside.

Finishing up, he sits in a small pocket of sun that finds its way to the otherwise shaded area. Now, he realizes it has been well over an hour since Paul has gone off. Nicholas begins to wonder and decides to go a bit further beyond the falls. *Perhaps Paul's on the other side of the waterfall and can't hear me*, he thinks as he gathers the backpack and makes his way up the steep path. Reaching the highest point of the path he cries out, "Paul!"

He scans the area below, and finding no sign of Paul, begins to grow a bit worried, knowing the sun will set in about an hour. Thinking Paul may have gone back to the point where they crossed paths, he decides to comb the trail back down. Jogging down the rocky path, he quickly makes his way back to the water hole where they last saw each other.

He must be there, probably already dressed and looking for me, he thinks, nervously laughing. The sun begins to make its final descent behind the high hills in the west. As he reaches the reservoir, he is disappointed when he sees Paul's clothes folded, untouched, on the rock where he had left them.

"Paul, where are you!?" he yells out. "Yo-o-o-o-o-o! Dude, where are you?" he continues screaming, frantically, as the sun lowers almost out of sight.

Nicholas knows it will be dark in about an hour and that if they don't start to head back now it will be a dangerous hike back down the mountain. His heart races up into his throat as he puts on his clothes and shoes. Assuming the worst, he wonders if he should run back down and hurry back into town to find help.

"Paul!" he yells out again, in one, last, desperate attempt.

The sun is now behind the hills, and the faint light of dusk slowly begins to fade. Nervously hustling down the rocky path, anxious to get to the road, his right foot snags the side of a rock, throwing him into a fall. His left leg catches him, springing him back into balance as he keeps speeding down the trail.

Finally reaching the opening of the trail, he jets out onto the street. Short of breath and trembling from nervous excitement, he begins to run toward the village. The muffled sound of a vehicle grows louder, from behind him. He swiftly spins around and runs to the center of the dusky, dark road, anxiously flailing his hands to flag the vehicle down as what seems to be a small motorbike comes to a slow stop at the side of the road.

"Hello!" the young driver calls out in an Indian accent as Nicholas runs toward him, panting.

Nicholas blurts out a sentence that seems like one word, "PleaseIneed-help myfriendislostinthewoods!"

"Your friend is in the woods?" the young Indian driver tries to confirm, not fully understanding him.

"Yes, lost in the woods, I can't find him. I need to get the police or, I need some help!"

"Oh, this is very dangerous! Please to get on the back and I will take you to the police," the young boy says, patting the seat behind him on the small motorbike.

Getting on the back of the bike, Nicholas feels it speed off, passing blaring headlights of cars in the now dark, winding road. As they rush through the twists and turns, Nicholas's mind races with fear for his beloved friend. His mind creates all kinds of scenarios of what has happened. How will he tell his family back in New York? How devastated will he be if Paul is dead? Catching his fear-driven mind, he swallows past the rock in his throat and takes a deep breath as he trembles, holding onto the young boy who precariously weaves in and out of cars.

Taking a few more deep breaths, he begins to think positively, *He is probably looking for me and on his way back right now, he must have taken a wrong turn on his way down the other side of the hill.* These thoughts are feeble attempts to cover up the great fear that consumes his body and mind.

Finally reaching the outside of the town, which is lit up and busy, they swerve in and out of meandering cows, jeeps, mopeds, pedestrians, and dogs. The carnival of traffic grows thicker as Nicholas's patience wanes thinner. He often drops his foot to the ground to counter the near falls on this crazy ride for help. Flying past a small shop, the driver pulls to the side of the road, where Nicholas can make out a small, painted sign that reads, *Police*, translated under Hindi writing.

Hopping off the motorbike, they rush toward the small, blue, concrete building. A single officer sits in his dark-tan Rishikesh Police uniform. He stares at a wall as an ashtray still smokes from his lazy attempt to put out his last cigarette. Crashing through the door in a huff, they startle the officer to his feet.

"Hello, please I think my friend is lost in the jungle, we got separated, I need help please!" Nicholas' words come out in rapid fire as the officer does his best to understand.

The motorbike driver, a young Indian boy about seventeen years of age, exchanges some words in Hindi to Officer Anil Singh.

"Oh, this is not good," the officer replies, looking over at Nicholas.

"Oh, thanks for that confirmation, I wasn't sure," Nicholas sarcastically fires back.

Officer Singh picks up the small, black phone that sits on his desk, and dialing, turns toward the wall in seeming secrecy. After exchanging some words in Hindi over the phone, he places the phone back onto the receiver and says calmly, "Please sir, have a seat and please to be waiting, more officers are on the way to help."

Nicholas takes a deep breath. Feeling light headed and nauseous from all the excitement, he decides to take the officer up on the offer. Pulling a small, white pouch from his breast pocket, the officer pulls out a *bidi*, an Indian cigarette rolled in brown, dried betel leaves, and offers it to Nicholas.

"So much for quitting," he says as he takes the *bidi* from the officer, who simultaneously hands him a pack of wooden matches. The three men sit for a moment in silence and smoke.

"Where are you from?" the motorbike driver asks, breaking the silence.

"United States, U.S.A." Nicholas mumbles distractedly.

"Oh, U.S.A. number one!" he says with a smile.

"America!" the officer confirms.

The calmness of both men is unsettling to Nicholas, who wants to go quickly to find his friend.

"So, how long until the other officers arrive?"

"Yes other officers coming," the officer says sitting back down in his black chair, which squeaks into a slight recline.

"No, how long until they come, how much time?"

"Soon, they coming, and we find your friend," the officer says authoritatively.

The officer's calm demeanor somehow comforts Nicholas as he draws in the last bit of hot smoke from his *bidi*, finding that what had quelled his nausea at the onset seems to now make it worse. He crushes it into the round, wooden graveyard of an ashtray that sits on the officer's desk.

"You have girlfriend?" the officer asks, as the motorbike driver leans in to hear the answer.

"No, no girlfriend."

"Wife?"

"No wife," Nicholas politely answers, noting the absurdity of the questions— given the circumstances.

"So, how is this gonna go down? Flashlights, dogs, what?"

"Officers coming," the officer answers, not fully understanding the question.

Nicholas stares at a clock as it ticks away on the wall. It reads 7:15. He grasps his head, sinking his fingers deep into his scalp and lowering his eyes toward the floor. He closes them, trying to sooth his frantic mind. Fidgety and unsettled, he quickly pops to his feet and notices the motorbike driver pulling a pack of Gold Flake cigarettes from his pocket.

"May I have one?" Nicholas asks, thinking it may calm his nerves and help shake the harsh taste of *bidis* from his mouth.

Handing him a cigarette and a small box of wooden matches with a cartoon man on it, he extends some comfort, "Don't worry, sir, we find your friend."

Nicholas smiles as the flare of a match ignites the cigarette.

"Name?" the motorbike driver asks.

"Nicholas, and you?"

"Simple name, Ragesh," he says standing proud.

Nicholas takes in a long drag of cigarette. That old, familiar burn of smoke fills his lungs, rushing his head with nicotine. He realizes that having that first smoke had been a bad idea, having quit over a year ago.

The door opens, and as a flood of smoke pours out, two other officers rush in, speaking Hindi to Officer Singh. One officer, who seems to be the one in charge, turns to Nicholas and walks toward him.

"Your lost you friend in the jungle?" he asks, seeming concerned.

"Yes, yes, about three or four hours ago."

After turning back to the others to speak a few more words of Hindi, he again turns back to Nicholas. "Where is guesthouse you friend staying?"

"We're sharing a room at Nishant Guest House, up over the hill."

"Maybe we check first there," the officer suggests.

Thinking it's a good idea, and realizing he should have thought of it in the first place, Nicholas follows along as all usher out of the station. Piling into a small, cream Jeep, Ragesh, Nicholas, and Officer Singh sit in the back as they drive off. The trip is quick, and upon arrival at the Nishant Guest House, Nicholas runs up to the room as the others wait in the Jeep. Getting to the room he notices the padlock is latched and locked. Opening the door he realizes that no one has been there since they left early in the morning. His towel still hangs over the bed where he left it, and there are no visible signs that Paul has been there. He latches the door and hurries back downstairs to the officers, who are smoking and talking with the guesthouse owners.

"Not here!" he yells out. Everyone rushes back into the Jeep.

"No one see your friend today," Officer Singh says, confirming his conversation with the guesthouse owners. Fireworks blast off into the night sky with loud, shotgun-like echoes, ushering in little Diwali, the first day of the two-day Diwali festivities. Ragesh explains the festivities to Nicholas, who understands them to be a sort of combination of Christmas and the Fourth of July here in India. Nicholas isn't very interested in festivities at the moment, leaning in to inform the officers of where he last saw Paul as they drive off toward the waterfall.

"So we will take torch and split me and you," Officer Singh explains, pointing to Nicholas and Ragesh, "and they two, and we will find your friend," he says as smoke pours out of his mouth from his last exhale.

The opening of the trail is dark. The officers grab flashlights, which they call *torches*. They distribute one to each person, exchange a few words of instructions, in Hindi, and begin to search into the pitch-black jungle.

The officers hold black, wooden sticks, which Nicholas imagines are for any fierce animals they may encounter.

"Oh!" the officers call out over and again.

Nicholas joins them, "Paul! Paul! You out there?"

Carefully looking in every spot they pass, they reach a split in the path, where they break up into groups. Two officers go off alone to investigate another trail as Nicholas's group heads toward the felled tree. Nearing the tree, they scan the area with their torches, but Paul is too deeply covered by the thick brush to be seen. Even in the light of day, they would have a difficult time seeing him. Moving slowly, they walk only a few feet from where he lies still unconscious, hidden from all sight. Only an owl, which sits high in the tree above, peers down into the opening of the brush, wondering what these strange men with lights are doing in the jungle at such a time. If the men could scan from the branches in daytime, like a bird in the tree, perhaps then would they see Paul lying perfectly still.

After searching for hours, they finally rendezvous back at the Jeep.

"In the morning we can again look," an officer says to Nicholas.

"He may already have walked very far, and maybe will come to the village and call you," Officer Singh says, trying to console.

Nicholas wants to keep searching, but the vast jungle is overwhelming, and so he reluctantly agrees with the officers to wait until daybreak. Piling back into the Jeep, they drive off, back to the Nishant Guest House, where they instruct Nicholas to meet them at the station at seven in the morning to begin the search again. Thanking the officers he confirms, "See you at seven then."

He turns to Ragesh and shakes his hand, "Friend, thank you so much for your help."

Still holding his hand, Ragesh replies, "Tomorrow I am coming and bring friend for help."

"Thank you!" Nicholas says, wishing words could express his gratitude as tears well up from confused emotions.

As the men pull away, Nicholas makes his way up to his room, where he briefly fantasizes Paul will be waiting for him. The fleeting fantasy shatters as he reaches the top of the stairway, noticing the padlock is still secured from the outside. Entering the barren room, heavy with burden, he collapses onto the bed. Feeling empty and alone, he feels tears fall from his face. He lies back, exhausted, staring at the ceiling as his eyes close. Burning with grief, his mind stirs in thick confusion, driving him deep into a weary slumber.

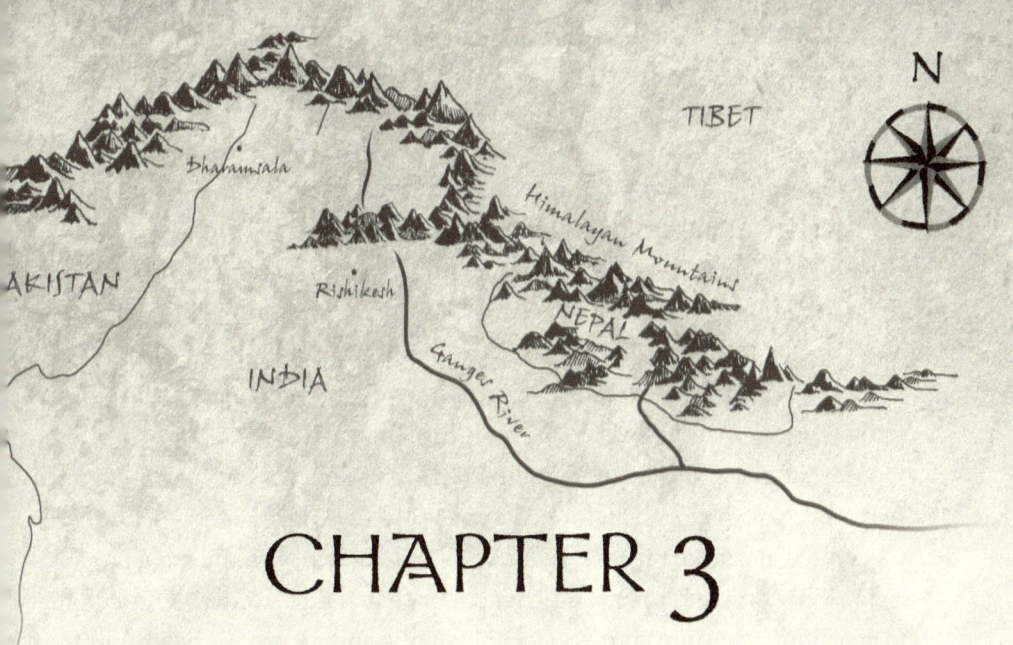

CHAPTER 3

THE DARKNESS OF early morning begins to brighten behind the shadowed foothills. A lone bird chirps in the jungle, soon followed by others. Paul still lies silent as consciousness dawns. Flies feast in a frenzy on the dry blood crusted onto his hair and the ground next to his head. As monkeys begin their day swinging through the treetops, searching for breakfast throughout the jungle, a small, dusty, monkey, tan, with a pinkish-red face, munches on some freshly sprouted leaves. The monkey rips off small, tasty pieces of branch with his little hands and eats them with delight, eyes half closed as the rapture of fine monkey cuisine fills him with every bite.

"Markat, Markat!" another monkey similar in size and age cries out as he swings from tree to tree.

"Markat, come look!" he says, jerking his head in the direction he wants to bring his friend.

"What is it, Bandar?" Markat asks, content to sit and eat his breakfast.

Bandar excitedly pulls at Markat, and the two descend the tree in skillfully controlled falls, to the sandy ground. Bandar cautiously pulls away the brush for an unamused Markat, finally revealing the body of Paul. Markat's mouth instantly pops open, forming an *O* with his lips, as he jerks his head, astonished.

"Is he dead?" Markat asks, getting a closer look as Bandar breaks away the thick brush and sits upon Paul's chest examining his face.

"He is still breathing," he notes, feeling the man's chest slowly moving up and down.

"Careful, Bandar," Markat warns, as he draws closer, "is he sleeping?"

Bandar begins to poke at the face with his hand. "I have seen him before, on the road yesterday," Bandar explains.

Markat just stares at the face, inspecting in amazement, never having seen a human so closely before. "What should we do?" Markat asks.

Getting no answer from Bandar, who is fascinated with the man, he asks again—this time with concern, "Bandar! What should we…?" And before he can finish, they are startled as Paul coughs and moves his head slightly. Quickly, the monkeys hide behind some of the thick brush that surrounds them. Paul regains more and more consciousness and begins slowly to open his eyes, realizing he has a massive headache. He rubs his face, which cringes in agony, and slowly raises up his stiff body, sitting up with a look of massive confusion. His eyes, blurred, strain to look around at where he is. His headache begins to dull as he sits rubbing his hair, feeling the moist blood on the back of his head. Bandar and Markat are softly talking.

"Look at his face. He looks ill," Markat says.

"What's that, who's there?" Paul calls out, hearing voices, but not seeing anyone.

"Hello?" he calls out as he lifts his stiff body to stand, face wincing with every movement.

Bandar leaps up onto the felled tree, startling Paul. They stare at each other for a moment.

"Yes, this is definitely the man I saw yesterday," Bandar says to Markat, who is keeping his distance below, behind the trunk, not feeling as brave as Bandar.

"Yesterday?" Paul asks, rubbing his arms to ward off the chill of morning as Bandar's eyes widen with amazement.

"Can you understand me?" Bandar asks slowly.

"Yes, oddly enough, I can," Paul answers, amazed himself.

Markat leaps up next to Bandar, "You can speak to monkeys?" he says dumbfounded.

"Apparently so," Paul says, still in a great deal of confusion.

"What is your name?" Bandar asks.

Paul thinks for a moment and the answer is not there. "I, I don't know," he answers perplexed by the simple question.

"Surely you know your name," Bandar says, going on, "where are you from?"

Again Paul thinks hard, his head throbbing as he walks out from the thicket and brushes himself off. "I can't remember. I don't remember anything," he says, searching inward for answers. Getting lightheaded, he sits on the gravely sand as Bandar and Markat leap down beside him.

"Don't remember your name. Maybe you don't have a name," Markat entertains.

Paul sits in silence. Sounds seem to grind into his brain as he twists and turns his throbbing head. Tightly clasping his skull, he closes his eyes as a loud ringing and voices intrude in on him from all around. Small voices of insects buzzing past, a distant voice in a bird's call, and finally the ringing in his ears, which overwhelms all the other voices. He bends over like a child, holding his ears tight in an attempt to quell the sharp ringing.

"Are you OK?" Markat asks concerned.

The ringing suddenly stops, and he opens his eyes. "What is happening?" he asks.

Bandar looks at Markat perplexedly, then back at the mysterious man before them. From a rustling above drops down another monkey as young in age as the other two. Dropping down, she stands in awe at the tall man, who looks at his body in wonder of where his clothes might be.

"What is going on?" she asks Bandar in a whisper.

Bandar turns with a playful smile. "Hi, Kamala," he bashfully greets her. "I found him lying here asleep," he says, leaning in to whisper for no apparent reason other than to get closer to her. "He doesn't know his name or where he is from."

"Should we tell Rakesh?" Kamala asks, concerned, with a puzzled look on her face.

"Who is Rakesh?" Paul asks as Kamala gasps in shock.

"Oh, and he understands us, too," Markat interjects, noticing Kamala's shock.

"Is this a dream?" Paul wonders as he rubs his face, baffled about what's going on.

"Rakesh is the leader of our clan. He would have to know about you. He can help you," Bandar explains.

Paul is confused what to do next. Feeling helpless and bewildered, he says, "Can you take me to him?"

The three monkeys look at each other with concern, as if they are bringing home a stray to their parents, "Do you think it's a good idea?" Markat whispers with trepidation.

"Sure it is, we can't leave the poor guy here. At least Rakesh can help point him in the right direction," Bandar argues.

Agreeing in a huddled whisper, they come to the conclusion that it would be best to bring him to Rakesh. "Follow us, it's not too far from here," Bandar instructs, pointing out across the jungle.

The three monkeys lead the way up a narrow path behind the waterfall. Stopping to drink some water, Paul dunks his head under, washing away some of the blood crusted into his hair. A blunt throbbing in the back of his head frequently shoots sharp pains down his neck. Feeling uncomfortable, he follows the monkeys as they move on. They make their way up over the hill that runs behind the waterfall.

Paul notices something in his checkered, blue boxer shorts. Pulling out the piece of paper, he reads it, with no recollection of where it is from: "Who are you? I am that person when you have forgotten me you look to your peeping in self soul/spirit you will find there all that. Can you please give me all your troubled pain? I give to you pleasureful of human life." Having no idea what these words mean, and with a brain to distraught to think, Paul folds the paper and wraps it back into the elastic band from where he found it. Three words from the paper run over in his head again and again as he walks: "Who are you?" He tries persistently to remember.

The sun has risen over the hills. In Rishikesh, Nicholas makes his way to the station to begin the hunt.

Meanwhile, back in the jungle, Bandar instructs, "Stay here, we'll be right back," as they come to a lush area densely populated by tall trees.

The monkeys quickly swing about, disappearing into the vastness of the jungle. Watching how quickly they travel through the trees, Paul marvels as they swing and swoop through the branches, which seem to interlace one tree into another. Waiting patiently, he sits on fallen leaves that are browned and crisp, resting his feet from the morning journey. Hanging his head back, he stares up at the treetops that canvas the jungle in a green array of shelter. Searching his memory as he watches the optical illusion of swirling trees above, he feels his life is like a word that's on the tip of his tongue but cannot be recalled. He grows frustrated trying to remember.

Bandar pops his head down, holding the tree with one hand and hanging the rest of his body just within ear range, "OK. Come!" he beckons as he drops to the jungle floor to lead the way.

Crossing the threshold of this dense green sanctuary, guarded by trunks that stand like tall, protecting soldiers, Paul notices hundreds of monkeys going about their business. One monkey grooms another, and as he pulls mites from his mate's fur to nibble on, he notices the strange juxtaposition of monkey and man and halts to a frozen stare, letting the tasty mite leap free from his hand. Stopping mid-bite upon leafy branches, other monkeys watch in wonder. The whispers of questions from the monkeys in the treetops above can be heard as Paul passes through the sanctuary. It is not uncommon for a man to pass through this area, yet very uncommon for a monkey to be leading him through at such close proximity. They sense a strange encounter, a strange encounter indeed. Paul thinks of how the soft, fallen leaves of the trees are a far better cushion than the gravel that has cut up his aching feet. As they pass a few monkeys on the ground, Paul catches the eye of one who quickly squats in a pouncing position, showing his teeth and calling out a challenge.

"Yeah, yeah. We all know you're tough, Abhay," Bandar says mockingly as they walk by the monkeys, who stare in primordial dominance.

Nervous concern washes over Paul as they pass countless monkeys, all seemingly staring at him in discontent. Drawing closer to Bandar's lead, he feels more secure. Although Bandar is a smaller, younger monkey, his attitude and confidence ease Paul's nerves. Bandar's lanky stride rhythmically bounces along as he looks back every now and again with a smile of assurance to the concerned face of the man behind him. Paul trusts Bandar, who, with the spirit of an ape, confidently presses on. They stop as they come to a massive tree that sits at least three meters wide, spilling immense roots above the soil, digging deep into the Earth. Looking up, Paul imagines the tree reaches the heavens in its endless ascent into the immense, flourishing treetops of the jungle. Still looking up, his attention is swiftly drawn to a large, overweight monkey that drops down with a heavy thump behind them. Five other elder monkeys, fur slightly grayed at the tips, surround Bandar and Paul in a swift silence that alerts their attention.

"This is Rakesh," Bandar says, swaying his open palm in the direction of the large male monkey sternly staring him up and down with a frown of disapproval.

The five elders stand, looking intently, as a crowd of monkeys fills the trees around them, awaiting to see what is going on.

"So you can speak to the monkey?" Rakesh says, seeming unimpressed.

"Yes, h-hello," Paul stammers, "I can't seem to remember my name or where I am from. I've seemed to have hit my head rather hard, and Bandar said you may be able to help me."

Rakesh stares in silence, with an almost irritated look, as he rubs the thick whiskers on his chin. He raises one brow in contemplation. "And you wish help from us?" he interjects, signaling Bandar to stand away behind the elders with the wave of his hand.

"Any help you could offer, sir, would be greatly accepted."

Rakesh draws closer, letting out a silent laugh through his nostrils.

"Was there help for the monkeys from your people when our great and sacred forest was laid to ruin so you could come from faroff lands and profit?" Rakesh says as the elder monkeys look on in approval, shaking their heads.

"I don't know about this, surely I would never . . ."

"Silence!" Rakesh interrupts. "I know your kind all to well. You love the monkey when we are for your picture taking and amusement, but besides that you take from the jungle, from the monkey. You cut our trees, and this is fine. The trees live to give, and give they will to all of the Earth, but you now take more than you need. You pollute our waters with your filth and plastic. You go off into our jungles and enjoy the love of our great jungle and give very little or nothing back except a stream of devastation. I speak for the jungle, for she gives and gives and never complains, but you take and take and self-absorbed in your silly little worlds of trinkets and such have forgotten about the balance. You have forgotten who you are indeed, you have forgotten that you are the jungle, you are the monkey who has lost his way."

He takes a deep breath as he glances back at one of the elders, who nods at him to go on, "Now you boast you are more intelligent than the monkey. The intelligent human, you know so much, yet can't even survive in the jungle one day. Intelligent human, bah!" He finishes, raising his hands up as monkeys begin to hoot and ha, shaking the trees above.

Swallowing past the uneasy lump in his throat, Paul looks over at Bandar, who now wears a look of concern on his face. The audience of monkeys grows louder as Rakesh orders, "Silence!" The trees fall silent, and all fix on his next words.

"So this is 'who you are' and you'd do well to join back with 'who you are' in town."

"But surely I am not this, I can't be, I know."

"You *know*, you know!" Rakesh emphasizes, silencing Paul as he now comes closer, staring at him in disgust. His dark red face now match his eyes, blaring in crimson anger, offsetting his grayish auburn coat. Taking a deep breath, he calmly says through his sharp yellow teeth, "Know this, 'man.' Humans have been given the great gift and have misused it for fleeting pleasure and cheap laughs. Your gift has become your curse." Bits of spit spew from the passionate words onto Paul as he looks down at Rakesh. "Many times I have sat in your towns observing, and with all these 'things' you are still miserable. You think more will somehow make you happy, so you consume more, you take from the jungle and don't give back. You kill the blessed cow and thank her not. You tie the donkey to do your bidding, you chain the monkey to turn a *rupee*, and all the while grasping at more, you have forgotten 'who you are.' This is a shame," he finishes, hanging his head with a shake of disapproval. "So go now. Bandar will take you back to 'who you are.'" He turns away, walking past Bandar, "Take him back to the main center. That is where he belongs."

"But, Rakesh," Bandar pleads.

"Rakesh nothing," he hisses showing his teeth and lowering Bandar's head in inferiority.

"But, sir, perhaps you can teach me, and I can help the humans to understand," Paul asks in his last attempt to smooth him over.

Walking away toward the tree with the elders, Rakesh comes to a halt before turning to answer. "Long have been the days when man and monkey saw eye to eye. Man rose up and forgot about the monkey, and now man is the lost monkey who pretends he is not. There is no hope for man. My only hope is that when you wipe each other out with your ignorance and wars you don't take the monkey and jungle with you. I fear that is a wish not to be fulfilled. You may mean well, man, but I know your species all too well, and soon will come the time when even you will want to rule the monkey. Yet the monkey is governed by a force far more powerful than any man, ridden with greed, could manage to be. So please, go now, there is no hope for man."

"But perhaps . . ."

"Go *now*, I said, before our clan has their way with you and scatters your body throughout the jungle," Rakesh yells, turning.

The trees again begin to shake, and the monkeys fiercely howl, hoot, and ha. Looking around, Paul begins to sweat.

"Quickly come!" Bandar demands anxiously as the two swiftly run off.

The sanctuary of jungle has turned into an asylum of monkeys that echoes out across the jungle. Dodging sticks and debris being thrown down, they quickly make their way out, finally stopping at a safe point just outside the shelter of thick trees.

"I am sorry, but perhaps Rakesh is right. I mean in town you can find out who you are. They will help you there."

"Perhaps," Paul says crouched over, hands on knees, catching his breath.

"Forgive Rakesh, many years back his family was taken from him, children and wife, for what he thinks was for research or some sort of profitable amusement. We know little about where the humans take us, but it happens often. Rakesh has much bitterness toward man for this."

"No worries, friend. I don't know what I expected to find there. From what I can remember and recall from my time in this world of humans, I can understand his concerns."

"What do you remember?" Bandar asks as they begin to walk.

"I remember the world, and life in general, but can't remember my life in it.

It's as if my past were a dream that upon waking I quickly forgot, yet remember the world around me."

"Well, in town I know you will find an answer," Bandar consoles.

"That, my friend, I am unsure of."

Suddenly Bandar scales swiftly up a tree, and with a loud thump a clump of green bananas falls next to Paul. Leaping down next to them, he rips one off and hands it to Paul, who smiles in thanks, noticing his enormous hunger. Sitting in the quiet solitude of the jungle, they finish the bananas. Paul gets up and makes his way over to a soft-flowing stream. Squatting down, he cups his hands, drawing water to his mouth and wetting his hair. Bandar squats down on all fours and, putting his mouth to the crisp water, softly sips. Looking up, the man smiles at Bandar and Bandar smiles back, remembering when they first met on the road.

"I remember I saw you yesterday!" Bandar says with revelation.

"Yesterday?" Paul enquires.

"You were with another man sitting by the roadside. Perhaps you will find this man in town."

Racking his brain, he still remembers nothing, not even the previous day.

Standing up, he rubs his face, noticing the warm comfort of the day's sun that pervades the jungle. He thinks of how Bandar must feel comfortably secure in his little, warm, fur coat, as he begins again to walk on. Reaching a roadside that runs along the jungle, Paul notices that the hours of walking have left him with a blunt hunger that shoots a sharp pain to his head. "Can you muster up some more of those bananas?" he asks.

"Be right back," Bandar says, puffing up his chest, feeling proud to help.

Sitting on a rock just before the road, Paul awaits Bandar, who quickly returns with some bananas. This time they are yellowish brown. Plopping them down, he runs back off into the jungle and quickly returns, holding a piece of tree that dangles small green pods among leaves.

Paul picks the beans from the pods and thinks of how grateful he is that Bandar is there. He thinks of the difficulty he would have had trying to find food on his own. He imagines trying to scale up the steep trees in an effort to get some bananas and laughs inwardly. They finish up and sit for a while, resting from the long journey. Evening is soon upon them and the sun begins to retire behind the far hills.

"It's not far," Bandar says as he rises up and leads the man across the road to a small path that overlooks the Ganga River.

Seeing the town not far off, they proceed on. They arrive at the back of a strip of small restaurants and shops that rests at the beginning of the busy village. Unseen, they continue down a back alley, following a concrete wall that blocks the alleyway between the building. Passing fly-infested garbage that smells both appealing and appalling, they come to a bamboo ladder, which Bandar climbs up quickly, signaling to follow. Grasping the ladder, Paul gradually makes his way up, coming to the top and stepping out onto the roof, where Bandar sits, watching the busy town below. They sit on the edge, hidden by the dark skies. Firecrackers ring out in strident and persistent bangs as people crowd the busy, narrow streets buying and selling, dancing, and drinking, snapping pictures of each other against a river ablaze with floating candles under a sign that reads, "Happy Diwali." Diwali, is the large festival celebrated in India signifying when Lord Rama came out of the jungle after fourteen years, victorious over the evils he battled against. A holiday of gift giving, of lights lining the houses and adding color to the towns, and torched candle lights that burn into the night amid battle-like fireworks that pop off in a constant fury.

"Here we are, friend," Bandar says, watching the fireworks spread across the sky in a stunning performance.

Smiling, but ill at ease, Paul holds his arms as the night winds chill his near-naked flesh. Bandar descends the roof. Paul as he sniffles a runny nose, watches the monkey vanish. A few moments pass and Bandar swings back atop the roof, heaving a tan, cotton, and long-sleeved shirt, with matching pants adorned with wooden buttons.

"Where did you get these?" Paul asks, in wonder of how his small body could even carry the clothes up to him.

"These people are so caught up, they are no match for the stealth monkey," Bandar replies, assuming a kung fu-like pose before dropping down again out of sight. A pair of nicely made, leather, sandals is heaved up, followed by Bandar. "Here. Now you can go off to your people nicely clothed, as they prefer."

Putting on the clothes and sandals, Paul feels warm and new, as if he had never worn clothes before.

"Thank you, Bandar, I can't express how much your kindness means to me."

Bandar blows off the compliment, "Monkeys are brothers to every-one," he explains as he sits next to Paul, who looks out into the crazy streets of celebration.

"Although Rakesh is old and bitter, most monkeys respect that all are our brothers: not just our fellow monkeys but humans too, and the trees and the rocks, everything. We live among our brothers always. Your people have forgotten this," he says, looking out into the sea of confusion.

"You are very wise for such a young monkey," Paul says, surprised to hear such wisdom from Bandar.

"This I have learned from the wise Kavi, who lives deep in the jungle."

"Kavi?"

"Yes Bahi, Kavi teaches us. Kavi is tapped into the source of all things and has great wisdom."

Looking out into the town again, Paul feels anxious. He sees beggars pleading for money, some missing limbs and some disfigured and sickly in other ways. He sees a look of desperation through a false joy that people seem to be wearing as masks. "I don't relate to these people at all. I am not this."

"These are your brothers, Bahi," Bandar says.

"What is Bahi?"

"You are Bahi," Bandar says with a smile. "You are my brother, and this you should teach to your lost brethren. "

"But I must find out who I am, truly, in order to do this, or else I fear I will be lost in this sea of suffering and confusion before me."

"Go, Bahi, be with your brothers. You will forever be remembered as my great friend, Bahi, the one who talked to the monkeys," Bandar says as he stands up and walks toward the latter.

"Bahi, I like that," he thinks as he rises up to thank Bandar, resolving to use this name. Descending the ladder, they come to the back alley once again. They peer out between the shops, and Bahi cases the hectic market streets.

Bang!

Startled by a firecracker, Bahi turns to see Bandar with a *samosa* in one hand and a round sweet in the other. "For you, Bahi," Bandar says, hand-ing the food to him, "Go now and teach your people."

Thanking Bandar, Bahi watches him walk off into the stark darkness behind the bright lights of the village. Eating the *samosa* and small sweet pastry, he slowly makes his way out into the street, which is inundated with men selling maps and postcards. "Hello, friend, Hello!" Bahi ignores the loud yells of the vendor, who follows him as he pushes past the suffocation of people. Firecrackers pop off persistently in a clamor that pierces his ears as he feels something pulling on his pants. Looking down, he finds a small girl, dirty with crusted snot around her nose. Her large, brown, pleading, eyes stare at him as she motions a sign of hunger, placing her hand to her mouth in an attempt to get food or money from Bahi. If he had either he would. "Sorry, I have nothing," he admits as he walks, but the girl is persistent and follows him. Bahi's heart is overwhelmed with the suffering all around him. Even the seemingly happy and well off seem to be hurting in some way, grasping at things all around them, as Rakesh had said. Besieged, he begins to run briskly, pushing through the crowd of people. Firecrackers blast off at every step. Vendors attempt to stop him, flashing things to buy in his face, but he persists onward, away from the village. He runs so fast and so far that when he finally stops to catch his breath, he finds himself on a dark roadside overlooking the Ganga River. He sits as tears begin to fall down his ruddy cheeks, cooling in the fresh breeze extending off of the river. Feeling alienated from the world, yet not belonging in the jungle or among his people, he truly feels lost, alone, and frightened.

"Who am I? What is my purpose here in this strange land? How do I return home?" These questions pain his mind as he weeps alone in quiet desperation. Feeling something on his thigh, he looks with a quick fright to see Bandar.

"Oh, Bandar!" he says, wiping the tears from his eyes. "You are truly the only one I know."

Bandar smiles in silence and sits in Bahi's lap. "Kavi," he says softly. "Kavi can surely help you."

"Will you take me to him?" Bahi asks, clearing his throat with a swallow.

"In the morning we will go. Tonight we sleep by the river."

Making their way to a small, empty cave that sits just above the river, they climb inside. Bahi lies down and Bandar cuddles up to him. They warm each other from the cool night chill outside. They both fall fast asleep, exhausted from an eventful day.

CHAPTER 4

O PENING HIS EYES slowly, Bahi begins to come back to the world of time, far from the deep, subtle world of sleep he was just lost in. He hears the river rushing as he looks over the boulders that stand like warriors praying to the sun. Looking around, he notices that Bandar is nowhere to be seen. He rubs his eyes and stretches his cold feet so that they protrude straight out of the small cave space. Shaking the stiffness from his body, he stands to a crouch, walks forward, and ducks out of the cave. *Where has Bandar gone?* he wonders, as a loud thump sends his attention behind him, where a branch of bananas has just fallen. Bandar drops down, holding two *samosas* in his tiny hand.

"Good morning!" he says, sprite like, as he hands Bahi one of the *samosas*, still warm, fresh off the pan.

"You know, Bandar, it's not nice to steal."

"Stealing, hmm, yes I've heard of this. If one man is hungry, should not another give him food? If one man is cold and naked, and another man has an abundance of clothes, should he not give to his brother?" Bandar asks.

"I suppose, but without permission or enquiring one may not know if the man has an abundance or is just working for another man with abundance, and therefore you may in fact be taking from the very one who needs the food or cloth," Bahi fires back.

"Just eat the food," Bandar says as Bahi smiles in amusement.

Bahi bites into the crispy, fried *samosa*. The potatoes, peas, and spice filling are warming. He enjoys every bite before moving onto several bananas.

"Thank you, Bandar. If not for you, I would be starving and perhaps dead by now."

"Friends don't thank. Brothers do for each other without the need to be thanked," Bandar says as a matter of fact.

"Well, it is my feeling of gratitude, then, to have you as my brother."

"Me too," Bandar says before ripping through a banana skin with his teeth.

The two sit in the silent morning as the sun dances upon the river. With bellies full, they settle into the warmth of the moment, drinking in the day.

"We better get along if we're to reach Kavi before nightfall," Bandar warns. They both rise up.

They walk up a narrow path buzzing with insects feasting on small, violet wildflowers that speckle the bushes. They reach the road and proceed to cross it once again—entering the jungle. Bahi looks back at the road, taking in a deep breath of confidence, before turning toward the vast jungle ahead.

They walk for hours, delighting in the beauty of the jungle, passing soft, gleaming waterfalls; massive, ancient trees; and numerous species of insects and other animals. They stop for a brief rest, enjoying some fruit Bandar has gathered.

"How do you know Kavi," Bahi enquires.

"All the animals know Kavi, the great black-face monkey mystic. He's a respected sage here in the jungle. Many times he has come to our clan to teach us the wisdom of the jungle."

"Monkey?" Bahi asks, still jaded from the last encounter with Rakesh.

"He is no mere monkey. He is wise beyond our imaginations. Some say he takes the form of a monkey only to relate to the jungle life, but is in fact the ancient spirit of the forest. But I don't know about all that," he utters, shrugging his shoulders.

Bahi feels content, trusting that anyone worthy of such reverence is worth a shot. *What else is there to do?* he thinks, realizing his options are limited to Bandar's help. Moving on, they come to an ancient forest where even the youngest trees look to be about seven hundred years old. Thick vines that put the trunks of younger trees to shame hang from large branches as the sun makes its way through treetops, dappling the jungle with serene light. Walking with admiration and awe of such sudden beauty, they come to a massive tree that melts into the ground with large knots that bubble out in all directions. Bandar stops to look up. Bahi fixes his gaze upward, squinting to see what Bandar is looking at. He notices a large, hollow opening far up, shrouded with thickly hanging vines.

"Kavi lives there?" Bahi asks with concern.

"Wait here," Bandar says as he climbs his way quickly up the wide trunk to the opening above.

Watching as Bandar enters what looks to be a carved-out hollow of the tree behind the draped vine, Bahi sits on one of the many large knots that protrude from the base of the enormous tree. He is quickly drawn to his feet as the tree begins to rumble, sending a vibration along the jungle floor. The tree begins to open slowly like a lion's mouth. Bahi does a double take, not believing his eyes, as he jumps back. The base of the tree stretches open to reveal Bandar, now standing in the entrance with a proud smile.

"Come on, quietly," Bandar waves him in.

Entering the immense hollow of the tree, Bahi marvels at a beautiful, carved, spiral staircase that leads up the trunk. Random holes beam in sunlight as the two climb the long steep stair, corkscrewing higher and higher. Bahi runs his hands along the inside of the trunk as they ascend higher, still boggled by this incredible experience. Reaching a platform about halfway up, Bandar knocks on a small doorway intricately cut out in curious designs of swirling symbols foreign to him. The dark, wooded door opens as a small, white-furred monkey with a black face softly waves them in. Bahi crawls through the miniature gap that opens up into a large room dimly lit by beams of golden sunlight. Squinting into the far corner of the room, he strains to make out what's there, blinded by hazy smoke that dances in the soft, late-afternoon light that seeps in from outside. They are instructed to sit at a raised lip on the floor, which separates the rest of the room from the smoky space ahead of them. The smell of incense infuses the air as they sit quietly. The small, white monkey leaves, closing the door behind him. They can hear the soft settling of beads as a shadowed figure seems to stand up in front of them. Bahi again strains his eyes as the shadow comes out of the mist and into the light of the sun, closer to where they sit. Bahi knows instantly that this is Kavi. White fur wraps his charcoal face, melting into a beard at his chin. Taller than the previous monkey and taller than any of Bandar's clan, he languidly moves toward them, slightly hunched with age. Shells and bone jingle from his necklace as he slowly reveals himself. His dark, complacent face looks wise with age, and they can feel the energy that pours off him like the dry mist that flows around behind him.

"I am told you can speak with the jungle," Kavi's soft, warm tone is inviting.

"Yes sir, I can," Bahi says in an almost trance state.

"What is it you wish to know?" Kavi asks, not wasting any time.

"Well sir, I seem to have been cursed with forgetfulness. I don't remember who I am. I hit my head quite hard and haven't remembered since. I come to you to ask if you can help me with this question."

The wise monkey stares in contemplation, and softly blinking his eyes, he begins to speak, "You do not wish to know who you once thought you were, however you seek to know the truth of who you are, am I correct?"

"Yes, I mean I think so, it's confusing to me as of now. Bandar had taken me into town to seek out who I was, yet I felt the answers weren't going to be there for me. Was I wrong?"

Kavi looks at Bahi with a humble smile, "Let me begin explaining who we all are."

Walking closer to the seated inquirers, Kavi slowly steps with his staff, which runs upward from the ground, curving like a question mark above his small, black hand, topped off with an iridescent crystal that sets firm at the head of the staff. His light brown eyes glisten as he sits in the lotus position, each foot softly placed on either thigh. "On this planet," he begins, "we share a brotherhood that excludes no one and no thing." Bahi smiles at Bandar, having heard this before, as Kavi goes on, "Those of us that live and breathe have the fire of creation more active in us. Therefore we must eat feeding the fire, enabling us to sustain our lives by keeping the fire active to run our vessels. Starting with the smallest plant on this wonderful planet, plants absorb nutrients from the fertile soil of our mother and drink the sweet waters given often by the Earth's selfless bounty. So we have water, Earth, and fire. We eat the plants, which convert these nutrients and give us proteins to build our muscles and so forth, or we eat animals that eat plants and we get a secondary source of this protein. Either way, whether we are going directly to the source of nutrition or eating the leftovers in the meat of animals, all living animals such as you and I get our nutrition from the plant, which comes from the Earth and is fortified from the heavens above with sun. Our bodies are composed of the food we eat, and whatever it is we eat can be traced back to the plants and vegetation of the Earth."

Bandar and Bahi sit captivated by Kavi's words as he goes on. "You are the Earth, you are a reflection of the Earth, and the Earth is a reflection of you. If you check with your science you will find this to be true," he says as he tosses a biology book from a small shelf, which lands perfectly in front of Bahi, open to a page of a human structure.

"Where did you get this?" Bahi asks perplexed.

"That's insignificant to the conversation at hand. You are composed of three quarters water, or liquid, and one quarter mass, exactly like the Earth. You have in your body veins, capillaries, and so forth, which are your rivers and streams, and just like the Earth you have energy centers that run various systems of your body. Some call these the *chakras*. Also, like the Earth, if you pollute your body, you will get sick. But luckily, like the Earth, your body can withstand much pollution and can clean itself out. Yet, with too much pollution and toxins, sooner or later the body will collapse just like the Earth. Therefore you are all things on Earth, and all things on Earth are you."

Kavi stands up and makes his way toward the mist. "Come," he beckons as the two rise.

Clearing the smoke with a wave of his hand, he reveals a cauldron, bubbling from the fire below it. Stilling the bubbles with another faint wave of his hand, Kavi smiles as images begin to appear in the dense liquid. Bandar sits on Bahi's shoulder as they peer into the cauldron. They behold people cutting down trees, images of missiles launching and exploding, people firing rifles, images of humans smoking cigarettes and drinking alcohol, followed by an image of a large dozer leveling trees, and another of oil burning in the ocean.

"We are not being mindful of our destruction. We are devastating our mother at a rapid pace. As we destroy the Earth, we are destroying ourselves, you see, because we are the Earth. And why does the human race do this?"

"For money mostly," Bahi whispers.

"Aha," Kavi says as his eyes light up. "Very good, only after the last tree has been cut down, only after the last fish has been caught, only after the last river has been poisoned, only then will you realize that money can't be eaten. Some say we can live without the Earth, perhaps on a moon. But that, I tell you, will be the end of living and the beginning of survival. The end of living draws near if we do not heed the warning. The end of living and the beginning of survival," he says softly to reiterate his point.

A stillness pervades the room. Only the sounds of the bubbling cauldron can be heard.

"And so you seek to know who you are, I have explained this to you, but this you must also find for yourself."

Bahi is still speechless.

"Do you have something to show me?" Kavi asks Bahi.

"Um, no, I don't think so," Bahi answers as he thinks.

Kavi looks, and with a nod of his head, looking down at Bahi's pants softly asks, "A piece of paper perhaps?"

Remembering the folded-up paper in his boxers, he quickly digs into his pants, anxiously taking it out and unfolding it as he hands it to Kavi. "This is all I have, I don't know where it came from."

Kavi looks it over pensively and runs his fingers over the *Om* symbol before handing it back to Bahi. "Only one other human I know can communicate with the animals of the jungle, and this symbol on your paper is confirmation that you must meet him."

Bahi looks down at the Om symbol as he listens attentively.

"I don't know where you came from, I do not know where you will go, in fact this is all up to you. I do know this: your journey has led you here, and now I must point you in the direction of the Baba who lives beyond the valley. Bandar knows the beginning of the path's location and will show you the way," Kavi says, lowering his head and turning his attention to Bandar, who stands next to Bahi. "After you show him the entrance of the path you must return immediately home."

"That is a dangerous path. I must escort Bahi!" Bandar interrupts.

"You must go home immediately, for if you step foot on that path you will never return. Death awaits you there, young Bandar, and this is not your fate. Your journey, young one, goes in another direction. It is one of great importance as is Bahi's, and therefore I warn you not to stray from the path you are meant to walk."

"But, but, I . . ." Bandar tries to interject being quickly cut off by Kavi.

"But, but, nothing, young Bandar. Now you listen and listen well. Your merging with Bahi is complete. You have been a crucial part of his path. And now, like the great river, which splits at eagle's rock, you must part ways." He notices a look of concern on Bandar's face. "Fear not, young Bandar: all rivers lead to the same place. Yet, if they do not stream where they are meant to stream, they will not carry the water of life where it is meant to be carried. Thus those who need, and await it there, will be without. There is enough disharmony, too many rivers and streams offtrack. Return home. Your family worries for you. Kamala cries as we speak!"

Bending down softly to Bandar's eye level, Kavi looks with compassionate concern. "Promise me this, young one," he asks as he places a gentle hand on Bandar's shoulder.

"Of course, Kavi. I promise." Bandar lowers his head in reverent discontent.

Making his way over to the small shelf, Kavi pulls down a small brown cloth tied with a thin piece of vine. Untying the cloth as he walks back over, he reveals three berries that lie gently inside and hands them, laid out on the cloth, to Bahi.

"These will protect you on the path to the Baba. If you encounter any danger, simply eat these, and protection will be at your back."

Bahi ties them back up and places them in his pocket. "Thank you for your help, Kavi," he says as he bows his head, hands in prayer position. "Will the Baba have the answers I seek?"

"Only you hold those answers. Yet the journey you travel and the people and animals you meet will unveil parts of yourself, pieces of the riddle that will be able to answer this. So in essence we all hold the answers to each other."

Bahi runs this over in his head, trying to make practical sense to it at a time where nothing seems to compute. Kavi summons the smaller monkey from the other room as he bids them farewell. Walking off toward the miniature door they came in, the small, white monkey stands, showing them the way out as Kavi disappears once again into the mist at the far corner of the room.

Making their way down the steep, wooden staircase, which spirals down the trunk, Bahi struggles in the small space to make his way down, in contrast to Bandar, who effortlessly makes his way hopping and even playfully flipping down the steps. Finally reaching the mouth, they exit the tree, and as the Earth once again trembles, they watch as the hole heals up until it looks as though there were never an entrance. Bahi leans on a wide bodhi tree in deep contemplation and awe.

"The wise Baba is who taught Kavi. Surely he will have the answers you seek," Bandar says sensing a still unfulfilled Bahi.

"Have you met this Baba?"

"Not I. Not many do here in the jungle, but he is known by many. It is said that he is six hundred years old and transmutes his messages by thought to all of the world."

"What of the path? You say it's dangerous!" Bahi enquires.

"The path that leads to the Baba is one of great lore among the jungle, full of danger they say, but we have many stories and I believe they are just that, stories."

"What if it's truth?" Bahi asks nervously.

"Ah, just a story to keep the young monkey from wandering off," Bandar says, trying to ease his fears.

"Kavi predicted certain death for you upon the path. Danger must be prevalent there."

"My friend, keep your wits high and your senses open and you will be OK. You have the berries from Kavi. If not, then maybe I would be a little worried," Bandar says, now expressing a small amount of the large concern he holds inside, knowing this to be a path of danger. "We should sleep here in the protection of the ancient forest and leave for the path just before sunrise. You don't want to be on the path at nightfall," Bandar suggests.

Bahi likes the idea, and sitting on fallen leaves he absorbs the energy that vibrates from the enormous trees all around him, lifting his spirits and calming his mind. Bandar drags over a large, fallen banana palm frond and lay it next to Bahi. "Bed," he says, as Bahi stands to help him out.

Gathering more fallen fronds that spread wide with browned leaves, they create covers for their bedding to protect them from the cool night winds that will soon be rolling in. The forest is especially beautiful as the setting sun dances upon the ancient trees, adding a golden hue to the massive trunks, which embody wisdom and stability. Sitting in wonder of this magical land, Bahi reflects on the lessons of Kavi. He internally thanks the forest, the trees, the fallen leaves they have used for bedding, the fruit above, and the soil below. For the first time in the past two days, he feels calm. A smile grows upon his face. The quiet dust of the forest sails smoothly in the warm, golden sunlight, settling into the Earth. A butterfly lands gently upon Bahi's knee as he sits. He quietly observes her exquisite wings, silky black, with one reflective blue circle filled with dark lavender on each wing.

"Hello," he delicately greets as the butterfly leisurely waves her wings as if doing a light stretch.

"Hi," she replies to Bahi's amazement.

"Can you understand me?" he asks.

"Why, yes, I can, I'm not an idiot, you know."

Bahi laughs at the revelation that he can talk to insects too, scaring her to a delicate pounce a few feet away on the tip of the palm bed.

"You are quite possibly the most beautiful butterfly I have ever seen," he says in truth, drawing her back to his knee.

"Why, thank you. You are a very beautiful. Um, what are you exactly?" the butterfly asks, never having ventured out of the jungle to see a human.

"They say I am a human being."

"Who is they?" she asks.

"Ha, ha, I don't know," Bahi laughs. "What is your name, little butterfly?"

"Kamini," she says as she gracefully flutters to his arm to get a better look at him.

"My name is Bahi, nice to meet you, Kamini."

Bandar comes rustling over, back from gathering some food for dinner, a variety of fruits and beans.

"Bandar, this is Kamini," Bahi introduces.

"Hello Kamini, you are welcome to join us for dinner," Bandar says, pointing to the food he piled on top of the dried palm leaves, laid out next to a large tree.

"Why I thank you, but I have just indulged of the sweet nectars of that flower," Kamini says, floating gently and landing on Bahi's shoulder as they make their way over to the food.

A feast of fruits and beans lies before them. Bahi smiles with thanks as they sit around the food.

"So, where does a human being come from, and where are you going," Kamini asks.

Finishing a mouthful of banana, Bahi explains, "Well, Kamini, where I come from is somewhat of a mystery, as is where I am going. I am searching for that truth of who I am." Bahi goes on to explain of how Bandar and he met and what brought them to the ancient forest.

Finishing the meal, they see the sky darken as they shelter themselves in a huddle under the dried-brown palm fronds. The coolness of night begins to settle in. Silently they lie, all in contemplation of their own lives, and with minds as full as bellies, they drift off to sleep. The subtle sleep of dreams quickly consumes them, easing their tired bodies from the busy day.

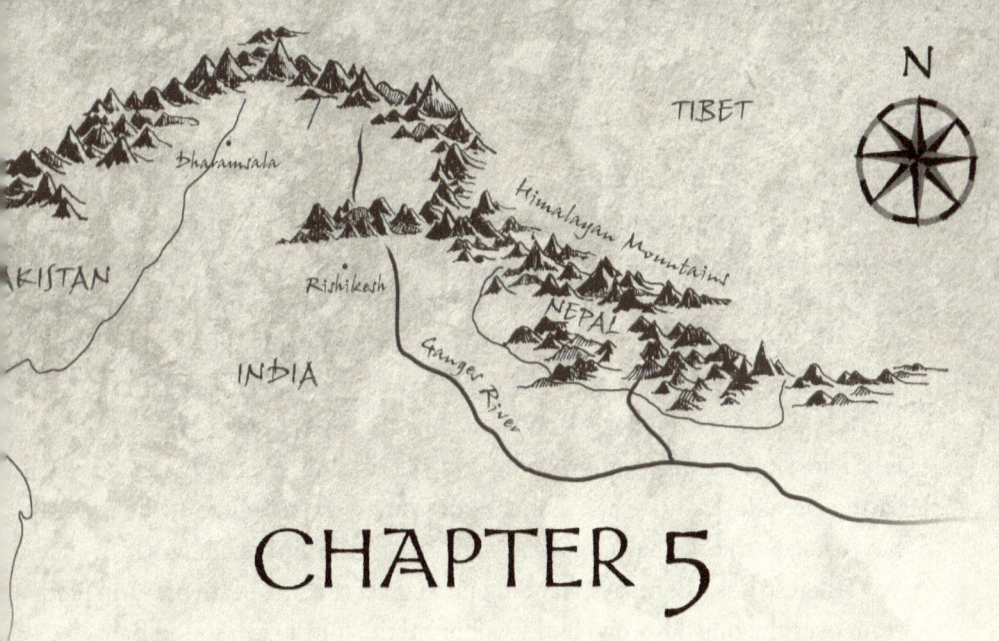

CHAPTER 5

"**B**ANDAR, BANDAR!" A voice softly pokes into the darkness of sleep. Opening his eyes, Bandar sees Kamala nudging him to wake up. He smiles. "Am I dreaming?" he asks playfully.

"Bandar, the clan worries about you," she says with urgency as Bandar sits up, bringing his mind to the present.

"The clan . . ." Bandar trails off, unconcerned.

"I worried about you," Kamala says lovingly, looking into his eyes.

Bahi begins to wake, slowly stretching up, pulling his knees to his chest, huddled in a sitting position and trying to contain his warmth. The sun has not yet risen, but light softly illumines the forest as Kamini makes her way to a fire-orange red marigold to feast upon its nectar.

"Today I will come back to the clan. I am showing Bahi the way to the trail that leads to the Baba," Bandar explains to Kamala.

"Who is Bahi?" she asks.

"Who indeed?" Bahi says with a chuckle.

"I named him Bahi, my *brother*," Bandar explains proudly as Kamini softly alights upon his head.

"Hello," she greets Kamala.

Kamala smiles back, "The path to the Baba is forbidden, Bandar," Kamala whispers.

Bahi listens in concern.

"Kavi has assured us he will be fine," Bandar says, noticing the concerned look on Bahi's face.

"I will come with you. I can fly above and see any danger ahead," Kamini offers. "and besides, I have heard much about this Baba, and I think he can help me."

"Help you, with what?" Bandar asks.

"I lost my family, my brothers and sisters—all gone. One day I was eating breakfast, and when I was done they were nowhere to be seen. I haven't seen them since. This was weeks ago," Kamini explains sadly.

"Then so it is," Bahi says, standing up to greet the first beam of warm light from over the hills. "Kamini and I will brave the forest path to the Baba."

"We should get moving so you can get an early start. One does not want to be on that path at dark," Bandar warns.

Gathering up, the four head out of the ancient forest, led by Bandar and Kamala. They pass great, rushing rivers and an array of beautiful foliage. They reach a large stone wall decorated with small, purple flowers that grow up its face.

"It's just over this hill," Bandar explains, pointing to a small path that fades into the incline of thick jungle.

Bahi begins to feel nervous, realizing that Bandar will soon leave him. They make their way up the narrow rocky trail, over a small hill. Reaching the summit, they come to another trail that descends into the darkness of the jungle. A wooden sign is posted on a tree. It points toward the trail. A large crow swoops down, its wide, black, silken wings lowering it to rest upon the sign.

"What does it say?" Bahi asks, noticing it's written in Hindi.

Bandar is busy looking up in a tree for food to give Kamini and Bahi for their journey.

"It's a warning," the crow says, staring down with solid -black beady eyes.

Bahi looks up. "A warning for what?" he asks nervously.

The crow turns his head toward the trail then back at Bahi, and from his sharp, black beak he speaks, "Better men than you have traversed this path and were never seen again. If you are smart, you will turn back now."

"I can't. I must see the Baba," Bahi says as Kamini floats higher to nervously look ahead on the trail.

"If the Baba wished to see you, he would come to you," the crow squawks.

Just then Kamala and Bandar descend a tree with some bananas and bean pods. Kamini soars down, landing on Bahi's shoulder.

"It doesn't look so bad, just trail," Kamini assures.

"Nothing is as it seems down there. Turn back now," the crow warns again.

"Don't listen to that old hag," Bandar says, brushing him off.

"You risk certain death, fools. I have warned you. You will never survive. If you step on that path I will be feasting upon your dead carcass come nightfall!"

Bandar pounces upon the sign, showing his teeth as the crow makes haste flying off.

"Nothing is as it seems, fools, turn back!" he warns as he squawks away into the forest.

Bahi is uneasy. "Do you think I will be OK?"

"You'll be fine. Just keep your wits about you," Kamala says.

"Yeah, don't worry about that old crow, he has nothing better to do than scare people," Bandar adds in an attempt to comfort.

"Well friends, this is goodbye then, huh?" Bahi says as Kamala hands him some bananas and bean pods.

"It's never goodbye," Kamala says with a smile.

Bandar jumps into Bahi's arms as he catches him with a startle and they laugh.

"Thank you, brother. One day I will return and repay your kindness," Bahi promises.

"Friends don't thank. We help without wanting back, brother."

Bahi feels a tear well up in his eye. His heart respects the brave compassion that Bandar has offered. Bandar bounces off of Bahi's chest and leaps upon the sign. Kamala pounces up to join him.

"Goodbye, friends," Bahi says, taking his first apprehensive step toward the trail. Walking further, with Kamini floating alongside, he is unable to see the opening of the trail through the thickness of the jungle. Already he misses Bandar.

"This isn't so bad. That crow's a kook," Kamini says, noting the air of peace offered by the trail.

"Not at all," Bahi concurs.

The sun splashes blessings upon the trail, which seems like any other they've been on. Feeling secure now, Bahi begins to whistle, quickening his pace so as to make good use of the daylight. Marching forward, they smile at the absurdity of fear they heard before entering the path.

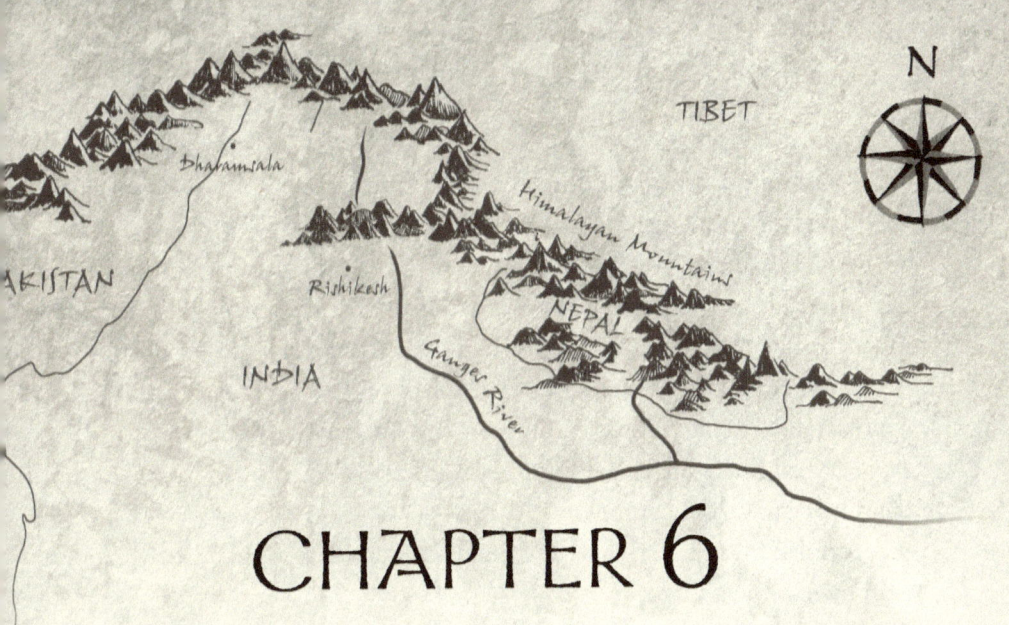

CHAPTER 6

S TOPPING BY A small stream that snakes along the trail, they realize they have been walking for at least a few hours. They drink some water and Bahi sits and eats some of the food given to them by Bandar and Kamala. Kamini rests on some flowers, sucking up nectar with her little straw of a mouth.

"So how did you loose your family?" Bahi inquires, bathing his face in the afternoon sun.

Kamini floats slowly to Bahi's leg, drenching herself in rays of sunshine.

"One day we were eating, just like we are now—my parents, me, and my twelve brothers and sisters—when all of a sudden a pack of monkeys came barreling through the jungle. We all scattered in the chaos. I was so startled that I flew and flew, and when I finally stopped I was in the ancient forest, where I stayed and feasted on the wonderful nectars in hopes that one day my family would find me. It's been quite some time, and my sorrow turned to depression. And that's when you came along."

"Why didn't you go looking for them? Why didn't you go back to your home?"

"We don't have a home. We roam the jungle and sleep where ever we are, under leaves, in the safe hallows of trees, wherever our rabble may be at dusk is where we make our home."

"That's a sad story, Kamini. I'm sure that the Baba can help you, I am told he is all knowing."

"I've heard only legends of him and never thought he really existed," Kamini says as she floats up, softly landing on Bahi's nose with a gentle kiss from her long tube mouth, "Thank you, friend, for this opportunity."

Bahi, cross-eyed as he looks at Kamini on the tip of his nose, smiles. "No, friend, thank you for coming on this journey with me."

Kamini floats off as Bahi quickly scratches the tickle on his nose from Kamini's small, delicate feet.

Kamini flies up high and descends back down to Bahi. "Looks like we still have a ways to go."

"Well, let us get on then," Bahi says, standing up with a smile.

Moving on once again, they come to a split in the path and Bahi stops to think, *Which way do we go?* Kamini flies up to have a look. As Bahi stands rubbing his chin in contemplation, he feels a pull on his ankle, and before he can look to see what it is, he is tugged down, falling hard onto his back. His breath thumps in his chest. A vine has wrapped around his leg and with force is slowly pulling him into a dense brush as he struggles to fight it.

"Help!" he cries out as he wrestles with the persistent vine.

Kamini flies down rapidly as Bahi grabs the end of the vine and manages to rip it off, but another vine has already taken hold of him, wrapping itself around his shoulder, and another around his other ankle.

"Bahi!" Kamini cries out, completely impotent.

Bahi struggles to keep his free foot in the gravel as the vines slowly begin to overpower him, pulling him into a thick tangle of vines and brush.

"Bahi, a rock!" Kamini yells out, landing on a large rock with a sharp edge just within Bahi's reach.

He quickly grabs it, loosening his footing, and with great force smashes the sharp side of the rock onto the vine, snapping it loose from his leg and sending the vine squealing back into the brush. The vine on his shoulder has tightened its grip and now pulls even stronger, overwhelming his strength. He notices a large, orange-and-yellow flower in the viney brush that opens like a mouth with sharp fangs. It salivates as he struggles. Bahi begins to panic, and with a forceful blow smashes down on the vine that straps his arm, not even penetrating the thick, jade attacker. Another vine catches his ankle again, and he feels overpowered as he draws closer to the salivating, monstrous flower that is almost as big as him. He can hear the flower open up its vines to reveal itself ready to consume him. In a snap of fear, he recalls memories of playing baseball, as he cocks his free arm back and hurls the rock at the monstrous flower, penetrating the hollow of the mouth as it quickly closes screeching with pain and releasing Bahi from its viney grasp.

Bahi, followed by Kamini, quickly scurries back and lunges to his feet, running away from the vines, panting as his heart races.

"What was that thing?" Kamini asks, still in a fright.

"I don't know," Bahi says, still shaken up, wiping dirty sweat from his beet-red face.

"You should have seen your face," Kamini says with a soft chuckle, lightening the mood.

Bahi laughs, shaking off anxious nerves, but still in fight mode. "Things are not what they seem," he says as he rubs his ankle, sore and slightly cut up from the vine.

Ahead, the path straightens. Bahi takes note of all the foliage. The trees seem to dance and the bushes to breathe as they proceed forward with caution. Walking for about an hour they come to a turn, where suddenly the path ends.

"What?" Kamini asks in confusion.

"We went the wrong way," Bahi says remembering the split in the path back by the monstrous viney flower. The panic of the moment took them down the wrong trail. Noticing their mistake, they walk back toward the split. As they near the man-eating vines again, Bahi gathers two large stones, and they proceed with vigilance, silently walking past the carnivorous plants that seem to rest like ordinary vines and bushes.

Proceeding down the other path and realizing they have lost a few hours of light, they begin to pick up the pace as Bandar's warning plays over in Bahi's mind: "One does not want to be on that path at dark."

The path grows narrow. Thick, dark-emerald foliage blocks out the sunlight. An uncommon silence settles over the jungle, unsettling both Bahi and Kamini as they precariously make their way about the path. The sun is low in the sky, and in only a few hours it will be dark. Nervous and uncertain, they move along.

"I am going to jog, so keep up," Bahi tells Kamini as he begins to jog in the hopes he can make up for lost time and reach the Baba before nightfall. The path finally opens up as he quickens his pace. After a while of running, he stops by a flowing stream to quench his thirst and rest for a minute. The sun has begun to make its descent behind the hills far off from the trail. Bahi kneels by the water's edge and washes his face as he drinks. Looking into the pool of water that gathers from the runoff of the stream, he notices his reflection. Looking deeply at his face, he thinks hard about who he is, and just then his reflection morphs into a demonic face surrounded by fire. He jumps back in fear. Slowly he looks back into the water, but only his reflection is there. He thinks he may have eaten a bad banana or something. He stands, noticing he feels fine. He crouches to grab a thick, fallen branch that lies in the running stream. The stick is about shoulder height, strong and pressurized from the many days of water flowing over it. He feels it will be wise to have a weapon in the dark. And jabbing it in the earth he notices it also serves as the perfect walking stick.

"Let's move," he beckons to Kamini, who is eating a piece of rotten fruit fallen from a tree.

Hungry and edgy, they move along the now dimly lit path as the remains of the sun fade away. As Bahi walks briskly, Kamini sets upon his shoulder. "Shhh, you hear that?" she asks in a whisper.

"No"

"Shhh, listen."

Bahi listens carefully and hears small beeping sounds that begin to grow louder. Almost instantly he feels something crawling up his pants as he jumps in fright, swatting at what feels to be a large bug in his pants. Looking up, he can see small gnome-like men coming out of the woods by the hundreds. Swiftly crawling up his body they knock his stick from his hand and skillfully trip him with vine ropes that they have wrapped around his walking legs. Thumping to the ground, he struggles to fight them off, swiping at some, sending them flying off into the woods. Like large ants working for a feast, they quickly take him and Kamini over and bind them in their viney rope. They call out in victorious unison, yelling up to the full moon, which has added much pale light to the otherwise dark path. Wearing an acorn shell helmet, one of the tiny men climbs up on Bahi's chest as he lies tightly bound, unable to move. His old, wrinkly face does not match his childlike exuberance as he tosses aside a hanging piece of his rat-fur jacket and stamps his staff into Bahi's chest, sending a piercing pain through his torso.

"Moo gai, gel thea," the gnome says as the others begin to frisk Bahi's pockets.

They pull the clothed berries from his pants, and he hears them call up, "Sip, don tik nee sleen."

Not understanding the language, he quickly realizes these little men are bandits, as they search him head to toe. Bringing the small cloth up to the man who seems to be in charge, still standing fast on Bahi's chest, they convene around it as two grasp their tiny hands on the cloth, pulling it open to reveal the berries.

"Seam nhat?" one of them says in wonder, as his beady eyes gleam in the moonlight.

"Seam nhat," the one in charge says in confirmation, plunging his tiny hand into one of the berries. All falls silent in anticipation.

As he pulls out a purple handful dripping with ripe berry, Bahi struggles and the others below tighten the rope.

"Sang heet!" the leader abruptly says, driving his stick into Bahi's chest once again.

Holding up the handful of berry that oozes from his hand he chants, "Sean nhat!"

All the others yelp and cheer, and with the raise of his small stick silence falls over them. Taking a large bite from the berry piece in hand he chews as the others watch in a hush. His eyes light up with delight, "Mmm." He stops mid-chew and grabs his throat, dropping his staff to Bahi's chest. The others look on with fear as he shakes and convulses and suddenly like a rocket is propelled upward, slamming into a tree and falling lifeless upon the dirt of nightfall. Several of the men run over to him yelling out, "Pwan Mei, Pwan Mei!"

Growing hostile, the rabble of banter sounds out, and Bahi can sense their anger and fears what they may now do. Kamini sits bound to the floor as a younger gnome taunts her with jabs of a stick. All the men jump up onto Bahi as he begins to struggle. Using all of his strength, he blows and spits at them, and trying to use his head as a weapon, jabs his chin as they come closer. Coming at him with small axes and spears, they seethe with anger. Fearing death, Bahi struggles to break free when a sudden gust of wind blows in oddly, knocking several of them to the ground. Bahi notices that the mango tree above him seems to be moving and lowering its branches. The tree swipes a large branch across Bahi's chest, knocking gnomes to the ground. Branches swoop down to pick up gnomes and fling them into the jungle. They begin to run in fear, retreating into the darkness of the forest. Bahi breaks free of the tangle of vine and liberates Kamini, who struggles on the ground, entangled in panic and vines. Picking up his staff, he swings it wildly in all directions as the gnomes scurry off crying out, "Meep meep meep!"

Realizing they're all gone, Bahi looks up at the tree as it appears to bow down slightly, revealing a face that seems to be smiling at him, through it's rough, barky trunk.

"Thank you," Bahi says, lowering his head in gratitude as Kamini floats up to his shoulder.

"The Baba awaits you," the tree says with a deep, commanding voice. The tree slowly creeks its branches down toward them, dangling a couple of ripe mangos. "Take, please," the tree offers with a comforting voice.

"How can I repay you for your help?" Bahi asks, plucking the mangos from the branch as the leaves shake like a splash of water, "Shhhh." The leaves ascend and the tree again stands upright.

"How can I repay you, tree," Bahi again asks.

The tree lets out a deep-bellowed laugh and says, "Remember me, remember the generosity of the forest, and you will more than pay me back. I ask for nothing but mutual deference." The face in the tree disappears into the trunk, and the tree stands still as if nothing has happened.

Kamini folds the berries back into the cloth, and Bahi puts them back into his pocket. "A talking tree! Now I've seen it all!" Kamini says.

Staring in wonder up at the tree, Bahi turns to place the two mangoes on the ground and brushes the leaves and debris that cover his cotton beige shirt and pants from the tussle. Sitting in the shelter and security of the great tree above him, he peels the mangoes in layers, revealing their glistening orange fruit, which Kamini sits upon, slurping the sugars. Bahi's mouth waters before he sinks his teeth into the juicy, sweet fruit, still warm from the day's sun. Gratitude overwhelms him as he stares up at the tree, enjoying its fruitful offering.

Finishing the mangoes, he stands up, cleaning his hands on his pants as he takes a deep breath, knowing there is more to journey in the darkness of the jungle. Not a thought even remotely entertains the idea of sleeping here.

"Shall we?" he asks.

"We shall," Kamini answers.

Patting the tree with appreciation, he picks up his staff and heads off down the dim, moonlit path. Approaching the darkness of the trail, forms move and breathe; vines are feared to be snakes; swaying trees could be ogres. As the knots in their throats tighten, they round a bend, where a hazy fog begins to seep in from the ground, illuminated by moonlight as it rises and thickens. Coming to an open area, Bahi notices stones skillfully set about the ground. "Is this a graveyard?" he whispers.

"What's a graveyard?" Kamini asks, with no answer from Bahi, who is on high alert, softly stepping through the dense mist, which rises up in a damp, eerie cloud.

The sounds of faint growling just ahead of them alert Bahi to grasp his staff extra tight. Palms sweating into the wood, he cautiously steps forward. The trees are old, and many look as though they have been dead for quite some time, hanging askew with naked branches randomly jutting out in ghastly directions. Kamini holds tight, digging her tiny, fearful, feet into Bahi's shoulder. The ground is moist to the step, and the moonlight casts ghoulish shadows that move as they walk. The fog thickens, undulating like campfire smoke, lighting up in the moonlight as it swiftly rolls by. The growling grows louder, and as they draw closer, transforms into snorts. Bahi can make out the form of a dog-like animal ahead as he takes a step backward, to avoid being noticed. A pack of six striped hyena tear apart the remains of a corpse they have excavated from a poorly dug grave. Standing stout and dog-like, with striped coats and long moustaches like cats, they gargle and growl as they tug of war the body, pulling it in either direction, their muscles flexing as they tear bone and flesh. Their forelegs are longer than the hind, affording them good leverage for ripping apart their prey. Bahi stares out at the beasts, noticing their dark manes, which run all the way down their necks and backs, ending at a their bushy, short, tails. Bahi's heart flutters in his chest. His entire body tenses, but he knows this is the only way to the Baba. Looking over at a large tree behind him, off to the left of the trail, he decides to crouch and stay there until they finish eating and go away. Slowly he back steps, and without notice steps on a stick, which echoes out a loud cracking sound.

The hyenas all look up in unison. Their dark eyes catch Bahi as he freezes in terror. Kamini floats up into the tree, "Bahi, climb up here!" she shouts.

Still frozen, the animals slowly advance, coming so close he can see their coarse, rough, coats dull gray, with black stripes that shadow vertically on their bodies. Their eyes look ravenous as their blunt teeth flex inside their bloodstained mouths. Bahi grips the staff, realizing he can't climb the tree and that to run would be futile. He envisions a scenario quickly through his survival mind: *I will aim a firm blow to the leader's head and keep on until I hit all six.* His legs tremble. Butterflies well up in his stomach as sweat beads his face. He remembers the berries and quickly rips them from his pocket, almost dropping them. He shoves them into his mouth, dissolving the sweet taste he thinks may be his last. One hyena is so ravenous as he crouches and moves slowly in for the kill, that his mouth stutters and drools as he growls. Kamini is speechless. She wants to yell and scream, but nothing will come out. Her little heart beats so fast that she thinks it will beat right out of her.

Eyes fixed on the predators, trembling hands firmly gripping his walking stick, he raises the wooden staff in front of himself like a samurai sword, ready to make the first blow. Adrenaline rushes his body. His eyes widen and instincts sharpen. The world falls away, and all he can see is six ravenous beasts ready for a fight. The leader lunges forward, attacking, and Bahi screams out, ready to strike. There is a sudden halt. Screeching forward in the dirt with their claws, all six crouch down, looking ready to retreat. Bahi feels the presence of something behind him, and as he turns to look, a giant cobra stands tall above his head. He falls to the ground in fear of such an enormous creature and scurries to huddle against the tree in a fetus position, holding his stick tight. The cobra jolts forward with a loud hiss directed at the hyenas. They swiftly turn and run. One tries to grab a final piece of the corpse, but the cobra lunges again with a commanding hiss, sending him crying and yelping closely behind the others, his bushy tail bobbing up and down as they retreat into the pitch-black trail ahead.

Retracting his hood-like head, his long, thick, scaly body gracefully slithers forward, making a U-turn back toward Bahi, who is still curled up in fear next to the large tree. The cobra's black head, decorated with yellow-speckled marks, shoots in front of Bahi, staring at him with beady eyes. The snake hisses as he moves his forked tongue in and out, rapidly sensing this clump of human terror. Bahi notices the snake's fearsome beauty. Refusing to look the snake in the eyes, he trembles, hoping it will just slither away. Never has he seen a cobra, or any snake of such grandeur. *I must be dreaming*, he thinks, as he tightly closes his eyes and opens them, in the hopes that he'd been in bed dreaming, far from this nightmare. Yet, there he is, still face to face with the enormous cobra, whose head is bigger than his.

Cobra's don't exist this large, he thinks, still trying to convince himself it's a dream. Kamini stands fast, digging her feet into the tree high above, careful not to even breathe too loudly in fear of being noticed.

"I am a sssservant of Lord Kavi," the snake softly hisses, head floating in the space before Bahi.

Remembering the berries, Bahi's heart calms. "Kavi, Kavi!" he screams in hysterics, followed by an uncontrollably nervous laugh.

"Yessss. Kavi. You have summoned me through he."

Bahi is still very intimidated by this enormous creature, but rises to his feet as the cobra swivels up to meet him eye to eye.

"What is your name?" Bahi asks, as Kamini floats down with apprehension.

"Muchalinda," he says with a grin.

"I am Bahi, and this is Kamini," he introduces, still a hint of trembling in his voice.

"Yesssssss, I know. How may I be of assistance?"

"Thank you so much. You have saved my life already."

Muchalinda gives a humble nod to his effortless feat. "This trail is full of dangers. Where do you wish to go?"

"I am on my way to see the Baba. Is it very far?"

Muchalinda bows his head, hearing the Baba's name. "Not too far. Come, I will protect and lead you there, for thisssss foresssssssssst is no place for sssssssssuch a delicate sssssssssssspeciessssssssss," he hisses melodramatically, tongue slithering in and out smelling Bahi.

"Thank you, Muchalinda. I am forever in your debt."

"I sssssssssserve Lord Kavi. The debt is all mine. Come," Muchalinda beckons as he slithers his smooth scaly body next to Bahi, who wonders at the immensity of such a snake, thinking he must be some sort of illusion, as he pokes Muchalinda softly.

"Zookeepers would have a field day," he thinks.

"Get on, hisss."

"On you?" Kamini asks, seeming concerned.

"Yesss, pleassssse."

Kamini sits upon Bahi's head as he mounts Muchalinda and grasps his smooth, scaly body. He has never felt an animal such as Muchalinda. The skin is like some sort of high-tech material, as each scale shifts in perfect unison with every movement. Feeling they're secure upon his body, Muchalinda swiftly slithers about the jungle floor along the trail. Bahi smiles like a child on a roller coaster as the cool night breeze whips through his hair, prompting Kamini to strengthen her grip.

The jungle is dark, and at this quick pace not much can be seen. Bahi holds tight, wrapping his thighs and arms around Muchalinda, his chest firmly pressed upon the scales. Blessed with night vision, Muchalinda smoothly sails through the darkness.

"Wooo, hooo!" Bahi yells out, with one hand shaking a fist in the air. Their speed is swift, smooth, and focused, and within thirty minutes they come to a halt.

The sun begins to rise as Muchalinda wraps his head back toward Bahi and Kamini. "Here you can walk. It's very clossssssssse," he hisses, pointing his head toward the opening of what looks like the end of the trail.

Bahi dismounts, hair puffed and straggled from the ride's winds, "Thank you again for our safety, Muchalinda."

Closing his solid, black, beady eyes, he bows his head before them. The yellow speckles of his head reflect the morning sun, which glows soft upon them now as the night fog slowly lifts, burning into the air. "It's an honor to sssserve," Muchalinda says before swiftly turning his body in the other direction and cutting through the jungle floor like smooth butter. In a flash he is gone, leaving Bahi and Kamini standing in the silence of morning break.

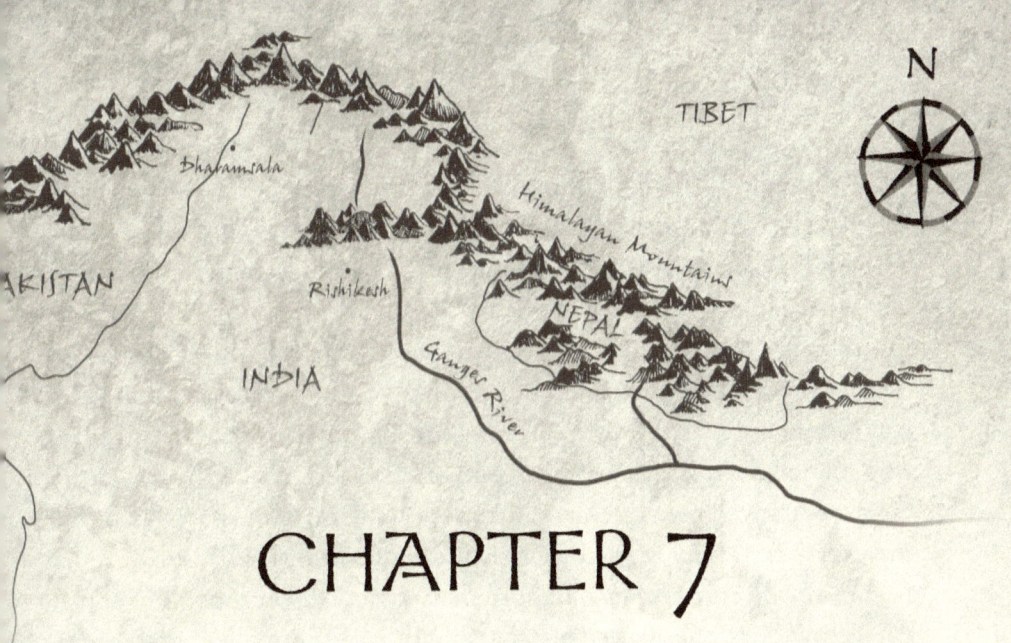

CHAPTER 7

D UST DANCES WITH small bugs in the thick of morning, which seems to rise up toward the sun that shines down softly upon the jungle. Looking forward, Bahi notices a white-stone archway that stands out among the darker stones, which rise up tall around it to create a wall that juts off into the jungle in either direction. The fragrances of sweet flowers permeate the air, and colorful berries dot the exotic foliage that lead to the stone entryway. Birds sing to the morning sun, and a peaceful air gently sifts through, carrying the scent of lavender, relaxing all in its path. Making his way to the entry, Bahi wonders at the beauty of precision in each stone that seems to be perfectly cut out to fit into the jungle that grows harmoniously around it. Noticing a smooth, silken-black bird with a boxed-orange tail, his gaze fixes on her as she pops her tail up and down, almost beckoning him into the entryway. The bird looks back and flies forward out of sight as Bahi sticks his head into the entryway, which leads into a large cavern.

"Hello," he calls out as his voice echoes through the seemingly endless cave.

"Should we go inside?" he rhetorically asks, already inwardly resolved to do so.

"I suppose we should," she says watching as Bahi steps in.

The cave is plain, softly lit by sun that reflects beautiful, colored crystals inlaid in the grayish cave walls.

"Hello, Baba?" Bahi calls out, and as they go deeper in, the entryway closes off behind them as a light shines down from an opening in the ceiling.

"Sit," a voice calls out as a fire magically ignites a single, thick log, lying in a small clay cylinder molded to the floor.

Bahi sits close to the fire to warm himself from the chill of morning. *I can't see anyone*, he thinks as he squints to search the small area around him.

"Sometimes what we see isn't necessarily what is there," the voice says, as a man materializes across from him on the other side of the fire, sitting in a meditative pose. The man looks very modern, with short, black hair, wearing jeans and a white, collared, buttondown shirt.

Surely this isn't the Baba, Bahi thinks, expecting someone different.

"How does one believe a Baba should look?" the man asks, reading Bahi's thoughts, and in an instant he morphs into Bahi's expectation of a wise-looking Baba, complete with a full grayish beard, long black hair, dark Indian skin, and a gaze of green eyes that set upon an infectious smile evoking peace with a single look. "Is this better?"

"Uh, yes, I mean no, I don't know," Bahi says dumbfounded, nervous and now feeling a bit silly to be judging who is obviously a powerful being in front of him.

"Be aware what your mind sees, for what we perceive as real is mere illusion. The wise take many forms, and to discount one on looks is to overlook the sweet nectar life has to offer. All are your teachers. The truth is one, although it takes many forms." Smiling, the Baba looks directly into Bahi's eyes.

"Yes, Baba, I understand," Bahi says, learning already a great deal in the first few minutes of their meeting.

"Say, child—What brings you through certain danger to arrive at my doorstep?"

"Baba, I have forgotten who I am, and even that which they tell me I am I do not relate."

"Mmm," the Baba listens and thinks deeply.

Not hearing a response, Bahi insecurely speaks again. "I have this paper but don't remember where I got it. It's all I have. I somehow hit my head rather hard and passed out, and when I woke up I had nothing but this paper and a pair of light shorts." Standing, he hands the paper to the Baba, who looks at it in silence.

"Hmmm," he thinks for a moment. "This is the Om, the sound of creation. Out of the ethers comes existence, beginningless," the Baba explains.

A bit cosmic, huh? Doesn't really answer my question, Bahi thinks in confusion.

The Baba stands, "Come, we will have breakfast. You must be famished after your long journey."

Bahi and Kamini smile in unison, noticing the aroma of food, which invites their rumbling stomachs from afar. Following the Baba to the back of the cave, he exits through a small door into the sunlight. Entering a beautiful garden area, a small table sits decorated with breads freshly steaming, fruits, juices, curds, and sweets—a feast fit for kings. Bahi's eyes widen and mouth waters as the Baba calmly points him to the feast before them. Kamini gently bounces from flower to flower along a smooth, washed-out, stone wall that encloses them. One flower is more delicious than the next. Bahi dips a buttered roll into some banana-honey porridge and washes it down with fresh papaya juice. He hasn't had a proper meal in days. Finishing the meal, he wishes he had two stomachs to fit more of the delicious food. The Baba sits quietly gazing and sipping tea from a small porcelain cup, not a morsel of food has he eaten.

"Kamini also wishes to ask you something," Bahi says, with a full and happy belly. "She has lost her family and thought you may be able to help."

The Baba's smile puts their minds at ease and attracts Kamini to land upon his hand. He drinks in her beautiful, silky-black wings, admiring the iridescent blue circles, which surround dark purple dots, one on each wing.

"Come, we'll walk," the Baba says, rising up and exiting the garden through a small back entrance that leads into the jungle. The Baba walks slowly, his every step seemingly purposeful as his white linen cloth gently dances with every movement. Barefoot, he places each step down in gratitude and mindfulness, "So you wish to know who you are? This question man has sought since beginningless time. You tell me you have amnesia, and I say even if I tell you who you were, still your burning desire would seek the truth you're after. All things are beginningless and never die."

"But things die, surely," Bahi says.

"You are correct, and every moment this is happening, yet there is the truth, which is endless and beginningless. We like to believe we have a creation, a beginning, but if you check, it's all beginningless, all formless, always changing. There is no part of you that is not Kamini and no part of Kamini that is not you."

Again, quite cosmic, Bahi thinks, trying to grasp the Baba's enigmatic speech.

The Baba looks at him directly in the eyes, "and the cosmos follows the same law," he says, sternly humbling Bahi.

They stop near a large spiderweb. Kamini has fallen behind as the allure of a beautiful feast of flowers has slowed her pace. A large, bluish spider with two even yellow lines on her back is busy weaving her web.

"Take this web. Each part connects to the other, and what looks random is all created by the spider. She is responsible for every piece, and each subsequent piece arises out of the one before it."

Bahi watches intently as the spider, weaving intricate patterns together, turns out a silky web. "This is like our existence, each connection. The very reason she is seen as a spider is due to past actions. Surely she is a spider as much as you are a human. There is order in this web of life, and we create it. We are stuck in this web of life, and we have woven, by our own actions, each fiber of it. I tell you this: we can free ourselves from this web, and when we do we will realize their never was a web. We spin our web with our actions. When we harm others, when we lust and crave and desire, we spin thick the web of desire and entangle ourselves in a web that holds us back from the very things we thought we were after. To enjoy the fruits of life we must be aware of this web we are weaving."

Just then Kamini comes flying in, excited, unmindfully snagging herself right into the spiders web, high up out of Bahi's reach.

"Oh, no! Help!" Kamini pleads as she struggles to break free, only further entangling herself.

"Help her!" Bahi calls out as the spider runs toward her in a flash to inject her poison, rendering Kamini paralyzed. Eyes glazed over, she lies lifeless upon the web.

"You must do something!" Bahi pleads, trying unsuccessfully to scale the tree.

"This is the fate Kamini has created. It's all in order," the Baba says, standing in calm reverence.

"Nooooo, we must!"

The spider has wrapped Kamini in a thick, cottony web of death. Tears fall down Bahi's cheeks as his feet rip bark from the tree in his last attempt to get at the web up the tree.

"We have to help each other, this I am sure of. Please, Baba, please do something."

"Yes, we must, and as we notice the suffering and ignorance of us all, our compassion and wish to help every sentient being free itself from the web that consumes us all gives us the power to release ourselves. Only then will we have the power to release all others."

"You are all-powerful, surely you can save her!"

"Her fate is inevitable. Even if I were to save her, she would die sometime. And this death she has created by her past actions. This may seem harsh, but it's a harsh web we weave. And I tell you this: who you know as Kamini can never die, just as the 'Who am I?' you seek is beginningless and endless, always changing form, dying every second, being reborn into the web thicker and thicker."

"How do I release myself from the web? How do I save Kamini?!" Bahi asks in desperation. "Please, teach me!"

"Bahi, calm your mind," the Baba says with a hypnotic gaze, dropping Bahi's mind into a calm state. "Look up at this spider. Can you see her young?"

Bahi squints up past the now cotton outline of Kamini and sees tiny spots of spiders moving around, "Yes, I see them."

"These spiders are all in the same web. They too need to eat and they too suffer day in and day out trying to live. The answer does not lie in gaining freedom for ourselves and the ones that only relate to this sense of *I*. It is only found when we release that sense of *I* and truly want to gain freedom from this web in order to help all beings, Kamini as well as the spiders."

"Can you teach me how, Baba?"

"I know of a place you will find all the answers you seek, a place where Kamini still flies. You wish to answer your question and save Kamini? Then it is there you will achieve this."

"Please tell me Baba. Oh, I can't look!" Bahi says, turning his head from the web where the spider now begins to drain Kamini's blood.

"Come, Bahi," the Baba says, walking away towards the garden.

"No, I can't. Kamini!"

"Let her go, Bahi. Only then can you truly free her. Let it go, move on, we all die, this body will wither away and decay, and one day change form and melt into the Earth. I assure you that the *I* you seek does not exist, and the truth of your existence can never die."

Entering back into the garden, Bahi wipes the tears from his cheeks. "Please, Baba, I can't take the pain all around me any longer. You must teach me the way."

"I can teach you much, but you must lead yourself out. Only you can do this. High up in the mountains of yourself, walk North and find Shambhala. There you will find the answers you seek."

The Baba puts his arm around Bahi, comforting his pain. "Bahi, you will find the answers you seek there, I promise. Try to remember there is a cycle of life. We chose our tales in this web we weave, distracting ourselves every day, pretending we will not suffer the same fate as Kamini. And this I tell you: Kamini, will soon be born again into this web of life, and the suffering will still be there. Go, Bahi, liberate yourself and help your friend. Don't let the pain overtake you. All is impermanent and in perfect rapture. You choose how you want to experience it all."

Bahi's head spins, exhausted from no sleep and the morning's drama.

"It's OK to feel sad, cry, be who you are. If you are happy, smile. If you are sad, cry. This is the beauty of life. Allow yourself to feel it," the Baba gently says to Bahi, who is holding back his tears. "Please lie, sleep, and in the morning you will leave when you are refreshed."

Bahi lies on soft white pillows that seemed to manifest at his feet. Lying in the sun, he rests all day, drifting in and out of sleep.

Evening has come and the Baba has prepared some rice and *dhal* for them, which they eat in the silence of Bahi's uncertainty. After the meal, the Baba speaks, "I wish to teach you something for your journey. It will bring protection in the face of danger." The Baba closes his eyes and opens his mouth, letting out a beautiful mantra. "*Om namah narayanaya*," he sings over and again. The vibration consumes everything as Bahi's eyes close and he begins to sing in unison, "*Om namah narayanaya, om namah narayanaya*." He becomes the vibration as all worries, all fears, all pains cease to exist. And when they stop, he opens his eyes, pervaded by peace.

"Say this with a pure heart in the face of certain danger, and safety will guide you."

"Thank you, Baba," Bahi says, lowering his head in reverence, keeping the catchy mantra in his mind.

"You sleep now, for tomorrow you begin a long journey."

"Yes, Baba," Bahi says with respect as he lies on the soft, white blankets that again seemed to have just appeared next to him.

"Goodnight. Tonight you die to be reborn in the morning, like every second that exists."

"Die?" Bahi says, sitting up in nervous excitement.

"Yes, Bahi, every second we die and are reborn. This is how it all works. If not, things would be fixed, like a photo. If not, I wouldn't even be able to complete this sentence, for the next word to be uttered, the one before it, must die, bringing birth to the next. Likewise as you fall deep into sleep you regenerate with the peace of death to be reborn fresh in the morning, have an auspicious night, young one," the Baba says as he makes his way into the cave. Bahi lies staring up at the stars that pour down upon him. He misses Kamini and Bandar, and thinking about the day, he begins to drift off to sleep. The smell of incense guides him deeper, and the mantra, *om namah narayanaya* sooths the pains that cut his heart, as the deep bliss of slumber washes over him. The world he thinks he knows melts away, his body still, like a corpse, dies into the night.

CHAPTER 8

THE SUN WASHES a warm greeting upon Bahi's face as he slowly opens his eyes to see Kamini floating about flowers, *Was it all a dream?* he thinks, rubbing his eyes and realizing it's just a butterfly that looks similar.

"Yes, it's all a dream, Bahi," the Baba says, again reading his thoughts as he sits meditatively behind him.

"So then, none of this exists, Baba?" Bahi asks, stretching up to face the Baba.

The Baba laughs, "Sure it exists. You see that butter dish?" The Baba points to the table set with yet again another feast.

"Yes, I see it," Bahi confirms, noticing the elaborately carved wooden dish.

"Well, we look at that collection of parts and we say *butter dish* because to say pass me the *round circle brown thing with the carvings on it* would be absurd in our conventional world, wouldn't it?" Bahi nods in silent agreement. "So we label things, and then we are convinced that they exist from their own side, just like you."

"But I do exist. Look, here I am," Bahi says playfully lifting his left arm up with his right hand and dropping it down.

"Yes, Bahi sits there, and I see a collection of parts and say *Bahi*, but the way my mind sees Bahi is different than how Bahi actually exists."

"I don't follow, Baba."

"Come. Sit and eat. I will explain."

Bahi sits before the great breakfast feast. A large piece of delicious chocolate cake overflows with dark icing on a plate in front of him.

"Now take this cake for example. Your eye sees the colors and forms and sends that signal to your memory storage, and all your past experiences of cake come up and says *chocolate cake*, and you assume to know how it's going to taste because of the past experiences. Yet, in reality it may taste completely different. Perhaps the baker left out the sugar. What a different experience, indeed, huh?" Bahi studies the cake, hoping the baker did not leave out the sugar. "We even go so far as to think that this cake will bring us happiness."

Bahi begins to grab at it, and it disappears, leaving a grimace on his face as he looks up to the Baba in surprise.

"But take the cake away and you suffer, because you attach to it as a source of lasting fulfillment and happiness. Grasping for something that does not exist from its own side. Now the level of suffering is different than in other scenarios, but it's still there."

The cake reappears in front of Bahi. "Now, sure this cake exists, but the attachment and craving that you blindly follow thinking this cake will bring you happiness is an illusion. For you may eat it and feel temporarily elated, but keep stuffing your face with it, and soon you will feel sick, and it will become a source of pain and suffering. So I ask you: is the cake a source of happiness or is that feeling coming from within?"

"I like cake," Bahi says, missing the point.

"This alone proves this logic. I do not like chocolate cake, so when I see it, it creates an aversion in my mind and I think, 'yuk', but this is not how it exists. So who is right? You, who thinks it's a source of pleasure and happiness, or me, who thinks it's a source of disgust and pain?"

"Uhm, we are both right?" Bahi concludes.

"We are both wrong," the Baba goes on. "This cake is just a cake, and the attachments we place on this cake are lies, stories our minds have created, great fantasies of how we believe this cake to exist. And we are doing this with everyone and everything."

Bahi thinks deeply now as the Baba goes on, "We think this cake inherently exists. We think it's *cake*, a fixed thing, but, Bahi—point to the cake for me."

Bahi smirks and points, dipping his finger into the rich chocolate icing.

"So is it the icing? If I put icing on a plate and say, 'Here's your cake,' would you agree?"

"No, Baba, I wouldn't. That would be silly," Bahi says before sticking his iced finger in his mouth. "Mmm, didn't leave out the sugar," he says in delight as the Baba goes on.

"If I put the top, breaded layer on the plate and say 'Here's the cake,' it would be quite different from this, wouldn't it?" Bahi nods in agreement. "So we see a collection of parts: we see the top layer, bottom layer, and the icing, and we call it *cake* and assume to know everything about it. But if the cake were fixed, then it would always be here, but it is only here depending on causes and conditions."

"How do you mean?" Bahi asks, now fully engaged.

"This cake was made by my servants, who spent all morning making the batter, making the icing, both of which contain numerous ingredients that have come from other places, traveled from faroff places to reach here in vehicles that probably killed millions of bugs and sentient beings, just like Kamini, in their travels. Let's look at just the batter, the grains, the sugar. We can trace them back. They once grew in a field that was cared for by a farmer, gaining nutrients from the sun, watered by the rains, fed by the soil that consists of countless living organisms that decayed to create its nutrients, and all of them can be traced back like this as well. Before it was growing, it was a seed, and that seed came from another plant, and so on and so on, beginningless, one thing connected to the next in an endless cycle of interconnection. All things depend on other things to exist. So the causes and conditions for this cake to sit before you are endless. And in fact, if you check, this cake can be linked to everything. It can all be traced back, and you will never find a beginning, like you, Bahi. You think you were created by your parents, but trace it back starting with you now, your body is a compilation of all the massive amounts of food you have eaten in this lifetime thus far, and as we know all that food can be traced back like an infinite web too. At one time you came from your parents, fed by the food your mother ate, composed of the DNA of your father and mother, who came from their father and mother and so on and so forth. It's all interdependent, everything depends on everything else to exist, nothing is separate from this, and so all you are is due to the kindness of others. Your language, your genetics, your name, all given to you by others. Those who made your food that composes your body, the bugs and animals that died for it to come to your plate, and so on. And so I ask: 'Who is Bahi?'"

Bahi sits trying to make sense of it all, "I, I am just a collection of things due to the kindness of others?"

"Well that's a start, young one. Take it slow. This is the opposite of what your modern world beats into you every day: the separate self that we perceive. We're led to believe that the self is not dependant on any-thing to exist, and so we breed depression, loneliness, and a slew of other sufferings, feeling separate from our happiness. You are fed these lies day in and day out, and what's more is you believe them. Now eat up and be grateful for all the sentient beings that brought this meal to you. All the beings that died when the grain was picked, and so on. So, to repay the kindness of all sentient beings, we will enjoy this meal, because there is nothing wrong with enjoyment or pleasures. It's the lie that it will bring us lasting happiness, that it's the source of our happiness, when in fact the source is within you. So enjoy each moment, not attaching to it, be-cause attachment is illogical and will bring suffering and separation and will cause us to worry when it will be gone. And when it is gone we will fret, so unattach and just enjoy each blissful moment in being completely present. Renounce the past and the future. Renounce, meaning to relax in the present and truly enjoy, truly experience pleasures. What we call pleasure in our world is mere attachment and fear: mind out of the pres-ent moment. This is not pleasure. Those who unattach truly enjoy the pleasures of life. Bliss is now."

Bahi focuses his mind in the present moment, and colors seem deeper, the air smells sweeter as he picks up the piece of moist cake, opening his mouth—when in a flash it disappears, "Be willing to give it all away without any sense of loss, and know it is not the answer you seek. It's all impermanent, and in perfect rapture. The answers to your happiness and peace are not external."

Bahi sits frustrated and hungry. The Baba lets out a deep belly laugh as the cake reappears. "And so all beings can enjoy such pleasures, let us feast to repay the kindness of others. Renunciation is to stop constantly searching and seeking objects and things outside of ourselves as a source of happiness, because we have been doing this for eons and still haven't found the answers to lasting peace there—have we?"

Bahi nods his head "no," content with the piece of cake again in front of him. The Baba continues, "So we abide in the bliss in this moment, enjoy, savor, and be OK when it's gone, be present, young Bahi."

Poking the cake to make sure it's real, he quickly bites it. The sensation of pleasure and deliciousness runs down his tongue. A smile washes over his face as the Baba sips his tea and watches him devour the cake.

"I can tell you this for a hundred years, but you must experience it in order to make it true, and at Shambhala you shall experience this and more," the Baba explains.

"Please, Baba, do you have a map or directions to follow?"

"Every day close your eyes and try to find the *I* you are so concerned about. Try to locate the body first. Ask yourself: Am I the hands? Am I the head? If there were just a head here, could I call this *Bahi*? Am I my legs? If only my legs were here, could I call this *Bahi*? Picture yourself cutting off all your parts in search for your *I*. Then notice the pile of parts, and blood, and bone, and still none of these is Bahi. Then contemplate the following question: Am I my mind? Well, the mind is said to have six consciousnesses, so if you were this, then there would be six of you. So you conclude you are not the mind either. So you have found an entire collection of parts now and none of them is Bahi. So you can't put together a bunch of parts that is not Bahi and get Bahi. That is not logical. That's like having ten horses and putting them together to get a sheep. Illogical. Ten things that are not sheep can't become a sheep. This is a bit boggling at first," the Baba says, watching as Bahi's mind struggles to keep up. "Go slow and remember the interconnection of all things."

Bahi looks tense as he follows. The Baba goes on. "This will bring you to find there is no *I*. Like the cake, it's there. Bahi definitely exists, but just not the way you perceive Bahi to exist. This is liberation. The self you grasp at, the separate, fixed self that suffers in seperation from it's happiness, does not exist. So practice in this way. And when you get to that space, that space of truth, the space of limitless possibilites, stay there in that empty space that was once occupied by delusions of a fixed self. In this space, you will see Shambhala. You will gain the map and be led to this land of pure bliss where all your questions will be fulfilled.

Bahi stops in mid-chew. "Soooo, OK then, but I do exist, right?"

The Baba again laughs. "Yes, Bahi, you exist conventionally, just not the way you or others perceive you too. When we see others, we have all these notions of how they exist or how they should exist, like when you met me at first and I didn't fit your mold of a Baba. Bahi, this is the surest way to Shambhala. Wise masters have secreted away maps. Yet this technique will be sure to guide you there. The map will be clear to your mind, I promise."

"What if it isn't?" Bahi asks, uncertain.

"Stop relating to your doubts and fears. You are not your doubts and fears. You are a limitless, unbounded being. Creating a mere map of Shambhala is at the very least of your vast abilities. Practice this meditative technique and trust me. I would not lead you astray. When you realize you are not a limited, fixed self, that fixed *I* you always relate to, you realize you are constantly changing—limitless with limitless ability. So don't limit yourself with your thoughts. You are not your thoughts. Now come, the morning grows late and the journey is long."

The Baba stands up and walks toward a beautiful, flowered bush that grows out of a soft fountain running water into a koi pond with purple and white lotuses. Bahi walks comfortably over to him and observes the beauty. The Baba gently extends his hand. "Take this grain of rice, for when food is scarce, this will sustain you." "I don't think a grain of rice will sustain my hunger," Bahi says laughing, knowing his appetite.

"The only reason you have even a morsel of food, a grain of rice, is because you have been generous and have given in the past. Action begets action. Now trust when you smash this upon a surface. A great feast will lie before you. And this, Bahi, is your doing, for what we do now we create later, and what we have now we have created from the past. And you, my friend, have been very generous in the past, I assure you."

"If you know my past, please tell me who I am!" Bahi pleads.

"I am talking about the lives before this one. You have been in this web for a long time, struggling in different forms, and now you struggle as Bahi in this life. As for who you are, only you can discover this. And when you reach Shambhala, all of your questions will be fulfilled, I assure you. Be like this lotus," the Baba points out a white lotus growing from the small pond. "This lotus needs mud to grow. You can not plant it on the concrete. Yet, this lotus rises up out of the mud to shine its beauty upon the world. The mud is much like our suffering or struggle. Suffering plays an important role in bringing about your compassion and understanding, but we can't stay in the mud, we must rise up and extend our beauty to the world. So rise up, young Bahi, and go now. Shambhala awaits you."

"Thank you, Baba, I cannot. . ."

"Shhh. . ." the Baba interjects. "We speak many words, but words are empty. Actions, my friend, actions of generosity, compassion, and so forth . . . one action of kindness is worth a million words. Go now and remember this, compassionate one."

Silently Bahi walks toward the back exit way, directed by the Baba. As he moves further away, he can hear the Baba call out, "Remember, the Bahi you perceive to exist does not exist the way you believe it to."

Entering the jungle, Bahi's mind swirls, trying to grasp the lessons of the Baba. Realizing he does not have a clue where to start his journey, he turns back to ask, but the Baba is gone. The cave and garden are all gone. All that is there is the vast jungle, overgrown as if there were no cave, no garden, no Baba. His heart thumps as a bolt of anxiety sinks into his stomach.

"Go North, follow the path North, follow your heart, contemplate existence, and you will find your way to Shambhala. When all else fails, stay northward toward the high mountains," the Baba's words echo softly in his mind.

Bahi stops and notices three trails ahead, one lit up by the rising sun. *This must be East.* Bahi remembers. *The sun rises in the east.*

Looking left, Bahi sees there is another trail. He thinks, *If this is East, then this trail must lead North.* And with confidence he starts toward the northward trail. His sandals rustle the rocky path below his feet as the sun warms his body from the East. Placing the rice grain deep down into his right pocket, he notices butterflies meandering about the jungle and smiles remembering Kamini. He vows inwardly to find Shambhala for Kamini, for Bandar, and for all the beings of this Earth—for liberation.

He steps onto the dusty path and breathes in the morning air. Contemplating the words of the Baba, he thinks about his body as he looks at the trees that line his path. *I am here, they are there, surely this is I*, he thinks.

The path is straight, with a slight, persistent, incline that goes on a distance beyond sight. Walking upward for quite some time, he sits to rest for a moment. Taking off his sandals, he rubs his feet. It has been awhile since his breakfast, and his stomach feels empty. Remembering the rice given by the Baba, he thinks it's best if he waits until dusk. This way he can save a bit for morning. He hears the melody of soft, running water not too far off the trail. He puts his sandals back on and follows the soothing sounds of flowing water. His hair is dry and straw like from the arid mountain air. His mouth feels like the dust he kicks up as he nears the water. Squatting down, he scoops up two handfuls of water and slurps them into his mouth as the rest runs down his chest, wetting his shirt and pants. The water in the stream rambles South over a chorus of brownish rock lit by high-noon sun. Smelling his body, he takes off his clothes and bathes in the shallows. The cold stream invigorates him as the sun shines down upon him. Sitting naked in the middle of the stream, face warmed in the sun, he washes his body. He wets his hair, and several strands break off into his hands from the dryness that has been inflicted on them. Bahi next dips his face into the cool stream and gulps the refreshing water before standing up. As the water flows through his legs, he looks around at the trees and bushes that line the stream. A sense of freedom comes over him as he walks off to the edge of the streambed, where he sits, drying in the sun and gentle breeze before putting on his clothes and proceeding back to the path. Walking again for several hours, he thankfully thinks of how this path is seemingly less dangerous and murky than the one leading to the Baba.

Monkeys scurry past overhead, dropping remnants of sticks that fall down onto Bahi's head. He realizes the sun will soon set and wonders where he might find shelter from the night. Sitting upon an opening in the trail, a tree hangs down, spreading its lanky, straight branches like an umbrella over Bahi. He reaches deep into his pocket and pulls out the small brown grain of rice, and looks at it. He wonders how this small grain will become food. This leads him to ponder all the unfathomable things he has witnessed on his journey so far. He laughs and smashes the grain on a rock with his hand. Lifting up his palm, he sees the grain is still there: just a single grain of brown rice on a slate rock. He stares befuddled. *Perhaps this is a lesson in itself from the Baba*, he thinks, hoping he is wrong. The grain begins to slowly wiggle on the rock, and with a pop bursts into the air, dropping down a vast feast before his astounded eyes: rolls; ripe fruits; hot, steaming tea; and freshly cooked noodles. Bahi laughs hysterically, dancing foolishly around the food in astonishment. Sitting back down in disbelief at this grand feast set before him on a cloth that has also manifested before his eyes, he pokes a roll to see if it's real. Again he laughs as he stares into the noodles that steam from a blue, ceramic bowl. Grabbing a piece of bread, he breaks it, noticing its warmth, as if it has just been baked. *How is this possible?* he thinks as he stuffs his face. A small fly lands on a piece of noodle, which has precariously fallen from his grasp. Bahi smiles to have a guest for dinner. "Hello, little friend," he says, bending down closer to the fly. The fly stagers back and forth in a nervous dance, checking out Bahi, not sure if he should fly away or stay for the feast he has discovered.

"Buzzzzz hello," the fly answers back, his tiny voice barely discernable.

Bahi laughs again, realizing that this is far more fantastic than any dream he has had. "Please, little fly friend. Help yourself to any of this."

Buzzing up to Bahi's shoulder, the fly sets down. "Bzzz, thanks, bzzz. You are kind." The fly buzzes back down to sit on the noodles.

Finishing up, Bahi takes the uneaten food, namely a few rolls and un-peeled fruits—apples, mangoes, and bananas—and wraps them up in the cloth, tightly bundled. Bahi smiles at the fly, who walks almost frantically in sporadic patterns, as flies do.

"What is your name?" Bahi asks.

The fly zips up to his arm as Bahi lifts it to his face to talk closely, "I don't know what this meanzzzz," the fly says.

"What do they call you?" Bahi asks.

"I do not know."

"I am Bahi. They call me Bahi, and you have no name. I know what that's like."

"No name, sorry."

Bahi chuckles, "That's OK, a name is not important."

Buzzing, the fly asks, "What is it you call me?"

"I call you *fly*."

The fly stops for a second from it's almost constant movement, and looking up with his big red eyes sees Bahi in a pattern of many faces. "Bzzz. I am Fly."

"Well, hello, Fly," Bahi chuckles. "Looks like it may be dark soon. Where can I sleep tonight, Fly?" he asks, not expecting to get an intelligent answer.

"Bzzzz yes. Follow, please." Fly bounces off of Bahi as Bahi quickly stands, grabbing the cloth of food.

Proceeding through some bushes, he steps quickly to keep up with Fly, who barrels through the unbeaten path of the jungle. Losing him from his sight every so often, Bahi stops to look as Fly buzzes back into his sight. "Come, there." Fly buzzes quickly over to a small rock wall with a carved-out entryway.

Bahi pokes his head inside, "It's not the comforts of the Baba's, but it will be safer than out there," he thinks. "Thank you, Fly," he says as he ducks into the small opening.

The cave is dark and cool. As he settles on the cold, ground, he wonders if he will be able to sleep. Sitting in silence, as Fly buzzes around the cave, he takes a few deep breaths. "So, Fly, do you have family?"

"No family, no name, now we are friends, yes?" Fly questions back.

"Yes, now we are friends," Bahi says, settling into the cave.

After a few moments in the small cave space he steps out to observe his surroundings. He listens as the jungle begins to settle in for the night and is glad he has some shelter from the darkness. The sun is now completely gone and he retreats into the cave, noticing Fly is gone. Lying on his back, he reflects on the day, and closing his eyes, he tries to find his *I* as the Baba had instructed. *Am I my hands?* he thinks. *Well if I were then if I cut off my hands I would no longer exist.* He searches his entire body in this way and decides, *Perhaps I am just the entire collection of these things.*

He pictures all his body parts piled up, and laughs, thinking, *What if Fly came back and just saw a mound of body parts piled up in the cave? Where am I? Who am I?* he wonders. *Am I the mind that thinks this? If I am, what mind am I? Am I this peaceful mind now or the frightened one from the other day. My mind is always changing, so which one might I be?* He decides he is neither the mind nor the body and rests in the absence of both, noting that both are constantly changing. This *I* he believes to be fixed and set does not really exist the way he perceives it to. He thinks how wonderful this is, because he constantly creates himself anew, like the Baba said, limitless and changing, not limited and fixed the way he often believed. He rests in the absence of that which he thought he was. The peace of that space calms him, and he drifts off to sleep as he hears an echo that says, "Shambhala," ushering him into a deep sleep.

CHAPTER 9

IN THE DEPTHS of the cold, black night a strident rustling out-side the cave awakens Bahi. His bleary eyes come to focus in the night's darkness. He sees the shadow of a large snake just outside. His heart lifts from its slumber, beating faster, bringing him fully awake and alert as he scurries toward the back of the cave. Trembling, he tightly holds the cloth of food and watches with trepidation as the snake gently sways from a nearby tree.

Perhaps if I am very still, the snake will not see me, he thinks. Cautiously, he sits up. He hears the sound of his own breath and fears even that is too loud. His breath trembles as he listens to the rustling of unknowns out in the trees above the cave. The snake becomes very still. Bahi worries that the serpent may be waiting to strike at him any moment. As he sits in great fear for hours, the jungle begins to brighten from the rising sun. Bahi begins to make the snake out and sees it's none other than a vine hanging from the tree. He looks closely to make sure, and untenses his body. Laughing in relief, he ducks out of the cave and grabs the vine. "Oh, snake," he says outloud, swinging the vine around. "You had me for quite a scare." Laughing at himself, he dissolves the fright of the past few hours.

"Buzzz." Fly lands on his face.

"Morning, Fly!" Bahi says, now relieved.

"Morning bzzzz."

Bahi pulls an apple and roll from his cloth. "Come. Eat," he invites, as Fly buzzes over to eat a small speck of bread.

After eating, Bahi picks up a tall stick from the ground, ties the cloth with food around one end, and props it over his shoulder—holding it at the other end.

"Fly, I must move on, I have much journeying ahead."

"Buzz, I will come with you, friend."

"Please do. I would love the company."

And to that resolve, they enter the northward path, where they trek on for several hours. Along the homogeneous path, they've seemingly passed the same group of trees several times. The trail has led them to a wide field of grass and brush that lies in between gray, jagged rocks. Looking around, Bahi notices it closes off again into the jungle northward, just across the field. He sits down on a stone protruding from the ground that has seemed to invite him for a rest upon its flat surface. Taking in the innate beauty of this open land, he ponders how far he must be from any city, and again begins to think who he is, where he comes from. It often frightens him to think of this, for his uncertainty is unsettling. As he stands up and stretches in the deep silence of the jungle, he kicks a rock playfully. Fly buzzes ahead as Bahi slowly walks toward the northward trail, just on the other side of the field. He breathes in the beauty of the open land nestled among trees that line it in an almost perfect circle.

Bahi heads toward the northward trail. But an uneasy feeling, as if he is being watched, creeps into his consciousness. Proceeding with caution, he grasps his long stick, which holds what's left of the food. Fly now sits on the cloth, buzzing on and off, constantly moving. Suddenly, from a disturbance in the treetop above a large tiger pounces down only a few feet in front of them. Bahi's entire world comes to a sudden halt. As if in slow motion, his focus sees every move of the massive, burnt-sienna cat. His heart races and palms sweat as he drops the food and stick. The tiger opens his mouth, exposing large, white, knife-like teeth as he lets out a roar. The force of the roar hits Bahi, knocking him trembling to his knees, washing him in waves of dizziness. The tiger's nostrils flare. Smelling Bahi's scent, the beast contemplates devouring him for lunch. Bahi sits paralyzed with fear, sweat soaking his shivering body. He knows that an effort to run would be useless against a cat of such speed and vigor. Closing his eyes, he begins to chant *Om namah narayanaya* over and again. He begins to come to terms with certain death as the tiger again roars out in domination. Bahi's voice trembles as he chants. Fly precariously buzzes around the Tigers face, fearless in knowing he would never be a feast for a tiger.

"*Om namah narayanaya!*" Bahi becomes the vibration in the darkness of his closed eyes. After some time he begins to wonder why he is even still able to chant this mantra alive. Opening his left eye, he notices the tiger is now tamely sitting right in front of him. The tiger's broad, white chest and irregular black stripes are eye level as Bahi sits opening his eyes. The tiger lets out a playful, soft roar and lies on the gravel as if he wants to be petted. Bahi, still soaked with sweat and uncertainty, continues the mantra as he puts out his hand, slowly and in awe, to touch the tiger's chest. Grasping the short, close hair of the chest, he rubs in a petting motion.

"Oh yeah, right there, that's the spot," the tiger says in a calm, relaxed tone.

"*Om namah narayanaya,*" Bahi still calls out, afraid to stop.

"*Om namana* who?" the tiger says while rolling over to sit on his belly, his large paws facing Bahi.

"*Om, namah, narayanaya,*" Bahi says with a nervous smile.

"Never heard of him," the tiger says with a smile as he stands up and reaches out his paw, "Raja's the name."

Bahi looks at his massive paw, burnt sienna on top, fading into a pale yellow and finally to a fluffy white fur that holds his retracted claws as they rest in the rough pads of his paws' bottoms. Reaching his hand and placing his palm in the rough pad of Raja's, still cautious, Bahi says, "B-B-Bahi."

Raja stands quickly and pats Bahi on the back with such force it knocks him over. "Now that wasn't so hard, was it?" Raja says as he nears the food sack next to Bahi. "Whatcha got in here, chap?"

"Food. You want some?" Bahi gladly offers, grateful to still be alive.

Fly settles on Bahi's shoulder. "That's one big pussycat," Fly says in observation.

"Sure is," Bahi says quietly as he opens the cloth, laying the food out. "Bread, apples, and a mango. That's about it. Help yourself, Raja."

"That's it? Have you seen how big I am?! I may just have to eat you, then, roar roar roar!" Raja says audibly, roaring in a semi-dramatic fashion, shaking his head.

Bahi begins to tremble again, swallowing past a stone in his throat. "Well, I-I-I-I'd like it if you didn't."

"Well I-I-I-I'd like it if you didn't," Raja says mockingly. "Lighten up, kid. I'm just having fun with you. You don't smell very tasty anyhow, I-I-I," Raja says again, mocking Bahi as he laughs.

Bahi begins to laugh along with Fly, and the three laugh away the tension that was as thick as butter.

"So what brings you to my kingdom, Bahi?"

"I am traveling to Shambhala in the North, I am not sure exactly where it is, but I assume it's a great distance from here."

"Shambhala, huh? Never heard of it. I have a friend a bit North of here who can understand the human language, even read bits of it, result of some black magic gone awry. Say, how do I understand you?" Raja says noticing the conversation. "Oh no, they got me, they got me," Raja frantically says as he paces nervously talking to himself. "Mama said not to hang out with those leopards. Darn it! No ma, I'm King of the Jungle. No black magic spells can hurt me." Raja says mocking himself. "Oh woe is me, they got me!" Raja gets down on his belly with his paws in prayer toward Bahi. "Please take the curse from me, please!" He pleads with eyes tightly shut.

Bahi laughs, "It's not a curse. I can talk to all the animals. It's my curse, I assure you."

"That's true buzz," Fly says as he sits on Raja's ear.

"Are you sure? Ha ha! I knew that. I was just testing you," Raja says pointing one sharp claw at Bahi before standing proud. "Black magic, Ha! Ma, I told you no black magic can get your boy!" he yells almost insanely into the thick of the jungle. "King of these parts I am!" Raja says, strutting proudly back and forth. Bahi and Fly laugh at the antics of Raja as he comes to face Bahi with a cocky puffed-up chest. "What were we talking about? Oh yeah. So I was headed North to see my buddy anyhow. The spotted deer are delectable this time of year," Raja says, raising one eyebrow like a connoisseur. "You want to come with?" he offers.

"Please, if you think he may know the whereabouts of Shambhala."

"You would be surprised the useless stuff he tells me from his observations of the humans in the city close to where he lives. I always tell him, humans are good only for one thing, Tendwa—lunch!" Raja says it while licking his lips and staring fiercely into Bahi's eyes in a serious gaze of instinct. All falls silent, then a smile cracks his face. "I'm joking!" Raja says as he lets out a belly laugh. Bahi forces a laugh, letting out his nervousness in the form of a tight cackle.

"Here, get on, I'll ride you up. It's quite a distance North and may take up until tomorrow. It'll be quicker this way."

Finishing up the leftovers from the Baba, they climb atop Raja. Bahi takes hold of his massive, warm body. "Hold tight, Bahi. Don't worry about me! Skin's as tough as a rhino. I'm the King!" he yells out as he bolts off into the jungle. Bahi holds tightly with a smile from ear to ear. The warm jungle air whisks through his hair as Fly secures himself in Bahi's shirt pocket, snug as he rests along the journey. Raja runs full speed for a long while, amazing Bahi with his stamina.

Coming to a stream that runs along a low valley, the tiger slows as a dusky sun shimmers white diamonds along the flowing water. A few drinking gazelles sense Raja as they jolt off into the distance of the valley's plains, leaving a smoke of trotted dust in their path. Coming to the water's edge, Bahi dismounts Raja, shaking out his stiff legs. Fly buzzes out of his pocket to sit on a piece of dung left behind by the fleeting gazelles. Silently drinking from the river, Raja looks up at Bahi. Water saturates the tiger's white beard. It drips down as he smiles, "We'll ride into the night and stop for rest before dawn."

"OK," Bahi says, glad he doesn't have to walk this great distance.

Raja lies in the warm glow of the setting sun, rubbing his back in the gravel, then with a quick spring to his feet he instructs, "OK. back on, boys!"

Bahi mounts once again, and fly tucks away into his pocket as they whisk off along the valley's plain. Animals scatter in all directions at the mere presence of Raja. Bahi feels privileged to ride upon such a king of kings in this immeasurable jungle. They journey into the night, up the sides of steep rock cliffs, Raja's awesome strength easily hoists them up as Bahi grasps tightly to his body. They run along vast, open fields and narrow paths, passing all types of animals, who stare strangely at such a scene of man riding tiger. A large deer-like animal stops mid-chew upon some tall grass that falls from his mouth, raising his eyebrow in disbelief as the strangers swiftly pass by. They stop once for a brief rest and some water in the thick jungle night before rapidly heading off again into the darkness. Raja seems to have an unlimited source of energy that propels them through the night at such speeds.

Reaching a rock cliff, Raja stops suddenly as the sun begins to crack upon the dusty mountains afar. A pinkish orange mat lines the soft mountains as Raja bends down to let Bahi off. Stretching out, Raja lets out a deep yawn that echoes softly upon the dusty mountains, almost beckoning the sun, which creeps over the top of a far peak, extending a stream of warmth, dimishing the night's coldness. Raja lies down and Bahi sits back. Head rested on Raja, facing the sun, Bahi gazes off into the distance at birds that usher in the day, swooping around the sky, plucking insects out of the air. Closing his weary eyes, he falls swiftly asleep. The warmth of the sun now blasts them fully from over distant mountains as they recline high above the valley below. They snooze on a precipice of flat, rocky cliff cushioned with grass.

A few hours pass, and Bahi opens his eyes in the afternoon sun. Squinting, he gets up to go to the bathroom. His face burns from the sun as he stretches and rubs his cheeks. Bahi watches as Fly buzzes around aimlessly. He wonders if Fly ever sleeps. Stepping off into the woods, Bahi begins to go to the bathroom, smiling inwardly from such an amazing adventure. Finishing, he scratches the beard that has begun to form on his face. He closes his eyes and stretches. When he opens them he is face to face with a Himalayan Black Bear. Standing tall in his smooth, short, black hair, which adorns a white crescent on his chest, his white chin drops open as he lets out a roar, leaving Bahi speechless as he feels the warmth of this beast's breath. Quickly, Bahi recites the mantra *Om namah narayanaya*, but it doesn't seem to be having any effect. The bear swipes his large claws at Bahi, who quickly ducks behind a fallen tree that leans on another, standing erect by its side. Striking the fallen tree with such force that he nearly breaks it in half, the bear hops around the side as Bahi swiftly backs away, tripping on a root. He lies helpless as the bear lunges forward and—like a flash of lightening—Raja pounces down between them, letting out a roar that echoes through the mountains. The bear roars back as Raja growls, slowly moving toward him. Keen that he may be no match for Raja, the bear growls in disgust and runs off.

"That's right! King of this here jungle! Tell your friends!" Raja roars triumphantly as he walks back towards Bahi.

Bahi gets up and brushes the dirt from his clothes. "Thank you, Raja. That was a close call."

Stretching his back in a cat-scratch manor, forelegs down, back legs erect, shaking off his nap, he strains to say, "All in a days work for," standing proud, "King of this here jungle! Come on, Tendwa lives close, hop on."

Mounting Raja, they quickly head off toward the valley below. En route Bahi notices a village or town in the distance. Smoke billows quietly from a white house that sits softly, surrounded by a few others that seem to be built into the mountainside. The sky is a rich blue. Puffy, white clouds pour over the mountaintops, often casting shadows on the small homes that dot the spaces between trees in the green of the hillside. The jungle has turned to a fragrant pine forest. Monkeys swing above them as they slow to an open area, shadowed by large pines that jut out of rocks in odd directions.

"Tendwa?" Raja calls out as he pops up onto a steep rock, which flattens at its summit.

"Yeah, thanks! Maybe leave a bit for the rest of the forest," a leopard shouts up to a monkey, who mocks him with a hoot and ha as he throws a bare stick down from a tree above. Hearing Raja behind him, he quickly turns. "Well, isn't this a pleasant surprise?" he says, smiling in his white fluffy face as a stick comes flying down from the monkey above, knocking the leopard on the head. "Yeah, thank you, come again!" he shouts up condescendingly as the monkey mocks with a laugh. "It's no wonder we're not vegetarians, Raja. These damned monkeys eat nearly half the forest in one sitting, speaking of which, I see you have brought a feast for us. Well done," he says, noticing Bahi standing on the rock above him, where Raja stands proudly peering down.

"Ha, ha, no, no, Tendwa. This is my friend, Bahi."

"Well well. Has the king gone soft or just mad, paling around with humans?" Tendwa asks as he effortlessly pounces up the rock to sniff Bahi. Bahi cautiously stiffens to alert.

"A bit of both, I suppose," Raja quickly fires back. "Besides I've come for the spotted deer. My palate doesn't fancy a distasteful human. No offense, Bahi."

"None taken," Bahi says in relief.

"He is looking for a place called Shambooz, Shamlala, Shamalama-dingdang."

"Shambhala," Bahi interjects.

"Oh, sure sure. I know of it," Tendwa says with certitude.

"You do?" Bahi asks, eyes lighting up.

"Sure. It's not far from here," Tendwa says, walking closer, sniffing Bahi again.

"Can you please take me there?"

"Sure, but why you wanna go there anyway?"

"It's the sun and moon, the place of wisdom, where I can find the answers to all my questions," Bahi says excited.

Fly feels his excitement, "Sun and moon buzz!"

"Oh sure, sure it is, lil' buddy," Tendwa says, turning to Raja and making a kookoo face that alludes to Bahi's seeming insanity. He then looks serious. Before turning back he looks into Bahi's eyes, his topaz leopard eyes twinkling in the silence as he sizes him up.

"Sun and moon, buzz!" Fly circles in the air in hysteria, breaking the awkward silence.

"Well, if you're a friend of Raja's, you're a friend of mine," Tendwa says quickly, changing the mood.

"Sun and moon, buzz!"

"Alright already, you're worse than the damn monkeys. I suppose this is your friend too," Tendwa says referring to Fly.

Raja shrugs and smiles in affirmation. Tendwa walks close to Raja. "You will have to explain this odd turn of events at a later date," he whispers to a smiling Raja. "Well, come on, then. It's only a few minutes from here."

"A few minutes! That's great, thanks!" Bahi says in excitement.

"Yeah yeah, sun and moon, stars and fairy dust. C'mon, you freak," Tendwa says, murmuring the last part under his breath.

Tendwa leads the crew as they all walk along a winded path, twisting upward. Small rocks lie upon the fine, dusty dirt laden with brown, fallen pine needles. Trees shoot out horizontally from the roots on the rock-and-dirt wall to their left, then shoot straight up to the sky, some twisting in unique patterns. To their right, the path steeply drops off, lined with trees that seem to hold the path up, probably the only thing that keeps it in tact during the monsoonal floods. White sun makes its way through the otherwise cool, shaded path as they walk.

They come to a flat overlook were the trees drop off into the valley, visible below. An empty road can be seen in the distance, and just below, a busy street. People walk back and forth, often stopping at the many street vendors set up along a row on one side. Small tables propped up with thick, wooden sticks are laid out with golden statues and jewelry. Some sell colorful clothing and wool socks. Shops and cafes tightly pack the narrow street. They can hear the commotion of the town from above. Horns honking, people talking, music flowing through the air.

"Well, here you go: sun and moon," Tendwa says.

"Where? I think you are mistaken," Bahi says thinking there must be a miscommunication.

"You see that blue sign?" Tendwa says, pointing his furry paw.

"Yeah, I think so," Bahi says, squinting.

"Next door. Now follow it up." Bahi looks to the café next to the blue sign and scanning up a couple of flights sees a sign that reads, "Shambhala." Steep stone steps lead to the top of the building, where the sign points with a red arrow.

"What is this city?" Bahi asks.

Raja shrugs unknowingly, keeping quiet as he has since they began to walk.

"They call It Dharamsala. I sit and observe these whacky characters often. I can read your human language, you know—even speak to humans. You're the only one I've talked to in years. The last guy I said hello to ran off in a craze, and I think he is still under psychiatric help," Tendwa laughs and stretches as the rest look off onto the city street. "Yeah, it's my curse, black magic," Tendwa says completing his stretch.

"It sounds more like a blessing or a gift. I can speak to the animals, I have that gift, like you," Bahi smiles.

"That's what I say. You hear that, King?" Tendwa says to Raja, who is deep in primal stare a few feet away, looking down into the valley below. "What's that?" Raja says, turning back toward them.

"It's a gift I have, not a curse. I agree with the human here. I am talented, indeed," Tendwa says proudly.

"Yeah, we'll see how much of a gift it is when those witch doctors who cast the spell come looking for you again."

"Come on, why you always have to steal my thunder, Raja?"

"Cuz I'm the King, and the King is late for stag-and-spotted-deer feast, so I must bid you all a fond farewell," Raja says, stalking back to the tree, where he watches grazing stag below.

"You're gonna kill those stags?" Bahi asks, looking down then over at Raja.

"I'm going to eat, Bahi. It's how I survive. Tendwa and I don't have the good fortune as you do to be able to survive otherwise," Raja says looking back to the stags.

"Well then, how do I get down to this road?" Bahi asks, figuring he'll waste no time in investigating this Shambhala below.

"Follow this trail down and the first road you see. Make a right. That leads right to it. That's this road here."

"Thank you so very much for everything, Raja," Bahi's hands are in prayer position and his smile exhibits the deep gratitude he expresses. "Thank you, Tendwa for showing me here. Good luck with your reading and human communications," Bahi says to end on a good note.

"Yes, yes. I hope you find what you've been searching for down there. I have always wondered what it was like in those places," Tendwa expresses.

"Well if it's what I have been told, I will come back and welcome you. All are welcome at Shambhala."

"I don't know about that," Tendwa says, laughing as his mind flashes back to the last time he crept into a café and escaped near death from the hysterical locals. They chased him out with pitchforks and sticks, as the owner let loose a shot from his gun, just missing Tendwa as he swiftly ran off. "I visited a café like this once. Once!" He laughs again. "OK, we're heading this way, good bye, friends," Tendwa concludes.

"Good bye, buzz!"

"Good bye, my good friends."

"See ya around, little buddy," they all talk over each other saying their goodbyes as they part ways.

Bahi and Fly make their way back down the winding path. "I am pretty excited to get down here, Fly," Bahi says, covering up his wariness of finding Shambhala so easily.

"Sun and moon?"

"You're a creature of few words aren't you?" Bahi says as he lets out a laugh.

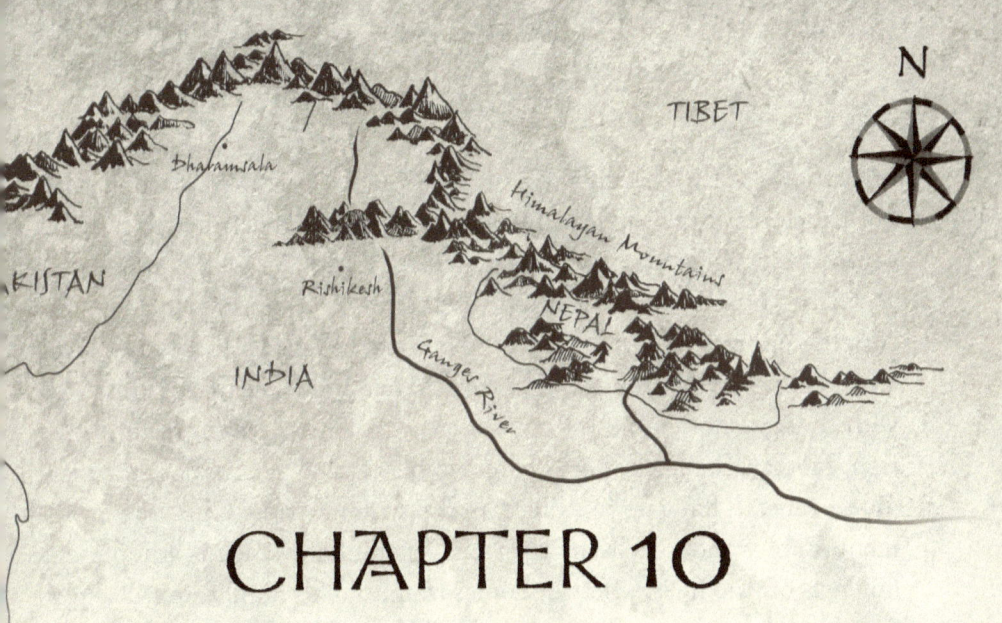

CHAPTER 10

WALKING JUST A short distance, they step onto a crossroad, where men stand in relaxed banter around small, black-and-yellow auto-rickshaws awaiting customers to usher through the city. One driver notices his prospect in Bahi as they draw near. "Hello, friend, where are you going?" the rickshaw driver asks.

"Shambhala!" Bahi says proudly, prompting the man to quickly give up his pitch, as he turns away in the realization that a rickshaw is unnecessary for such a short distance ahead.

The busy flow of energy floats down the small city street. Except for the Baba, Bahi hasn't had much human interaction in a while. The stimulation is inviting as he takes in the surroundings, noting that the main center they pass through is a far cry from the patient bliss of the jungle. Slowly he makes his way up the slightly inclined street, taking in the goings on around him. Two Caucasian men with beards stand tall, next to a white jeep. They carry large backpacks. Bahi passes a small liquor store on his left and diverts his attention to a little pastry shop that seems to be out of place, smack in the middle of a crossroad section that shoots dirt roads in five directions. He stares through a glass showcase that exhibit cakes, rum balls, and other delectables. He remembers what the Baba taught him about how our minds jump to conclusions thinking it will know exactly what this will taste like, when in fact we have no idea. He fantasizes it will melt in his mouth and taste much better than his automatic craving response tries to tell him. Moving along, he passes a vegetable shop that spills out onto the street. A Tibetan man sits under hanging oranges and bok choy on the lip of his shop's entryway among an array of colorful produce. The strong Asian influence of this city mixes with those of noticeable Indian descent. Looking up, Bahi reads a shop sign, Tibetan Thangha Shop. He remembers that Dharamsala is the place of the Tibetan refugees in exile from the tyranny of the Chinese government. Bahi wonders why most of his general knowledge is still present, but facts of who he is, where he comes from, and his family are still a mystery. He remembers certain facts: can add one plus one, but can't remember how or when he learned to do so. He passes a momo stand that sits just in front of a yellow temple decked out with red prayer wheels, which make up the temple walls. He watches as a Tibetan woman fries doughy dumplings next to others that she steams in a small, silver steamer sitting upon a green table that reads in yellow paint, *Veg. Momo*. The woman seems humble. The crow's feet near her eyes give away her long past of sitting in the warm sun, day after day, selling *momos*. Fly sets upon one of the doughy dumplings cooling on a plate. He has a quick taste before being shoed away by a potential customer wearing a camera on his neck. Judging by his straw-like brown hair and white complexion, Bahi guesses he is European, one of many tourists along the tightly packed street with shops selling everything from books and statues to socks and radios. Bahi wishes he had money so he could eat some of the fragrant food all around him. Looking down, a dark Indian woman sits frail and skinny as she straddles an empty cup. "Hello, sir," she says, with her mangled hand propped out to beg for money. Great compassion wells up as Bahi wishes he had even one rupee to give the woman.

"Sorry, I don't have," he says with a frown.

"Sir, please," she begs as he walks away with a sorrowful heart.

Many a crippled man and woman beg for money along this street frequented by tourists. Contemplating his body and general health, Bahi feels grateful for all he has, wondering why some are born into this life of beggary and degradation while others are born into a world of money and health. Walking more quickly, he begins to doubt that a place of wonder such as Shambhala could even exist in a city like this. *This journey has turned up the most unexpected at every turn, perhaps this is the home of Shambhala.* Thoughts battle as he tries to convince his misgivings. *Why wouldn't these people just go there?* he wonders. Finally he reaches the small café that sits at the bottom of the concrete steps leading up to Shambhala. Looking at the sign that guides him up, he begins to feel that there has been a mistake. He has quick flashes of doubt for the Baba, for Tendwa, for himself. Stroking the soft beard on his face, his fingers run slowly from cheeks to chin as he contemplates.

"Hello, hello," a soft voice calls. He feels someone pulling on his shirt.

Turning, he notices a woman carrying a baby boy about one year old. She wears tattered clothes wrought with dirt that finds it's way to her face, blending into her dark skin. "Please. Baby," she says, putting her hand to her mouth, motioning for food.

"Sorry, I have nothing," Bahi honestly says.

"Please!" she pleads, looking as if she will soon cry. The baby stares at Bahi, crusty snot fills his nose. Bahi's heart, feels their pain of hunger, the jungle has seemed to attune him more with his feelings. Knowing there is nothing he can do for this woman, he turns his back and heads up the steep, cold concrete steps while resolving in his heart that he will help all of these people, if he can obtain the answers from Shambhala. Passing a small café on his left, he proceeds a few more steps to the top, where he reads, painted on the concrete wall, *Shambhala Café.* Stepping in, he is quickly disillusioned, realizing it must have been a coincidence in name and not the Shambhala the Baba told him about. Coming inside, two men, one of Tibetan decent, young, wearing a t-shirt and jeans and another looking almost a mix of Indian and Tibetan, also wearing a trendy t-shirt and jeans, greet him. He walks in toward the back feeling the upset he began to feel when he first saw the place and suppressed the doubt in the hopes that he had found the true Shambhala. Four western travelers sit on the cushioned floor by a window overlooking a short table, preparing to eat. He heads out the back doors that lead to an overhang seating in the afternoon sun. A girl sits and reads as he settles on a steel seat fixed to the wall. One of the men from the entrance drops a menu on the table that shoots out of the railing in front of him. He smiles and looks over at the reading girl, who looks strangely familiar. Looking up, she smiles then looks back at her book. Then she looks up again as Bahi looks off onto the green hills in the distance.

"Where do I know you from?" the girl's sweet voice softly catches Bahi's ear as he turns to her.

"Uhm, I wouldn't know," he says, deep in thought.

"Where you at Tushita?"

"I just arrived here today. Where is Tushita?"

"It's just up the hill. Oh, it's amazing. You have to check it out. I did a re-treat there recently," she says, as Bahi now engages her greenish-brown eyes.

"I know where I know you from. You were in Rishikesh, right?"

"That's right!" Bahi exclaims remembering the sign where he and Bandar sat on the rooftop.

"Paul. You're Paul. We met at that café. Remember? I didn't recognize you with the facial hair."

"Please forgive me. I don't remember," Bahi says searching his memory.

"No, no, it's definitely you. You were with that other fellow. What's his name?"

Bahi shakes his head, not knowing.

"Nicholas!" she says with a smile, awaiting confirmation. "Surely you remember, Eva, the Irish girl, you guys were going for a hike to the falls."

"Eva, you may be right," Bahi says, now intrigued that she may know him. "I've since gotten amnesia from a blow to the head and haven't re-membered a thing since."

"Oh my God! Are you serious? What are you still doing traveling?" she asks with concern, moving closer to the edge of her seat.

"Well, I don't know. Good question, Eva. I've forgotten everything it seems, well not everything. I mean, I don't remember who I am, where I am from. You tell me my name is Paul, and you might as well have said Picasso because I draw blanks on my entire past."

Fly sets upon the woman's uneaten meal as she is distracted in conversation.

"Are you serious!" she says with alarm. "You need help? I can help you. My father has friends at the embassy. You're American, right? This is pretty crazy. Let me help you. We can go straight away." She begins to rise up as Bahi nods her calmly back down.

"Even though I can't remember my life, I would bet money that this has been the craziest and most fantastic journey I have ever been on. I am on a mission to find out who I truly am. You say I'm Paul. This means nothing to me, and the more I search for who I am, the closer I feel I am coming to the truth, although today I feel further from it."

"Are you feeling OK?" Eva asks, looking at him strangely. "You need to seek out some help. You may have an aneurism or something. You sound a little off."

"Look, I realize I must sound pretty crazy, but me losing my memory may be one of the best things that ever happened to Paul," Bahi says passionately to Eva as the moment slows down. Five seconds of silence feels like five years as they stare into each others eyes. "I am searching for Shambhala."

"Well congratulations, because here it is," she says pointing to the inside of the café as she softly laughs.

"No, no, the true Shambhala. This is why I must keep moving on."

"I think you should see a doctor and get some help. Amnesia is serious business and not for nothing, but you don't seem to be making a whole lot of sense."

"It is very serious Eva," he says placing his hand on hers. An uncertain awkwardness about this familiar stranger alarms her. Bahi says, "I look around me and see all these people—everyone: all of them, you, me, everyone is suffering. From the homeless man with no legs in the street to you and me. We think we know who we are, grasping onto this self we perceive to be real, all the while distracting ourselves from the reality of our suffering minds. You ask me who I am, and I tell you I have no idea, and in fact I believe this is a better idea than most. We are all journeying, reaching for answers to explain the truth, reaching for happiness at every turn, hoping the next reach will be the final answer to our lasting peace, but it isn't and so I tell you, Shambhala is the place where I will reach last. Shambhala is where I am headed, and when I get there I vow to lead everyone who wishes to go."

Eva pulls her hand out from under the ranting Bahi, "OK let's just pretend for a moment that you're not stark mad and say there even is a Shambhala outside of the fantasy and fairy tales. What makes you think that you will be able to find it? Do you know how many men have tried? I've read stories of people devoting their lives to this search and never even coming close."

Bahi stares in an awkward silence as insecure butterflies rush his stomach, twitching his face muscles with doubt. Eva's stern manner turns quickly compassionate. "Look, I understand your passion, I truly do, but we have to look at the reality, use fact. What do you have to go on that this place even exists?"

"I have journeyed a long way since Rishikesh, met with some amazing beings far beyond the scope of normal intelligence, the embodiment of wisdom. They have assured me that it exists. Eva, beautiful Eva," Bahi says now, lightening the mood, "Have you ever felt something so strongly that you know it's right, that's it's real. Something you can't explain to others without sounding a bit crazy but you just know?"

"I suppose I have, yes," she says in an attempt to placate him.

"Well let's say that you met some people, a wise man you just know you can trust. Everything about him embodies truth. And this wise man tells you that this feeling you have inside is true and in fact directs you where to find it, concrete and real. Would you ever be able to stop looking?"

"I guess I wouldn't, unless of course I had amnesia and forgot," Eva says in comic relief. "Do you even have any money or food?"

"No, not at the moment."

"Please order some food. I'll pay."

"No, I couldn't."

"Yes, I insist. Look, I admire your courage and resolve. I question you only out of concern. Please order something. I'll pay. I insist. It's the least I can do for an old friend," she says, realizing he doesn't even know the fleeting nature of their meeting in Rishikesh.

"Thank you, Eva," he says from the heart. "You said I was with a friend in Rishikesh?"

"Yes, the two of you were supposed to meet me after your hike. I know now why you hadn't. Here, use this pad to write down your order. Don't be shy. Order whatever you like. The food here is great."

As he peruses the menu, Bahi thinks hard to remember his friend, but only shadowy figures appear in his mind. "Look, I don't mean to have come off crazy or delusional. It's been a long day. I promise. I'm harmless."

"Well, you're lucky you're cute," Eva says with a flirtatious smile.

"Do you have any recommendations?" Bahi says, diverting her attention from his blushing face.

"Get the falafel, it's amazing."

Following her recommendation, he orders the falafel and some ginger lemonade. The two sit and talk long after the meal is gone. Looking off into the valley, they watch as the sun shifts over the building, casting rays down upon the mountainous hills.

"You probably could use a good shower. Why not come to where I am staying? I could get you a room. You can clean up, get a good night's sleep."

"I don't. . . No, I couldn't," Bahi says, internally hoping she insists again.

"Look, Paul, I want to help you. It's the least I can do for you. I wouldn't feel right otherwise. I also know a good doctor here in Dharamsala if you want to see him."

"For what? I'm healthy as a horse," Bahi says flexing his muscles comically.

They both have a laugh, and after paying the bill they leave the café, descending the concrete steps as dusk pours in. Fly zips to follow behind them. As they walk in silence down the still-busy dirt road, Bahi reflects on the events that have led him to the café. *What are the chances of meeting her here? Perhaps this was the reason for me coming here?* he thinks.

Second guessing himself after the conversation with Eva, he looks up at the rising mountains, remembering the Baba's instructions to go North and about the meditation that will act as his map to get to Shambhala. A feeling of assurance wells up inside of him, almost as if the Baba were walking next to him.

"I remember you telling me you were from New York, you and your friend Nick," Eva says.

"Yeah? I don't know, it's weird, I remember things I must have learned throughout my life, but certain facts such as my name, my family and friends, pretty much my whole life, is totally lost."

"Is it scary?" Eva asks, stopping.

Bahi thinks a moment, "Yeah, sometimes, at first it was very scary, but now I believe it's somewhat of a blessing. Perhaps I would have just gone through life thinking I knew who I was, thinking 'I am Paul,' and that's it. Now I have an opportunity to search deep to find out who I truly am, and honestly, that may be the scariest part."

"What if after all you find out you are just Paul from New York?"

Bahi smiles, puffing a laugh from his chest through his nostrils. "You have a way of putting things in perspective, Eva. I don't know, the 'Paul from New York' doesn't sound like truth to me, but what do I know?"

"Well I like Paul from New York, even if he doesn't remember he's Paul from New York," Eva smiles and continues walking. "What if you never find Shambhala? What if it is all a fairy tale?"

"Well I guess I'll have to go back to the fairy tale of who I used to be then."

Eva stops to think for a moment. "Touché," she whispers as she begins to walk again, catching up to Bahi.

"I like you, Paul. You're different, and this whole new mysterious outlook may do well for you," Eva says smiling again.

"Bahi."

"What's that?" she asks.

"My name is Bahi. It's the name I was given by a friend I met in Rishikesh after I lost my memory. And lately I feel more like Bahi than this Paul character."

"Ha ha, OK then, Bahi it is. I like it. That means *brother* in Hindi I believe?"

"Indeed it does," Bahi says, remembering how he learned this for the first time from Bandar." Do you speak Hindi?"

"I wouldn't say *speak*, but I studied it at University, always had a fascination with this wonderful country. Bahi, the great brother of man in search of truth."

"Brother of all things," Bahi says remembering the great lessons of Kavi.

Eva smiles the infectious smile she effortlessly wears, and the two proceed walking, Fly buzzes around with a female fly he seems to have gotten entangled with over some cow dung. Taking their time, Eva and Bahi wander the streets of Dharamsala, stopping often to see what the vendors have to offer. Bahi wonders at the many woolen socks, hats, and jackets—thinking how handy they would have been in the brisk nights he's encountered.

"Paul . . . I mean Bahi, I'm sorry," Eva says stopping in humorous correction. "Why wouldn't you at least get yourself in order with your passport and money before heading on? Your family must be worried sick."

Bahi thinks for a moment. Family is a portrait filled with shadows, yet his heart aches at what they may think happened to him. "Perhaps they think I am dead," he says with concern.

"Yeah. It's not very nice to play dead, you know," Eva says.

"Eva, I fear that if I go back to the life I once knew, my journey to Shambhala will never continue. And I feel so close. It's been several weeks already. What's a couple of more?" he asks, feeling gray woolen socks that hang from a store front in order to avoid the disapproval of Eva's gaze.

"I'll make you good price," the shop owner says, noticing Bahi.

"Is free a good price?" Bahi asks with a smirk?

"I'll buy them for you," Eva offers.

"Why are you so nice to me? You barely know me?"

Fly lands on his shoulder, rubbing his hands together, dipping his big bug eyes into them rapidly before buzzing off with his new mate.

"We all need each other, right? Isn't this the course of your valiant journey, Bahi? Besides if it were me, wouldn't you do the same?"

"I honestly don't know. I mean, yes, now I would, Bahi would, but I can't speak for Paul."

"I'm certain Paul would too. I mean, you lost your memory not your heart, right?" Eva pulls out two hundred *rupees*. "How much?" she asks the short, weathered, Indian shop owner.

"Two hundred," he answers.

"One fifty," she barters, knowing that tourist season is coming to an end and two hundred *rupees* is way overpriced.

The shop owner silently agrees, and with a bobble of his head takes the money and hands her change.

"This is the thing, Eva," Bahi says as they begin to move along the street, "I don't know Paul, and it scares me to think he may be totally different from me. This is why I must go on to Shambhala. There I am certain I will find who Paul really is, who Bahi really is," he says with conviction.

"What are you really looking for, Bahi?"

"I don't know," Bahi says honestly. "I don't know. All I do know is that

I set out to find who I was, and maybe I thought that meant my name, but deeper inside I know I was looking for more. I think losing my memory may have been the best thing that has happened."

"There have been times in my life I wished I could just forget it all, start over. What makes you think you'll know all the answers at Shamb-hala? And I know I've said this before, but how can you be sure it's not just some fairy tale told by the locals?"

"If you had seen the things I have seen in the past few weeks you would not know the difference between fairy tale and reality. The more I look at this fairy-tale world all around me, the people suffering, this poor dog," he points to a dog limping past them, "the more inclined I am to believe in the fairy tale of Shambhala than this nightmare we call reality."

"But this is real, hence real-ity," Eva contends.

"Sure it is, I can see it, feel it, smell it, but I am standing in the same reality as this dog, as that homeless woman there, and all three of us see and experience this exact moment totally differently, so who's reality is the correct version?"

"Right, I get it, but we are all right, or wrong. I don't know. What's that got to do with Shambhala being real? You've gone off track."

"I'm saying that, because it's a far-fetched idea from our seeming 'real world' of pain and suffering, does not mean it doesn't exist?" Bahi says, struggling to grasp at the answers while in defense of an idea he himself is uncertain of.

"I understand. I don't mean to take you from your journey, I just wish you the best and want you to be safe," Eva says softly.

"When I look around, I wonder if it's 'safe' in the comforts of the 'real world'? Is it really safe or just a way for us to divert our minds from the inevitable suffering to come. If I can give answers, find a way out, help those suffering most, wouldn't the trip be worth it?"

"Of course it would," Eva says as she reaches deep into a glass container at a quaint, remote restaurant they have wandered across. She pulls a chocolate rum ball from the container and puts it to Bahi's mouth. "Take a bite," she offers. Bahi bites the ball, feeling an instant rush of chocolate through his taste buds "It's not all suffering you know, Bahi. Life is full of amazing, wonderful things, like rum balls," she says raising her eyebrows as she pops the other half into her mouth.

"You're right, Eva. I'm sorry to be such a downer."

"It's OK. I like your fortitude and resolve. It's sexy," she flirts.

Bahi smiles. "So what makes me able to enjoy a rum ball, but she can't even afford one if she wanted to?" he asks, pointing to a homeless woman sitting dirty on a curb, hand out, looking defeated in every way. Her desperate face tells a story of a woman beaten down by life. Eva silently walks over and gives her two rum balls and one hundred *rupees*. The woman's eyes light up with thanks as Eva turns and walks back toward Bahi.

"See, we can all enjoy a good rum ball. We just have to look out for each other, everyone, even, or especially strangers."

Bahi smiles as Eva has become even more attractive in his eyes at this moment. "You're an amazing person, Eva."

"Oh, no. I'm just a person. We can all do this in some way, but you Bahi, you are brave, and I know you will find what you seek at Shambhala. I kind of wish I could come with you."

"Well, you certainly changed your tune, huh?" Bahi chuckles. "You could come with me, you know."

"I fly back to Europe in a few of days. And unfortunately I do remember my family. No I'm kidding, they're brilliant, I love them. I have several family obligations to attend to or else I'd be right with you."

Bahi smiles at her with understanding.

Walking up a steep hill they come to a short, iron gate painted green. "Here it is," Eva says lifting the green iron latch atop the gates. They proceed toward the small cottage-like guesthouse that sits back behind a large lawn, nestled in the comfort of trees, off of a quiet road not far from the city streets. Coming to the small cottage, which sits before the strip of cottage-style rooms behind it, lined up one next to the other, Eva knocks on the door.

"We'll see if we can get you a room," she says, awaiting a response.

The door creaks open slowly to reveal a short, young, Indian woman with a pleasant smile, "Hello, is everything OK?"

"Yes, just fine, Rheta. I was wondering if you had another room for my friend here?"

"No, sorry, all filled. Maybe at guest house up street they have room," she answers directing them to a friend's guesthouse. Her soft demeanor and gentle eyes induce serenity in Bahi as she gently looks over at him.

"Thank you, Rheta," Eva says, hands in a quick prayer position as they walk away from the door.

"Bahi, why not just stay at my place for the night? It's already dark," Eva suggests.

"I wouldn't want to intrude. You have helped me so much already."

"It's more than fine. I would love the company, come on," Eva says as she walks off toward the cottages in the back of the field.

Coming to the white door of her room, she unlatches the padlock, opens the door, and waves Bahi in. Fly buzzes in quickly behind him. The room is moderate, with two small beds side by side. Her red hiking pack sits in a corner next to a small end table strewn with random travel needs.

"Feel free to take a shower. *Mi casa es su casa.*"

"No, thanks. You've been so kind already."

"No, Bahi. Stop being Mr. Humility. My pleasure is in helping others, so please, take a shower," she says taking a towel from her pack.

"No really, I'm OK," he says not wanting to intrude on her space.

"No really, do us both a favor and take a shower," she insists, hinting bluntly.

Bahi smells his underarms. "Is it really that bad?" he giggles.

Throwing the towel at him, she responds, "It could be better. I have to go down the street real quick. I forgot something. Be back in ten minutes. Take your time, soaps in the shower."

"Thanks!"

Eva exits the door as Bahi sits on the bed releasing a deep exhale. Sitting in silence, he thinks of Eva and his whole situation here in Dharamsala. Realizing he is well due for a shower, he heads into the bathroom. "You've been quiet," he says, noticing Fly on the wall, knowing he has been consciously avoiding any conversations with animals and bugs so as not to come off overly insane to Eva, who already has her reservations about Bahi's mental state. Fly just buzzes back at him as he goes into the shower.

He sits in the hot water as it runs onto his shoulders and down his back, soothing his tight muscles from the weeks of journey and sleeping on hard ground. The water goes from hot to warm and quickly starts to lose its heat as he finishes up, turning off the now cool water. Stepping out, he notices a sense of strength induced by the jungle. He feels that the elements of the natural world have put him more in accord with himself. Feeling a quality of strength and peace, he towels off and opens the bathroom door. Steam follows him out as he wears a towel around his waist. His hair is slicked back wet, as he feels refreshed and a deep sense of renewal.

"Here," Eva says as she hands him some fresh new clothes similar to his dirty ones: black cotton pants and white t-shirt with a soft, wool grey, long-sleeved shirt with a single button on the opening of the breast.

"You really didn't have to," Bahi says.

"Someone had to," she says kicking his tattered, dirty clothes to the corner. "And here. I figured you'd need one of these," she says tossing a toothbrush, which he fumbles to the floor trying not to lose his towel in the catch.

"I promise I will pay you back for everything," he says as he picks up the toothbrush from the smooth concrete floor.

"I know you will, I'm not worried," she says without any expectation of payback.

"It will be nice to sleep in a bed."

"Why? Where have you been sleeping?"

"You don't want to know," Bahi answers with a laugh.

"You've been sleeping on the streets. Please tell me you haven't been sleeping on the streets."

"I've been camping out so to say. It's been fun."

"In the woods? You're crazy!"

"Am I?" Bahi asks seriously. Looking into Eva's eyes, there is a moment of still silence broken by Eva, who turns toward the window.

"Come on, get dressed, I'll buy you dinner."

Bahi dresses, and the two make their way to a nearby Tibetan restaurant. They eat and talk, as the connection between them grows deeper with every word. Eva is very fond of Bahi, and his mysterious nature fascinates her. Finishing the meal, they make their way back to the room in the chill of night. Bahi puts his arm around her, drawing her close for warmth as they walk. She feels a comfort as if she has known him for years. Bahi, too, revels in the comfort of companionship after several weeks in the jungle.

Coming back to the room they sit on the bed in silence. Eva lets out a sigh of relief as she lights a white candle on her nightstand and turns out the light.

"I love candlelight, it's so relaxing," she says as Bahi smiles in confirmation. "Bahi," she says softly, drawing closer to him.

"Yes?"

"Nothing," she whispers, looking into his blue eyes, feeling a flutter of excitement in her heart.

Bahi moves his body closer to Eva and kisses her on the lips. She receives him with delight, returning the kiss, breathing in his freshly clean scent and holding his scruffy face. "I like your beard," she says as she caresses it and looks closely.

Bahi grabs the back of her head, running his fingers through her hair as he again kisses her lips. Fly mingles about the room with his newly found friend, as a cool gust of wind blows in through the slightly cracked window, flickering the candle. Eva and Bahi look deeply into each others eyes, holding each other, and as the soft wind blows out the candle, the room falls dark.

CHAPTER 11

S LOWLY OPENING HIS eyes, Bahi notices Fly walking about
on the far wall in a seemingly sporadic tribal dance. Yawning, he
turns to see Eva, who is fast asleep. Getting out of bed naked, he quickly
puts on his socks and clothes to combat the cold morning and icy concrete
floor as he walks to the bathroom. Coming out, he pulls the covers snug
around Eva, kissing her on the forehead as she opens her eyes smiling.
"Morning," she says as she stretches and pulls the covers closer, shielding
herself from the cold. She slowly rises, and they sit a while in the warm
sun of morning that blankets the front of the guesthouse. Deciding to go
for breakfast, Bahi feels most comfortable and contemplates staying with
her until she leaves for home in a week. They prepare themselves, briefly,
before going off for a walk in the calm morning, finding a small, quiet
café, perfect for a blissful morning such as this. It's early and they're the
only ones in the café with the exception of three Tibetan workers who sit
at a table in the far corner, talking, awaiting the customers who will soon
pour in. Bahi and Eva order as they sit next to a bookshelf populated with
books left behind by wayfaring tourists over the years.

"The Dalai Lama is giving a teaching today," Eva says as her cheese
omelet promptly arrives at the table.

"Oh yeah?"

"I signed up last week. I'd say to come, but it's a big process with security and all. They require passports and photos and such."

"That's fine, I sort of want to relax and do some contemplation on my next steps here," Bahi says as his eyes grow wide to the plate of eggs, potatoes, and toast in front of him.

"I feel bad. Are you sure? I can stay back if you like."

"Feel bad about what? You have done so much for me already. I would feel bad if you didn't go and missed an opportunity to see the Dalai Lama teach, all because of me."

Eva smiles, "Well it's over at half five, we can rendezvous here at six for dinner?"

"That sounds great."

In agreement, they finish their meals and quietly take in the stillness of the morning as they admire the quaintness of the café. Finishing up, they thank the staff and split ways, exiting the café. Bahi watches as Eva walks down a long, narrow road that ends at a large temple just a short distance away. He loses her in a sea of red robes as monks and lay people all funnel down the tightly packed, dusty, road in anticipation of the Dalai Lama's teachings. Bahi keeps on, after the large crowd has passed, and slowly meanders down the road, passing numerous cafes and street vendors, stopping often to check out what they have to offer. Bahi contemplates how he will ever find Shambhala. *Perhaps Eva is right: Who am I to think I can find this place?*

As he nears the temple, he can hear Tibetan being spoken on loudspeakers that seem to be broadcasting from the temple. He assumes it's the Dalai Lama. A side café offers small tables and chairs, partially bathed in the morning sun. A middle-aged European man tunes a small, grey radio to pick up a translation of the teachings. Carefully tuning with a slow turn of his fingers, ear close to the radio, he says, "Uh, there we go!" as he notices Bahi.

Bahi turns his face toward the sun, relaxing in the warm rays as his attention is turned to the English translation on the radio: "And so all the happiness in the world comes from wishing others to be happy, and all the suffering in the world comes from wishing happiness for ourselves alone. All beings want to be happy and don't want to suffer. It's the self-cherishing that is the source of our suffering. So selflessness is the antidote to self-grasping." There is a short gap in the translation as Bahi tunes his ears, now a bit more interested. "We must cultivate compassion because all of our conditions come from others, everything—all of it. All we are physically, all we have, it is all given to us or comes from, in some way, from others. Just check up on this. You'll see it's true, it's logic, it's science. And so if we are going to be selfish, we might as well be wise about it and help others."

Bahi slowly gets up from the chair and walks away, unable to hear the English translation. And as Tibetan spews from loudspeakers, pouring out onto the street, he notices a homeless man with one leg. Inwardly he develops a strong wish for that man to be happy. His heart begins to ache, and he is filled with great compassion. A tear drops down his cheek as he resolves to find Shambhala, not for himself alone, not only for his quest, but for all others: for this homeless man here, for Eva, for Kamini and Bandar, and for his family, whom he can't even remember but imagines must be suffering, especially if they have come to the realization that he is missing.

Selflessness is the antidote to self-grasping. Bahi contemplates these words of wisdom from the Dalai Lama. *Funny, we think the opposite is true. We think if we want something we need to hold onto it, grasp at it for ourselves—including happiness. If we want happiness we have to create it for others.* Bahi breathes in, feeling the strength of a selfless resolve to find Shambhala in order to lead all beings to the happiness they seek, the happiness he seeks, the happiness we all seek in whatever form.

He looks around and realizes that we are all suffering on some level, from the one-legged homeless man, to the people shopping and eating, the workers who brick the side of the building he passes, the shop owner dusting his shop. All of them on some level are reaching for happiness. Even if it's not an intense suffering, all are in the pursuit of happiness, of grabbing often at what they think is happiness. But then these things or people are soon gone, and we are left with more suffering. He reflects on the words of the wise Baba and of Kavi. An inner strength wells up from deep inside of him as the sun pours down blessings on his face, penetrating his being. Bahi sits for a long while on a quiet corner of the road near the temple. The sun moves across the sky, and before he realizes it, several hours have passed. A sea of maroon robes comes flowing from the temple teachings, pouring out in quiet contemplation. Bahi watches as he sits on a stump on the dusty, tan roadside.

"Bahi!" Eva calls out from across the road.

Bahi looks up, surprised to see her in the quiet chaos of people. Coming over to greet her, he sees that she wears a big, relaxed smile as the sun washes over her pale face. "So?" Bahi asks.

"Oh, it was wonderful. I wish you could have come. I realized while I was in there that you have no money. You must be starving. I am sorry about that."

"Don't be sorry. You have been more than generous, and besides that breakfast was easily three meals," he says rubbing his stomach and arching back to stretch in the sun.

"Well, let's get lunch, on me. I have to use up all these *rupees* before I fly home, so it might as well be on you," Eva says, softening her generous offer.

Bahi smiles and places his hand on her shoulder. "I want you to know I appreciate this immensely, and when I figure things out I am going to repay every *rupee*."

"Oh, Bahi, this is my contribution to your great journey. Come on, not another word about it, let's eat."

Eva grasps Bahi's hand as they walk off, both in contemplation of each other and simultaneously not knowing what the other is thinking they reflect, *How wonderful a world would this be if everyone thought of others first, free from selfish gain, even the pursuit of our own well being for others, changing the world by changing ourselves.* With a gentle smile their eyes meet, as if reading each other's minds.

They enjoy the day together, having lunch, walking the streets, getting closer and closer to each other with every step. As evening falls, they sit and partake of mushroom crepes with cashew sauce, overlooking the main square of the city in McCal Ganj, the semi-busy hub of the upper part of this city. Eva orders a bottle of Indian wine, which they enjoy over general conversations about life, each other, India, and how surprised they are at how good the wine is. They share many laughs as the bottle comes quickly to its bottom. Bahi feels warm for the first time in a while, be it the wine, the company, the food, or what have you, he cares not the reason and basks in it wholly. He has thoughts that he could stay in this moment forever, just stay with Eva in comfort. Shambhala, for the first time in weeks, is not the predominant thought in his mind. Fly and his new love interest mingle among the crumbles, which fall on the floor at Bahi's feet.

"I really like you, Paul, or Bahi, or whatever you name is!" Eva laughs, now feeling the wine.

"I really like you too, Eva, or whatever your name is."

The hour is late, and the second bottle of Himachal wine they have ordered sits empty before them. Bahi stands to his feet as the warm rush of red wine enters his head. His thinking pointed yet clouded, he thinks of the journey ahead, and pride born of alcohol puffs him up, though he is quickly deflated by the thought, *What am I doing?*

"What am I doing, Eva?" he asks, as she closes the billfold, paying the bill.

"You're coming home with me," she answers with a wink.

Bahi smiles, content with the unexpected answer as they leave the restaurant. Coming out into the chilly night, Bahi puts his arm around Eva, warming her from the cool Dharamsala winds that gently run up the street, pouring in from the dark forest. Holding Eva close as they walk toward the guesthouse, Bahi breathes in her subtle scent of flowers like a warm breeze over a spring mountain. Reaching the room they step inside and cuddle with each other, the world around far away. The Earth comes to a slow turn, as their time together seems infinite.

He can easily stay right here with her, holding her, smelling her fresh-scented hair, kissing her neck as she sleeps. He ponders this as he looks toward the ceiling, then turning over, he holds her closer, pressing his body warm against hers and as his eyes close, he drifts far away into a deep sleep.

Running through a field of flowers on a mountain hilltop with Eva in dreamlike bliss. Eva is playfully taunting him as he runs backward from her. Suddenly he slips, and the hill breaks away. He descends fearfully into a void. Falling, he reaches up to grab Eva, who moves further away with every second. Her yelling for Bahi from atop is silent and dreamlike, and as her concerned face drops away, Bahi falls deeper into darkness. He swims and struggles in the air and finally hits the murky ground as a vision of the Baba appears. "Bahi, all things end. To grasp at permanence is the path of the fool. It doesn't have to be a fall if you surrender."

Bahi is stuck to the ground, unable to move or speak. The Baba hovers above him and goes on speaking. "The happiness you seek outside of you is fleeting and will soon only make you suffer. The wine tastes good, the girl smells nice, the room is warm, but this will all come to an end, and then what? You have enjoyed the moments, and this is all you can do. Each moment you can turn the fall into a voluntary act, joyfully floating, abiding in each moment, accepting every step."

Suddenly all falls completely dark, and he hears the Baba fading, "Seek Shambhala. Leave soon, before it's too late."

The tunnel speeds back in reverse coming to the conscious world. In a flash Bahi wakes up, staring at the dark ceiling. Dark and cold, Eva has rolled to the opposite side of the bed. Getting out of bed quietly the warm feeling of wine has turned into a headache and thirst. Wrapping a blanket around himself, he then secures Eva in her warm, fleece blankets as she sleeps. He softly opens the door, careful not to wake her, and goes outside to sit on the small, front porch area. Looking up at the bright moon, in the crisp sky of the North Indian night, he thinks about his dream and ponders the truth of the Baba. Just a few hours ago he had felt warm, secure, and fuzzy, and now he feels cold, insecure, and has a slight headache. He thinks about the answers he seeks, knowing that he must move on to find Shambhala tomorrow.

"Buzz, bzzz, what are you doing?" Fly asks, setting down on Bahi's knee as the young philosopher, wrapped in a warm blanket, sits on the concrete porch of the guesthouse.

"Oh, Fly, I'm just thinking of how I have to move on tomorrow to find my destination."

"I staying here. I finding love here," Fly says, as Bahi softly laughs, feeling happy for him.

"I figured that. Good for you. I have to go alone anyway."

"Bahi? Is that you?" Eva says in a groggy fog of waking. "Who are you talking to?"

"Nobody. Myself," he answers, coming back into the room.

"What's the matter, honey?" she asks, closing her eyes and pulling the covers closer to her head.

"Oh, nothing. Just thinking. Go back to sleep," he says, curling up close to her to warm himself, kissing her neck, and whispering, "go back to sleep, beautiful princess." Eva smiles like a child hearing a bedtime story and falls fast asleep. Bahi drinks her in with his eyes, stroking her soft hair until he too falls off to sleep.

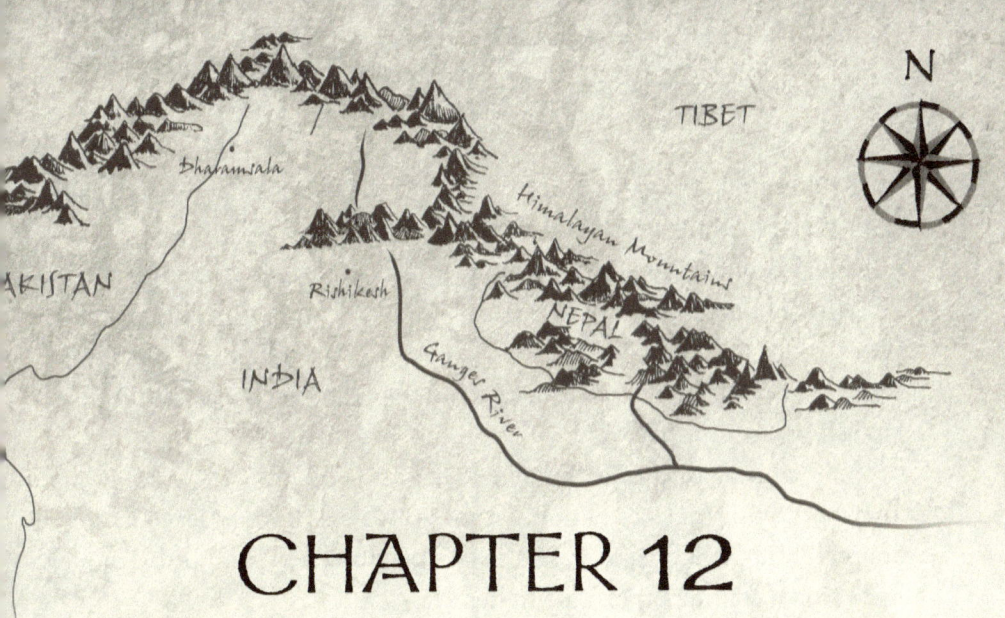

CHAPTER 12

MORNING POURS IN through the windows, bathing the lovers in a golden nimbus. Stretching to the day, Eva smiles, "Why were you outside last night?"

"I was thinking."

"About?" she further inquires.

"About you—how much I like being with you."

Eva smiles, leaning in to hear more.

"About how I have to leave, but don't want to."

"You don't have to, you know, you can stay here with me. You can come to Europe with me. I can take care of your passport and help you remember your life. We can locate your family. I told you my father has powerful connections, so we could easily." Bahi gently puts his finger on her rapidly talking lips.

"I have to find Shambhala, Eva, no matter what else I may want to do."

"Oh, Paul, you don't even know if this place exists," Eva says defensively, trying to sway him to stay with her.

"You're right. I don't, but if I didn't try to find it, I would spend the rest of my life, Paul's life, Bahi's life, wondering, fretting, and regretting the opportunity to possibly help so many."

Realizing her selfish intent, Eva quietly goes over to her small purse on the dresser. Pulling out a stack of *rupees*, she hands them over to Bahi. "This should help you on your journey."

"No, I couldn't. You've done so much for me already. Please."

"Please, Bahi, don't be silly. I am very well off. It's nothing, really. Please, Bahi. For me?" Standing with one arm extending the rupees, she adds, "I need to know you can eat and you can buy some clothes and provisions for your trip."

Bahi smiles, accepting the generous gift as he gives her a long hug. They both wish they could hold on forever. "I will have to leave in a few hours. I'll buy you breakfast," Bahi says playfully holding up the money. Eva's frown counters the smile in her eyes.

"I feel like I just won Indian Millionaire," Bahi says as he fans out the cash, lightening the mood.

Heading out for breakfast, they walk slowly, enjoying their final time with each other. Over breakfast they eat and gaze into each other's eyes as if they will never see each other again. "How do you even know where to begin?" Eva asks.

"I'll head North, as per the Baba's instructions." Bahi goes on to explain a little of his journey so far, omitting any conversation of talking animals so as to avoid a trip to the psychiatrist before leaving.

Finishing breakfast they walk to the main road. Bahi shops around, looking for anything that might be beneficial to his journey ahead. He buys a blue-and-black backpack, a classic name brand knockoff, from a small shop before moving on to a small garment shop next store. Looking around the small garment shop, tightly packed with hand stitched cotton, wool and linen wears, he greets the small woman busy at work with a large ball of yarn. Finding some warm wool socks and a warm black-and-white wool hat with fleece lining, he knows these will come in handy, especially as he goes further North. Eva comes over from the shop next door, holding up light orange-and-gray hiking shoes. "How about these?"

"Perfect," he says, leaving payment on the knitting woman's counter before going over to the shoe shop to fit his size. Putting on his new shoes, he secures the rest of his purchases in his backpack, and they walk off along the road, coming to a produce shop. After a short look around, he comes to the counter, holding apples, oranges, potatoes, nuts, and a small box of butter. Moving along on his shopping spree, he stops off at a shop where he loads up with biscuits, bread, a few packs of matches, a small pot to cook with, and a silver spoon. Feeling he is well prepared, he takes a deep breath as the two stop in silence at the edge of the road.

"Well, Eva, beautiful Eva," he says as a tear falls down her cheek. Bahi wants badly to stay, but knows that moving on is the right thing. He places the three thousand *rupees*, left over from Eva's gift into his pocket and hugs Eva tight. "Thank you so much for all of your kindness and love," Bahi says as Eva pushes back.

"I almost forgot," she says handing him a business card that reads, *Eva McCreary Wellness.*

"This is all my contact information, if you need anything, please call me," she says. Bahi looks down at the card in a moment of silence. "Call me after you reach Shambhala. I want to be the first to know before you become an overnight sensation," she says, lifting Bahi's head with a smile as he looks again into her eyes.

"Eva, I definitely will. Like I said, I promise to repay your kindness."

They stand in the stillness of the moment. "Well then, off with ya!" Eva says in quick Irish sternness, trying not to cry

"Yes, off I go." Bahi kisses her softly on the forehead, then on the lips, before turning to sever, walking away. After a few feet he turns back to see her, as she waves to him. He waves back, and as he turns a street corner, she drops out of sight. Passing the path where he had entered the town only a few days prior, he looks in on the forest and thinks of how he feels like a completely different person than the tattered man who came into this city. Refreshed and renewed, he passes the cross and walks on northward upon a road that quietens as it leaves the busy city. On the tranquil street, he encounters a woman holding her child on her way toward town.

"Sir. Baby. Please," she says looking down to the baby for sympathy.

He can see she suffers greatly. Her filthy, tattered clothes and skinny baby indicate her pain. He remembers this woman from the other day and is reminded also of his wish to help, but had no money. Taking the bundle of three thousand *rupees* from his pocket, he hands it to her as she quickly grasps in disbelief. "Thank you, sir, thank you." Her eyes light up, and thinking he must be mistaken, she quickly conceals the money in her tattered garb.

"Thank you!" Bahi says as he turns and walks the winding road North, breathing in the morning air.

The dusty road is quiet, except for the occasional truck and other vehicles that dip in and out of the sun on the twisting road. Noticing how the road quickly becomes chilly in the shade, he rejoices now, having proper clothing for his trek North. After walking for about an hour, he stops to let the sun shine on his face. A truck holding a large winch on its back presses around the corner and slows as it approaches Bahi. It hums to a stop with a hiss that seems to kick up dust into the streams of light peeking out from the hillside.

"You ride?" The Indian driver offers.

"Sure! Going North," Bahi says, pointing in the direction, noting the driver's broken English.

"Where from?" the driver, dirty from a morning of work, asks.

"U.S.A.," Bahi says, remembering his conversation with Eva.

"Oh, U.S.A. number one!" he says with a smile, as Bahi hops on the flat bed in the back and holds on.

"Where going?" the driver shouts back through the slim window in the driver's cabin as the truck begins to move.

"Shambhala!" Bahi yells. The passenger turns with a look of confusion, "North," Bahi says pointing upward.

"Oh North, North, we take you."

"Thank you!" Bahi shouts as the vehicle, now in full throttle, makes it near impossible to hear.

Bahi hangs on tight as the countryside whips by. Feeling the excitement of a small child, he enjoys the ride. They pass twists and turns of woodlands and jungles, the quiet landscape offers much to look at, from simple, small villages adorned with huts, to serene, lush fields. After an hour of driving, the truck comes to a stop at a crossroad. "Going East," the driver says, sliding the glass window open to talk to Bahi.

"Thank you," Bahi says as he hops down from the vehicle.

As they pull away into the East Bahi stretches his legs and looks around, making a quick calculation of where North is from where the truck pulled off. Noticing one road goes East, one West and the South road they came from which turns West, he looks North, where a steep hill stands devoid of road. A small opening into the forest hill has a sign with Hindi writing on it and an orange Om symbol painted on top. *How auspicious!* he thinks, noting the irony of where he was dropped off. "Back into the woods," he says outloud as he ascends up the small hill. Climbing the rocky path upward, his hands down as he crawls up the steep knoll, he reaches the top of the trail, noticing it flattens out a bit from there. Pieces of rock sporadically line the trail laid with pine needles, a bird chirps, and another hoots as monkeys quickly scurry through the trees above.

Taking an apple from his bag, he bites into it, slurping a big bite as he crunches and walks. Hearing a rustle up ahead, he can make out a goat, with yellow-stained fur and corkscrew horns, hopping up and down, its hind legs caught in some sticker bushes.

"You need some help?" Bahi asks as he draws closer, trying not to laugh at the old goat hopping up and down on her front legs in an attempt to kick the sticker bush from her entrapped hind legs.

"Would you be a doll and help a frail, old goat," she begs kindly.

Bahi takes hold of the sticker bush stick that must have clung to her and ripped it from its bush. Careful not to stick himself, he rips it from her fur. "Thanks, young man, that's better," she says shivering her legs in a tremble of freedom. "Back's not what it used to be," she notes as she leads Bahi with a slow hobble of a walk. "Where are you off to?"

"Shambhala, have you heard of it?"

The goat stops and thinks earnestly, "No, I don't believe I have, and I've been around awhile. I'm the eldest goat in these parts. Must be far from here, cuz I know every nook and cranny as far as the eye can see from these hills."

"To be honest, I am not really sure where it is. I am told it's way North, and if I keep on northward I'll find it. They say it's a pure land of perfect bliss, where the wise live and can answer any question," Bahi explains, feeling an excitement well up inside.

"Oh! Shambhala, you call it, ay?"

"You've heard of it?" Bahi asks eagerly.

"Oh yes, many times in stories. Most animals won't know what it is, but as a young goat, I hung around with a friend, another goat, who used to live on the small land of a very wise man who was able to communicate with animals like you," she says scrunching her brow and just now realizing she is communicating with a human. "The man would tell stories of this Shambhala, as you call it, or the pure land." The goat stops to engage Bahi in the nostalgia of the topic. "It is said there grows a wish-fulfilling cow and hills wrought with wish-granting jewels, but who knows, goats like to fantasize," she says, shrugging off the seriousness of it all.

"Do you know where this wise man lives?"

"I do, although there have been many stories told to me about this man through my dear friend, rest his soul," the goat says, bowing her head in reverence. "He told me he would gather animals who were doomed to be slaughtered and care for them, eventually releasing them back into the forest. My friend was one of them. He would tell us wild tales about this wise man who had great powers. And from what I gather, it may be difficult to talk to him."

"How so?" Bahi inquires.

"He told of how men would come to seek his wisdom, and he would not see them for days, weeks, and they would be left to sleep outside on the stoop. Many would leave, and even those who stayed night after night would seldom be let in for his great wisdom."

"I feel I need to try. Just going North is a broad destination, and my hope was that along the way I would meet someone who could guide me closer."

"Come, my deary, I'll show you the way," the old goat says, her slim, diamond pupils peering at him wearily before turning to lead the way.

Walking a short distance, Bahi keeps pace with the old goat, slow with age. They come to a hilltop and walk to its precipice, looking out over the land.

"I've spent my life here. I love these blessed hills," she says, sighing out a deep breath. "You see off beyond that large tree there?" she asks.

"I do."

"Where you pass that tree, there is a trail that runs all the way up to the wise man's cottage. It's quite a distance, maybe a few days by foot."

Bahi looks in contemplation, and noticing that the trail runs westward, diverting from his northern plans, he feels that it would be beneficial to seek this man out instead of aimlessly wandering North. "Thank you so very much!"

"Have you any food for your trip?" the goat asks.

"I do," Bahi says taking off his pack and unzipping it. "Apple?" he asks.

"Why yes, thanks," she says before biting into the apple, dropping the rest, which she eats after her initial slow chew.

Bahi joins in as he too crunches away at a sweet, warm apple. Finishing the apple, the goat walks over to a bush dotted with red berries and eats a few. "Come take some berries, they will give you strength." Bahi comes over, closely inspecting the bush as he picks one off and looks at the plump, red berry, rolling it around softly in his fingers.

"These are full of the life force."

"Life force?" Bahi asks.

"Everything is full of it. Just some have more of it. Some are tapped in unblocked. You see, there is an all-pervasive force, and when you recognize this you can draw from the most powerful and avoid the weaker, which draw the life force from you. These berries are ripe with power."

Bahi pops several berries in his mouth, enjoying the sweet gush, igniting his taste buds to send them down to his belly. "Interesting," Bahi says as the goat keeps on eating.

"An old goat like me has been around, seen a few things, learned a lesson or two."

"I rekon you have," Bahi says, eating more of the delicious berries.

"If you can tap into the high energy of the life force all around, you will always be protected. Yet know that one day you too will grow old and frail as I have. Everything arises and passes away, and that passing is peace, so don't grasp at even the sweetest berry. Just enjoy it and let it pass away."

"You're very wise for a . . ." Bahi stops himself.

"Go on, say it, 'for a goat,' right?"

"No. I mean yes," Bahi says embarrassed.

"While my friend was still alive he would transmit some of the wisdom to me from the Great Master. He taught me a secret and way of living so I might be reborn a human in my next life."

"You may be better off a goat," Bahi says softly.

"No, don't say that, we may seem to be doing well, but we suffer greatly. Most of us only eat, sleep and go to the bathroom, blind to any pleasure. I am fortunate to have been close to my goat friend, who gained wisdom from the Great Master. You, my friend, have a precious human life. Unfortunately, I often see in the villages that many choose to live like a goat or animal, simply eating, sleeping, procreating and making potty. This opportunity you have to use a mind of logic is a great one and should not be wasted with animalistic cravings. But who am I to say, just an old goat?"

"You're wiser than many humans I know," Bahi says with a laugh.

"Fortunate," she says, "plain and simple, fortunate."

"Well I thank you for the wisdom and direction and wish you well, but I should be getting on before it's too late," Bahi says.

"Yes you should, don't travel in the dark. It's dangerous in the dark," the goat warns.

"Thank you, friend," Bahi says as they begin to descend the hill and walk off across the plain toward the great tree that towers above the rest. He looks back, smiles, and thinks of how fortunate he is to have met the goat.

Coming to the large tree, he looks in wonder as he passes and steps onto the dirt trail washed with sun. The trail is open and dry, aligned with beautiful, vine-like bushes with small, oblong, green leaves that end at a pointed tip. The vines shoot straight up and hang over with the heaviness of bright, pinkish-red bell-shaped flowers that scent the trail as he kicks up a steady pace. He stops for water at a small pond and eats an orange, some nuts, and a roll with butter for lunch. As he sits silently, he listens to the sounds around him. Birds chirp, cicadas buzz, and the faint sounds of children in the distance lead him to imagine there is a small village close by.

Bahi notices the sun is about to retire. He resolves to find shelter for the night and build a fire. The pond is quiet, and as the white lotuses that decorate the water begin to close up for the night, Bahi gets up and walks on down the trail for a short while more, seeking refuge from darkness. The sun is now nearly gone from the sky. Finding a large rock that sits upon a dirt wall, standing tall, supported by tree roots from trees high above, he takes off his backpack. *It's not complete shelter, but it's better than the open trail*, he thinks, as he goes off to gather some wood. Digging a small hole and lining the perimeter with rocks, he skillfully places the sticks and larger wood pieces he has gathered in the hole before taking the small pot he bought to fetch some water from a nearby stream and wash up.

As the last remnant of light dissolves, he sparks a match, igniting some dry leaves he has placed below the sticks and wood. They quickly catch fire, and he smiles as the campfire crackles, growing stronger. Placing the pot with water on top of a large piece of wood he puts two potatoes in the pot. The water slowly comes to a rolling boil, and he lays back with his head on his pack, sighing in the relief of having some luxuries now. Looking up, he gazes at the stars, now visible in the clear black sky and wonders what Eva is doing. He imagines them cuddling up by the fire and talking about nothing in particular as they gaze at each other over some nice Himachal wine. The quick sizzle of boiling water flowing over into the fire, dissipates his fantasy as he uses his shirt to pull the pot from the flame, emptying the water. The potatoes smoke in the cool air, and he waits a few moments for the blazing-hot potatoes to drop in temperature. He mashes them up in the pot with some butter, and blowing off a bite, he plunges it into his mouth. Chewing the potato, he thinks of the delicious food he had in Dharamsala with Eva. He scrapes every last scrap from the pot. He adds more wood to the fire, shielding himself from the vast, dark forest surrounding him. The large rock to his back and the fire to his front give him a sense of security, as he lies in contemplation, gazing at the stars as he drifts off to sleep. He instinctually wakes up often in the night, adding more wood to the fire to combat the cold. The fire warms him to his core as he drifts back to sleep. Waking up a final time, he discovers he has exhausted all the wood. The fire sputters a final flame, which dwindles off of a charred log like a candle flickering to an end. Shivering, he wraps himself tight with his shawl. It's just before dawn. The hills are blue from the yielding of night to the subtle blush light that struggles to create the day. A crescent moon, slim as a fingernail, hovers over the hills. The sun softly rises, as a howl from the distance cries out and a lone bird whistles in the forest. As the sky brightens, gentle breezes caress the hills. Bahi's shawl, hat, and wool socks comfort the chill as he listens, still in a half sleep, to baby birds singing out in cadence to the morning's birth.

Bahi rises to his feet, still tired from a restless nights' sleep. He stretches and gathers his things to get an early start. Dreading another day of hiking, he rubs his face awake, wishing he had a warm bed to rest in. But, he makes the best of it, pressing on in the cold chill of morning. The hike warms his blood, and as the sun begins to gently heat the day, he sits to eat some fruit, bread, and butter. The tepid sun eases his depressed mind and body, still weary from yesterday's hike and only a few hours of sleep. He finishes his food and makes his way to a stream that runs along the trail and quenches his dry lips and throat. The smell of last night's fire permeates his clothing and mixes with the scent of the cool morning breeze. Giving himself a pep talk while washing his hands and face, he thinks of how wonderful it will be when he reaches Shambhala. The cold water ignites his mind, perking his senses as he lifts up and moves on, shaking the smoke of lethargy from his head.

Walking a good distance, he notices the sun is now high in the afternoon sky. He comes to a split in the path and contemplates which way he should go. He thinks it over, glancing down each path, and decides that because either way is unknown he should just pick a direction. Fear wells up. He does not want to choose the wrong path and stray from the direction to the wise man. Taking off his shirt in the hot sunlight, he decides to go right. He walks a bit and comes to a steep decline, where the trail drops off in an almost vertical slope below. Feeling cautious, he takes a step as rocks slip from under his feet, falling past the jagged rocks that stick out from the slope. It looks as though no one has traversed this path for some time.

Contemplating going back to the other path in the split, he considers that the path to such a wise man is probably one of great obstacles and decides to keep on. Sitting on his butt, he grabs hold of some well-rooted shrubs as he slides down slowly. Coming to his feet again, he jumps to a solid part of the slope before stepping off to another seemingly solid rock in the dark decline of the trail. The rock slips out, sending him flying down the slope, knocking him about. He catches his left leg on a piece of cold rock. In pain, he throws off his backpack and paces back and forth trying to limp off the piercing stab that shoots up his leg. A faint rush of cold sweat glazes his body. Mumbling obscenities to no one, he sits down to have a look at his leg. The rock tore clean through his pants, and blood soaks his sock. The pain is numbing, and his heart races in the fear that he may have done some serious damage. He sits and breathes consciously, not knowing his next step. He regrets the step he took that led him to the fall. "Damn it!" he screams out, his cry of remorse echoing through the hills, as tears fall down his cheek. Then, he notices a cave-like rock dwelling, and as the nausea that washes over him dissipates slightly, he hobbles over to it and sits in the sun for a while, just breathing, trying to calm his mind.

The continuing waves of pain make him realize that he won't be able to keep on hiking. He resolves to gather some wood, rest the remainder of the day, and spend the night in the shelter of this cave-like arch of rock, which opens up into a flat, dirt path just behind two trees. He hobbles to gather wood. As he lays a final piece of strong twisted branch, which he tries to break into kindling. But he gives up as sweat trickles down his face, leaving him faint. Feeling exhausted and queasy, he lies down for the remainder of the day, trying to divert his mind from the sharp, shooting pain. Both nausea and faintness plague him as the sun sets, leaving the day far behind.

Lying in darkness, he hesitates to light the fire, knowing the sooner he lights it the sooner it will go out and that the night will grow colder. He feels bouts of nausea and exhaustion and decides to light the fire. It takes him almost and entire book of matches to get it going. All the while he wonders why fate seems to have turned against him. Finally the fire blazes as he lays back, closing his eyes. Despite the throbbing pain, his dreams rush in like clouds in a storm. His mind tosses and turns, prompting him awake in the darkness of night, to turn back, to go home. Sweating now, in feverish delirium, he drifts in and out of sleep. The fire is out, and he shivers with the heat of fever that blazes within, due to infection in his leg. Waking up a few times, he throws up, off to the side of the cave, heaving an empty stomach. He manages to hobble to the stream to gather water in his pot. Scared and alone, he thinks he may die there and that even if he could listen to the promptings of his dreamlike fear, there is no way he can hike back, in this condition. After all, he practically had to crawl to the stream only a few feet away.

Waking up again, Bahi stares into the blazing sun, not having any sense of time or space, his lips dry and cracked. His leg is stiff, and as the blood dries around the puss of an open wound, he thinks over and again that he should wash out the wound, but dares not to touch it.

The cold night once again sets in as he drags in the remainder of wood he had piled up the day before. Barely able to light a match, he attempts to ignite a fire. Nausea and fatigue give him double vision as one last attempt sends the wooden matches flying in all directions. His head smacks down and he passes out once again in the fury of fever. The lord of death watches down upon him as he slips into a comma-like slumber. Opening his eyes in a dream, he finds himself in a beautiful, silent, tree-lined meadow adorned with sweet flowers and lush, green grasses. He stands painless and free and notices an image, like a mirage, shimmering toward him. Making out the white glow, he notices a beautiful woman gliding toward him. Mesmerized by her pale beauty and calming eyes, he surrenders to her energy, which captivates him. As she nears, his leg begins to throb as it opens up, pouring blood, dropping him to the grass, with pain. The woman swiftly catches him, almost falling at him, lying with him and holding him tight. He feels warm and secure as he stares into her endless eyes, which soothe his pain. "Fear not, Bahi, I am with you," she says smiling, as her long, golden-blond hair radiates light. She wears a long, pure-white, tunic that falls to her feet, outlining her perfectly formed body.

"I can't go on anymore. I can't," Bahi says without moving his lips.

"It's all going to be all right," she says as he stares at her full, red lips set upon her smooth, moon-pale skin.

Captivated by her beauty, he views his dream as an observer and sees himself lying on the grass coddled by this goddess of a woman. The sky begins to rain down flowers as she kisses him on the lips and holds him. He feels the wounds on his leg heal up almost instantly. "I'm scared," he thinks.

"Of course you are, but it's OK because we love you." he hears as they engage in still another long, soft kiss.

"Who does?" he asks in his mind as white light overwhelms his sight, flooding him in the warmth of its luminosity.

"Don't give up. Never give up. You will find what you seek. If you never give up, you will never fail."

He hears the soft wisdom of the Goddess as all falls black. The crackling of the fire opens his eyes from the dream. Flames rage in his haphazard fire pit as he notices his fever has passed. Looking down at his leg, he sees that he still has the wound, but it seems to hurt less. He lies in wonder of the dream, and in the warm glow of the fire, he now drifts off into a luxurious, dreamless sleep of deep healing.

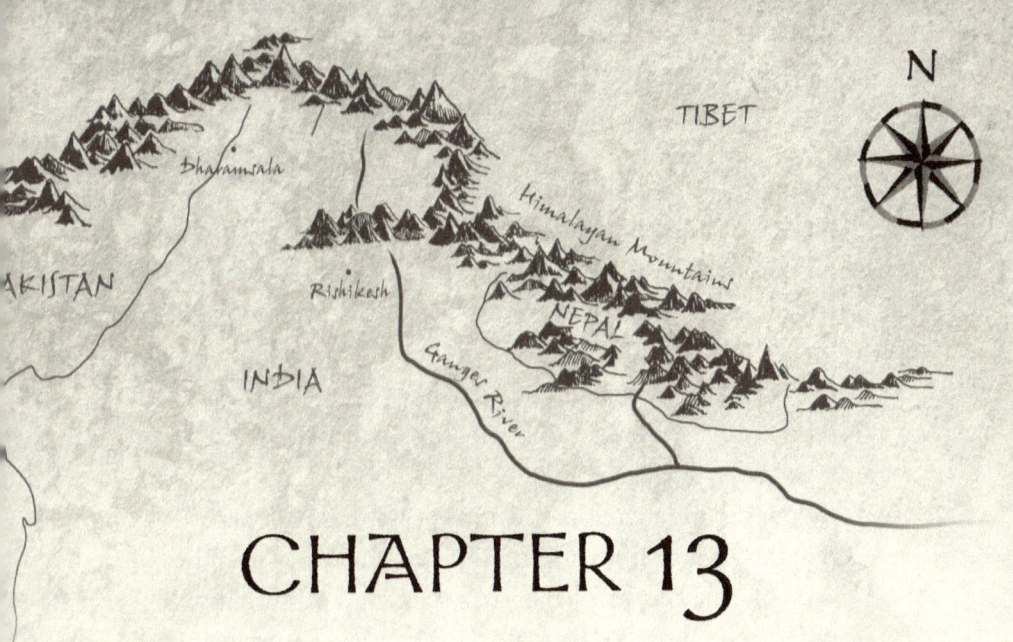

CHAPTER 13

I N THE MORNING Bahi feels much better and is finally able to
eat. He hobbles down to the stream for water and sits by its edge
and thinks, still in a daze after the incredible dream. He looks down and
across the stream. A wolf laps up water, peering at him with yellow eyes.
Bahi's heart stops as the wolf suspends his drinking—locking eyes with
Bahi. The animal's gray coat is clouded in black shrugs as he pulls his head
from the water and runs, crossing the stream near Bahi. Bahi leaps up,
dropping his pot, and with no regard for the pain in his leg, begins to run
to the cliff. The wolf quickly gains on him, tripping him with a bite of his
shoe. Bahi falls to the ground, quickly rolling onto his back. He can smell
the wolf lunging at him as he shields his eyes and face in defense. After
a moment he lowers his guard as the wolf just pants in his face, standing
over his chest.

"Hello?" Bahi ventures cautiously.

"Oh, me too!" the wolf says. Bahi cautiously sits up on the cold rocky
ground, with heart still pumping and beads of sweat forming on his body.
"Some wound you got there," the wolf comments.

"Yeah, I fell," Bahi says, still uncertain.

"You mind if I clean it up for ya? Looks like it might get infected."

"Sure." Bahi says hesitantly as the wolf begins to lick the wound.

"Ouch!" Bahi cries, pulling away.

"Don't worry, after this you'll be a new man," the wolf says between licks.

Bahi endures the pain, remembering that dogs have healing agents in their saliva. He smiles uncomfortably as the coarse tongue disinfects his wound. Finishing up, the wolf licks around his mouth and paws. Bahi looks down at his cleaned wound. "Thanks."

"Oh, nothing to it. Glad to be of assistance. Say, what brings you out here, anyway?"

"I'm looking for a wise man who lives not far from here."

"Oh, yeah I know him, of him. I mean, it's not far from here."

"Could you take me there?" Bahi asks, standing and brushing off his clothes.

"Sure. It'll be about a days walk with that leg. You're lucky I came this way. You could easily be dinner with that hobble."

"For whom? You?"

"Ah! No. Humans don't taste too good from what I've heard. But there are all types in this forest who would eat just about anything. In fact, I can hear them salivating now waiting for me to leave," his ears perk up.

Bahi looks around nervously, saying, "Yes, yes, I would be in your debt if you would show me the way."

"Ha ha, I am sure you would," the wolf says raising his head proudly and shaking his thick fur that covers his stocky fit body. "What's the name?"

"Bahi, what's yours?"

"Bahi, eh. Funny you don't look like a Bahi."

"Oh yeah? What do I look like?"

"You look like a Jack."

"What about Paul," Bahi asks.

"What about Bahi?" the wolf laughs, then strikes a serious tone. "I am Ajee," he says, lowering his head in honor.

"Funny, you don't look like an Ajee," Bahi fires back.

"Oh yeah? What do I look like then?"

"You look like a wolf," Bahi says as they both laugh.

"Jack and the Wolf," Ajee says, feeling a camaraderie.

"So, Wolf, who named you, anyway?"

"A wise old Baba with whom I would have conversations. In fact you are the only other human I've ever talked to. Say, are you a wise Baba too?"

"Far from it, Wolf. Far from it."

"Who named you?"

"You wouldn't believe me if I told you."

"You'd be surprised what these eyes and ears have witnessed in this forest, Bahi. Try me."

"A monkey."

"A monkey?"

"That's right, a friend, a brother," Bahi says proudly in a reverent manner.

"A monkey. Well then, I didn't see that one coming, but, hey, we've all got our stories don't we?"

"I presume we do. What's your story, Ajee?"

"It's a long one, and best told on our way to your destination before these predators have both of us for breakfast," Ajee says looking into the thick of the forest.

Bahi strains to look, but sees only wooded forest. An eerie feeling of being watched washes over him. "Let me gather my things, and we'll be off."

Bahi gathers his belongings, puts on his backpack, and urinates on the still-hot ambers of the fire. Smoke loudly pours out of the sizzling ambers as he finishes up and hobbles alongside Ajee. He feels safe in the protection of his new wolf friend. Walking off along the sunlit path, Bahi again asks, "So what's your story?"

"Ah, yes, the story. Well, where to begin? The journey has been long." As Ajee thinks where to begin Bahi picks up a tall stick he uses to crutch the weight of his bad leg. "I was born second in line to the alpha male of our pack. My brother went crazy and tried to kill me, yada yada yada. I left the pack as a lone wolf, tried to find a good female companion to no avail, fell in with a wise Baba who taught me great lessons, and now here I am."

"Certainly that was the abridged version," Bahi says.

"The what?" Ajee asks, confused.

"The short version."

"Yes, the short version. Hey, I figure it like this: if you have no story you have nothing to live up to, and every day is like a renewal," Ajee says, stopping by the stream to drink.

"I like that, Wolf. I like it a lot," Bahi says, bending down and cupping his hands. He scoops out some of the icy cold water into his mouth.

"What about you, Jack? What's your story?"

"I told you, a monkey named me," he answers with a smirk.

"And before the monkey?"

"Well, I was born somewhere that I can't remember and yada yada yada. I hit my head, monkeys, little people, a tiger, hurt my leg and now a wolf."

They both have a laugh. "I see you and I will get along just fine," Ajee says, walking off onto the path followed by Bahi.

"Hey, Wolf!" Bahi calls out.

"Yes?"

"What does Ajee mean?"

"Immortal."

"Oh, OK, cool. And are you?"

"Am I what?"

"Immortal, like your name says?"

"We will all die, Bahi. Everything ends. This is what the Baba taught me above all."

"Sounds like a fatalist, this Baba," Bahi says.

Ajee stops, looking up at Bahi. "If everything dies and ends constantly, then this is the true nature of things, and thus death is a mere word. What really happens is change of form, constantly. I am not the same wolf physically as I was when I was born—and you too."

"I am not the same wolf. You are right," Bahi says, adding some humor.

"Therefore, we never die. We are immortal in the sense that we just keep cycling back around into different forms, like the words coming out of my mouth: one ends to create another. This is the only way it can be, like the river that flows, stagnation is a myth, change is the only certitude my friend."

Bahi thinks a minute about how fortunate he is to keep running into these wise animals. He never would have thought that so many animals could pass down such wisdom. "Wow, that's profound, Wolf."

"That's not my words, it's the wise Baba's," Ajee says, again stopping to lower his head in reverence.

"Perhaps I should meet this Baba."

"You just have. His body has passed on long ago," Ajee says.

"So there is death," Bahi confirms.

"You, me, this tree: we will die. This body will wither and perish, and it will happen quicker than you think. This is why we must practice helping others and perform virtuous deeds, so our next form could be conducive to furthering the advancement of our minds. Or perhaps next I will be human," Ajee says proudly.

"I've been told it's the thing to be these days," Bahi says again, adding humor to the conversation. "I agree with you, Ajee, about virtuous deeds of helping others and such."

"It only makes sense. The energy we go forward with is the energy that creates the next moment, like a sentence. If I begin an angry sentence it throws that energy forward, creating anger. So too do all our actions. And since we never know when this body will die, we need to practice always, have a sense of urgency each moment, because that moment could be our last and that last moment will propel us into the next moment with whatever we have chosen."

"This Baba was wise, and I feel he was not the only one with wisdom. You too are wise, Ajee. I am looking for a place called Shambhala. Has the Baba ever talked about this to you?"

Ajee halts to a gasp, looking into Bahi's eyes. "And this only humans can achieve."

"How do you mean?" Bahi asks.

"The Baba talked about Shambhala, where the bread is always warm, the butter plenty, and rivers of nectar flow endlessly. Fires glow soft and strong and will never burn you. It's a pure land, Bahi. Yet animals will pass it by and never notice it. It takes only the mind of a human to find it, an exceptional human at that."

"Why is that?"

"I am unsure. Perhaps because of our minds. Not all animals think like me Bahi. I was blessed by the Baba. Before that all I did was eat, sleep, and hunt prey in almost constant fear. Now I still do this, but somehow am conscious of this and thus I am trying to live a life that will gain me a favorable rebirth so I can reach this Shambhala. It is here where one can be enabled to help all. The most virtuous life of all can be lived once one passes through its gates."

"Well, Ajee, if and when I find it, I promise you I will come back and show you the way."

Ajee's eyes and ears perk up. Then, remembering the teaching of the Baba, he sighs, "Perhaps in another life, my friend. Time is fleeting, and you are fortunate to be human and even more fortunate to be on the path to Shambhala. My path there is much longer than yours, but we mustn't give up."

"I won't give up, Ajee. I started out looking for this place for myself, to answer questions of who I am. And now I want to find it so I can learn how to help everyone. And in truth, if it were just a journey for myself, I may have abandoned it long ago. I now go on for the benefit of everyone: friends I've lost, friends like you, in fact I almost gave up hope that this place even existed and lost scope of why I wanted to find it, but now, my friend, you have renewed hope in me."

"Glad I could help, Jack, but you'll never find the wise man, let alone Shambhala, if we don't keep moving."

Bahi breathes in a breath mixed with laughter, and together they walk along the open plains. A cold mist sets upon the otherwise dry field dotted with pine trees. Bahi stops for a moment to rest his leg. The late morning sun quickly dries the dampness that permeates the air from the long night. Feeling the warmth on his face he can no longer see his breath as the day progresses. Ajee saunters over and begins to lick Bahi's wounded leg. "Hee hee, that tickles, ouch!" Bahi cries out.

"Sorry, Jack."

"No worries, it's just a bit raw still."

"Can you manage to go on?"

"Yeah, just need a few moments to rest here and there."

Ajee sits besides Bahi, biting at some bugs that land on his rear before letting out a yawn that ends with a squeal of relief. They sit in silent contemplation. Ajee happily pants, tongue askew, hanging out over his teeth, bobbing from his rapid breathing. Bahi ponders the amazing journey he has thus endured, *a talking wolf*, he thinks, as he laughs to himself. Getting up, he gives a pat on Ajee's hide, springing him quickly to his feet.

"Feel rested?" Ajee asks.

"Somewhat. Good enough, I suppose."

"Onward?" Ajee asks.

"Onward, Wolf, onward."

Bahi peers out across the field toward the thick of the woods. With each passing day and every step North it grows colder. He realizes that they are now traveling northwest, and he has a feeling of confidence in his path, confidence that had been lacking for a few days. The day's sun is as strong as Bahi's resolve as they enter a narrow path of a pine forest. Bahi begins to whistle a tune he feels is familiar but can't place the name. Ajee hums along as the two make merrily on their way for some time—before coming to a gorge. The crisp spray from the crashing gorge splashes off a felled tree. Ajee hops upon the tree, which acts as a bridge between the two sides of the gorge. Bahi joins him and sits in the noonday sun, watching the water rush below his feet. Falcons circle in the air above tall pines in the deep, bright blue sky adorned with thick, glowing, clouds. Crossing the water, they take in the beauty that surrounds. Bahi releases his pack, placing it on the brown pine needle floor, taking out the last two rolls. "Bread?" He extends his hand to a sniffing Ajee, who graciously takes it into his sharp fangs and then carefully places it on the tree, where he stands biting at it. Bahi follows the roll with a crisp red apple and nuts, which he shares with Ajee.

"I've never had these. *Nuts* you call them?" Ajee asks.

"Yes, *nuts*: almonds, full of protein, great for hiking."

"Hiking?" Ajee asks.

"Walking long distances as we are, humans call that a hike."

"Speaking of which we still have a long journey ahead of us. Shall we?" Ajee invites.

Bahi stretches and cautiously makes his way to his feet. He follows Ajee to the other side of the gorge, careful not to lose footing on the slippery parts splashed with water and cultivated with slick moss. Walking on, Bahi notices he is still hungry. Thoughts of the wonderful meals he had at the Baba's home fill his mind. His food has rapidly grown scarce now: only a couple of oranges and handful of almonds lie in his pack. *Why hadn't I bought more?* he worries, *I should have had an entire pack just for food.*

As they trek on and on, Bahi's leg swells, and he begins taking breaks more often. Sitting at one such break on a rock in the forest, Ajee runs off into the woods to relieve himself. Bahi notices him as he gallops back with a smile that seems to be always on his face. Optimism pours from his dark yellow eyes, a trait Bahi accepts easily.

"The sun is setting, and we still have a while to go. Maybe we should stay here until morning," Ajee suggests, pointing his snout toward a pine-tree-sheltered area behind them.

"Good idea. I'll collect some wood for a fire."

The two head out, collecting wood and sticks, which they quickly pile up. "This will be enough for two nights," Bahi says, noting the benefits of two wood gatherers.

Ajee squats down in a sudden hunting mode, "What's the matter?"

"Shhh!" Ajees' eyes are still. A rabbit springs from a bush like a bolt of lighting. Ajee gives chase, quickly disappearing from sight. Bahi internally hopes that the small gray-and-white rabbit can outrun Ajee as he squats to light the dry leaves he situated under a carefully piled stack of wood.

The fire hastily grows to a full blaze as Bahi sits on the ground, warming himself from the already cold air, the evening sun still ablaze. Ajee comes galloping back, the corpse of the rabbit hanging in his bloody jaws.

"Awww, Ajee, c'mon."

Placing the rabbit at Bahi's feet proudly, Ajee replies, "What? It's dinner, you don't want to starve out here, do you?"

Bahi realizes that this is the nature of the beast. Ajee is forced to murder his food for survival. He realizes that he would not last another day on an orange and some nuts. He is grateful for Ajee's skills in hunting. Bahi hasn't eaten meat in quite some time, in fact he can't remember the last time he had. Staring down at the bloody carcass of a rabbit, he looks up at Ajee. "Thank you," Bahi says. Ajee nods.

"You know, Bahi, it's the plague of the wolf. We must kill to survive. Humans have a unique advantage over us, but still they kill. I once asked the wise Baba about this. He never ate meat, and he explained it like this: every meal that has graced his plate was not without sacrifice. Bugs died while picking and caring for the vegetables and so forth. He said that the important thing was to be grateful for all the beings who were so kind to bring this meal to his plate, the farmer who cared for the seeds and crops, the workers who picked his vegetables, the animals and insects who died for it in each process, whether in growth or transportation or being run over by the vehicles bringing it to different locations, being grateful for the transporters who brought it, those who packaged it and prepared it, although he mostly grew and prepared his own food. You get the point?" Ajee inquires.

"I guess in this world we live in, Ajee, nothing is without sacrifice: no meal is without suffering," Bahi says again looking at the rabbit.

"But what is to be remembered, my friend, is the gratitude and mindfulness of all those involved in getting this to our bellies. Even this rabbit exists because he ate some veggies and grass that grew in soil, seedlings of others fed by the death of countless beings, insects and so forth, which fortified the soil. And so we can be grateful to all, and especially to the rabbit," Ajee bows his head.

"Ajee, you are truly wiser than most humans I have met. I gather you are well on your way and could accompany me all the way to Shambhala."

"You think?" Ajee says excitedly.

"Yeah, of course," assures Bahi.

"These are the words of the Baba, not me."

"Yes, but it's now your understanding that, like all the things that depend upon my food on a plate, so too is the wisdom from mouth to ear, and it goes back before the Baba. I assure you, those words are yours, Ajee, you chose to speak them."

Ajee thinks for a moment, looking to the sky where the sun now dances streams of orange and pinks across the horizon. "It's endless, beginningless," Ajee says in wonder.

Bahi begins to remember what the wise Baba had told him about how nothing exists the way he perceives it to. It all makes more sense now. Everything depends on everything else. And if you trace anything back, you will find it's beginningless. Looking down, he sees the rabbit lying lifeless before the blazing fire. Grabbing hold of a thick stick, he cringes as he stabs it through the rabbit and puts it over the fire.

"This is a weird technique. You won't ruin it, will you?" Ajee asks, concerned for his dinner.

"It's called *cooking*, Ajee. Surely you've heard of it. I think I was supposed to remove the fur first, though," Bahi says, watching as the fur singes off in the raging inferno.

"I have. The Baba would do it, just never saw it done with an animal."

After a few minutes, he pulls the charred stick and rabbit from the fire, tapping the meat, checking to see how hot it is. After it cools a bit, he rips off a hind leg. Streams of steam pour out as Ajee bites away at it, careful not to burn his mouth. Salivating, they both sink their teeth into the meat. *Doesn't taste too bad*, Bahi thinks, now wishing there was another. Finishing up the meat, Ajee continues to gnaw at the bones, and as Bahi peels an orange Ajee looks up. "To the sacrifice and kindness of this rabbit. Its life has let us endure a few more moments on this precious Earth."

"Here here, to the rabbit," Bahi raises his peeled orange, offering a piece to Ajee, who sniffs it and declines in disgust.

They both sit in silence in front of the raging fire, "Ajee?"

"Yes?"

"You're by far one of the most intelligent and unique animals I have ever met."

"Oh yeah? Well you're up there on my list of unique and intelligent animals too," Ajee replies. They both have a chuckle, and feeling the connection to the forest and elements, Bahi feels more like a wild animal as he strokes his full beard and pushes his hair behind his ears.

For the first time in several nights he feels comfortable and safe. Ajee's presence is that of a protector, allowing Bahi to fall fast asleep, drunk from the heat of burning flames before him. Ajee sits, eyes half open as he feels the comfort of his blazing-hot fur coat close to the fire. He sits so close that the intensity of heat is near burning as the smell of hot fur relaxes him deeply. They both drift off into a realm far from the forest floor, soon to be reborn in the morning sun, protected through the night by fire and comradery. The forest smiles down upon them as sparks float up from the crackling, dry pine that pops. Glowing ashes, which attempt to reach the bright stars, adorn the clear black sky. From high above one can see the glow of friendship amongst the cold, dark forest. An owl peers down in wonder, a dark-brown leaf bat points out the billowing smoke to his friend. They stare down as they swoop far above. The two lie dead to the world, in peaceful slumber, awaiting the morning rebirth.

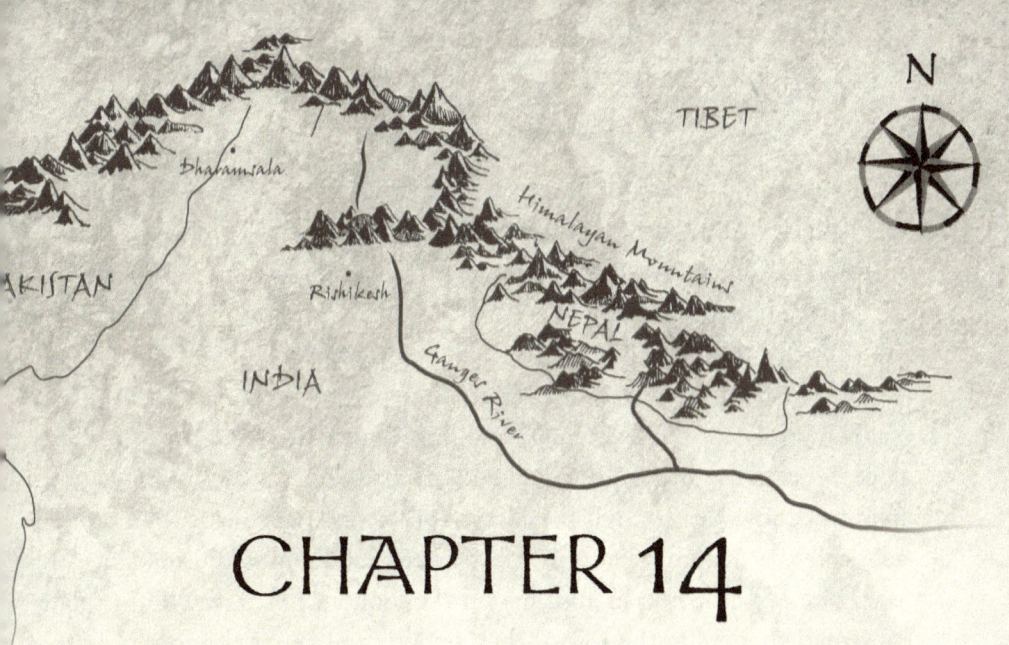

CHAPTER 14

BIRDS CHIRP IN the arrival of dawn's light as Bahi slowly opens his eyes, forgetting for a second where he is. Looking around, he sees Ajee nowhere as the last chars of wood smoke to completion.

"Ajee," Bahi calls out, standing to his feet to look around. "Ajee?" he softly yells into the forest. *Has he left me?* he worries, *I have no idea where to go from here.* The worried thoughts fill his mind as the minutes pass with Ajee nowhere in sight. Rounding a tree, Bahi heads back to the camp when a pounce on his back forces him to fall. Quickly turning from his belly onto his back, he looks up to find Ajee hovering over him. "Wolf! Where were you?"

"What? Are you the only one who has to go to pee around here?"

Bahi laughs, attempting to push him off, but he persists playfully, mock biting his arm. After a brief, playful tussle Bahi gets up and brushes off. "Most dogs I know just lift a leg when ever it's time to go."

"Most dogs?" Ajee says seemingly amazed.

"*Wolf* I meant," Bahi retorts realizing his words.

"Oh yeah, and how many wolves do you know?"

"Uh, none, I guess, well one now, forget it, it was a silly thing to say."

Ajee stares in a serious silence at Bahi, creating an uncomfortable air. Taking two steps to a tree next to them, lifts his leg and pees on the tree.

"Ahhh, I was just messing with ya. I was hunting for some breakfast, to no avail." Finishing up, he puts down his leg and walks toward the camp.

Bahi laughs to himself, relieving the tension and shaking his head.

"How's the leg, Bahi?"

"Better. Still hurts, but totally scabbed over now."

"Good, because we've got a bit of a hike ahead of us."

Bahi pulls out the last orange and bag of nuts. Splitting the nuts with Ajee, he eats the orange himself, and after packing away his shawl and hat, they move on through the forest, following Ajee's lead. Their stomachs, now even hungrier from the tease of a few nuts, prompt Ajee to keep one eye on the trail and one on the lookout for prey. Coming to a crossroad that splits the forest, they find several street vendors cooking chai, chapattis and chicken. The smell from afar makes their stomachs rumble. "I'll try to see if I can get some food for us," Bahi says, knowing he has no money.

"If you want, I can run out and growl as a distraction while you grab and run," Ajee suggests.

"Steal it? I don't know," Bahi says peering out at the three men awaiting buses at this remote rest stop in the middle of nowhere.

"What would the Baba say to that?" Bahi asks.

"Yeah, you're right," Ajee says looking down.

"Well, what would he say?" Bahi asks genuinely curious.

"He would say that what you do now will echo in eternity. He was always teaching of how our actions, both virtuous and not, will create results and start a wheel turning that is hard to reverse. And so he would say, 'based on the science of cause and effect.' He loved science, that stealing will cause us to have more lack in the future. And what may seem like a gain would be a fleeting ignorance that would create our fate later."

Bahi again is amazed at how this wolf can recall these teachings almost effortlessly. "Wow! Impressive! You were a great student of his I see, and yes that's my feelings too. Besides, I have an idea. Meet me on the other side just up the trail a bit," Bahi says, pointing out across the road to where the trail runs back into the forest.

"OK. I'll walk the higher road and meet you on the other side. If they see me, it may cause a stir."

"Good idea," Bahi says as he struts out to the road.

"Namaste," one man greets.

"Hello, Sir. Where you coming from?" the other vendor asks with a smile from ear to ear almost touching the small patches of gray hair on either side of his bald head.

"Just hiking, and I realized I have no money but am starving."

"Please sit," the balding man says pulling out a plastic chair from one of three tables upon the dirt road. "You no money is fine, I give you piece of chicken," the man says, removing a small piece of chicken from the smoking grill.

"Where you're from, Sir?" The other, shorter, darker man asks.

"America," he quickly says without even a thought.

"America! I love America!" the short one exclaims.

"Oh yeah? You been?" Bahi asks.

"No," he replies as Bahi gives a laugh.

"America, Obama, I like Obama, Black-man president," the balding man says, bringing over a small piece of chicken on wax paper.

"This is true," Bahi says trying not to laugh at the absurdity of the conversation.

"Say, I have a friend I am meeting down the trail a bit. He doesn't have money either. Could I trade you my backpack and this cooking pot for some food?" Bahi asks the balding man standing over him and the chicken.

Inspecting the bag on the table, Bahi removes his hat and shawl. "OK. Nice bag, I give you whole chicken for bag and hat," he offers.

Bahi thinks, knowing he is getting the short end of the deal being that the bag is new and costs about twenty times what a whole chicken costs. "How about two chickens for the bag and pot. I need the hat for the cold. I just bought the bag for two thousand *rupees*."

"OK, Mr. America." The man places two very small cooked chickens in a newspaper and rolls them up separately. "And have two *pani* for you," he adds, handing him two bottles of water.

"Thank you," Bahi says, cradling the small chickens in one arm and the bottles and hat wrapped in his shawl, bundled in the other arm.

"OK, friend, see you soon," the balding man says.

"Goot bye," the third man, who said nothing the whole time, speaks out.

"OK. Thank you," Bahi says, walking to the other side of the street. "Obama!" he shouts before entering the trail.

"Obama!" they echo back in sync.

"Boo!" Ajee pops out of a bush, startling a laughing Bahi.

"You really gotta stop doing that," he says as he sits on a rotting log, placing down the spoils of his barter.

"All right, brother, how'd you do it?"

"The good ole bartering system," he says, laying the shawl on the ground picnic style.

Unraveling the newspaper, he exposes the chickens. Ajee quickly grabs one instinctually and eats it on the dirt, practically inhaling it.

"Easy boy, enjoy it, there's no race."

Ajee just keeps on devouring until it's gone. Bahi, ravished as well, quickly finishes, and they sit with full bellies and a smile.

"Eating is weird, huh?" Bahi asks.

"How so?"

"I don't know. No matter how much we eat, we are always going to be hungry again," Bahi explains.

"Welcome to planet Earth, my friend," Ajee says with a chuckle.

Bahi thinks again about the Baba's words and of how this is what he means by not being led to believe external things are lasting happiness— and to just enjoy them as they pass, savoring the moment, not attaching, because soon you will be hungry again and again. *Two students learning the same lessons on different terms, now traveling together*, he thinks.

"All right, let's move. We don't have much further. We should be there by sundown if we don't stop again," Ajee rallies them up. They briskly move, now full of energy and food for thought. They walk the day and Bahi's leg feels stronger and less achy in the warm, energizing saturation of beautiful daylight that seems to pour in all directions.

CHAPTER 15

A S THE SUN begins to make its descent, they come to a small hilltop overlooking a short valley nestled in the hills. Bahi sees a modest hut-looking abode with a small, fenced farm beside it. Smoke pours out: a white, milky dance billowing from the chimney.

"There it is," Ajee says.

"That's where he lives?" Bahi asks.

"Yep. He will know how to get to Shambhala. The Baba would speak of him often in the greatest reverence. The Wise One in the valley, he who has gone beyond day and night, neither living in the lowest valley or highest mountaintop, free from duality, living in the middle," Ajee says staring in an almost trance.

Bahi is not really sure what that means, but it sounds good, and his excitement wells up as they descend the hill near the house. The evening air is thick with energy. Cold air swoops through the valley, pressing them back as if to slow down the nervous, rapid pace of Bahi. Standing now at the front of the hut, they feel warm as the sun burns a beautiful orange globe that lines the sky with a tangerine heaven. The woven, brown palm trees, which must have come from just south of there, glow in the orange hum of evening's show. Comfort pours from the chimney as the smell of burning mango wood finds their nostrils, leading them toward the front door. Slowly extending his fist, Bahi gives a few light knocks, and stepping back waits in anticipation, nervous to find what's on the other side of the door. A few moments of silence pass, and with another knock, this time a bit harder, he calls out, "Hello?"

The handle slowly turns as the door opens with a rustle of the leaf-covered opening. A short, white nun with a shaved head and yellow robes sticks her head out the half-open door, her round spectacles analyzing Bahi standing in front of Ajee. "Maha Bharat is not taking visitors at this time," her quick-mannered, Australian accent informs before she pulls her bobbly head back in and slams the door shut. Bahi can hear a chain lock being secured as he turns to Ajee with his hands up, shrugging his shoulders.

"Tough break, buddy," Ajee says.

"Break, nothin', I didn't come all the way here to turn back," he replies in a huff.

"What are you gonna do?"

Remembering his conversation with the goat about patiently waiting, he resolves to do just that. "She said he is not taking visitors at this time. I guess I'll wait until he is taking visitors."

"And you'll wait here?" Ajee asks looking around.

Bahi looks down at the small stoop before the front door, "Right here!"

"Sounds good to me." Ajee smiles and lies down as Bahi sits up against the house, holding his knees to his chest with a cross look on his face. After a few moments of silence, Ajee looks up. "And we wait."

"Yes Sir. We wait."

The sky turns black and the stars begin to bleed through the vast firmament above. The cold night forces them to huddle up, wrapped in the shawl, uncomfortable and stubborn. Ajee falls asleep and sleeps soundly as opposed to Bahi, who gets a few winks at best, constantly adjusting to the cold, hard ground, trying different positions to shield the brisk wind running through the valley. Growing envious of Ajee's thick fur and ability to fall fast asleep anywhere, he considers that perhaps they should have made a fire someplace close in the forest for the nights sleep. Yet his obstinance has kept him locked on this cold stoop of the small cottage. Bahi sits with his back against the house, watching as light projects over the hills in anticipation of the sunrise. He hears the lock unlatch and the door slowly creek open as he springs to his feet.

"You again. I thought I told you that Maha Bharat is not taking visitors at this time," the stout, bald nun says again, sticking her head out the doorway.

"I know, but if I can . . . ." The door slams before he can get the words out. Again he hears the chain lock secure from the inside. He lets out a sigh as he sits back down, frustrated, cold, and exhausted, wrapping his arms around his knees and resting his tired head on his arms. His eyes are heavy and burning from a bitter, sleepless night, yet his resolve is thick, like a stubborn ass that won't budge.

Ajee wakes up and stretches out, smiling from a deep and restful nights sleep. "I'll fetch us some breakfast," he says as he pops up and runs off through the valley.

Bahi can't even think of eating, although he knows he is hungry. One part frustration and one part exhaustion has baked a certain knot in his stomach. Ajee returns twenty minutes later with another rabbit hanging lifeless in his jaws and flopping around as he nears Bahi. Ajee drops the prey at his feet as he licks the blood from his mouth. "This place is full of them. Dig in, Bahi!"

"No thanks, I'm not hungry," Bahi turns away in disgust, looking off into the valley in angst, avoiding Ajee's cheery manner. His annoyance bred by sleeplessness and uncertainty is not in the mood to partake in conversation.

Ajee senses the uneasiness in Bahi, and clenching the hind legs of the inert rabbit with his jaws, walks a few feet away to eat his freshly killed breakfast. Bahi falls in and out of brief nods of sleep, and soon high noon shines warm sun from directly above. Bahi's dry mouth and throat crave water, but he does not want to move from the stoop. A few hours later, thirsty and now feeling the pangs of hunger, the door unlatches and creeks open, quickly springing Bahi once again to his feet. The small, stocky nun walks outside with a wicker basket full of feed. "You're a stubborn one, huh?" she says as she walks off into the yard, which is filled with dry hay and chickens. Bahi rounds his head, peeking out at her from the corner of the cottage as she tosses feed among swarming chickens.

Bahi walks over and approaches her. "Listen, please. I just need five minutes. That's all."

"Are you thirsty?" the nun asks.

"Yes, very."

"Well, help yourself to the chicken water," she points to a bucket of dirty water with feathers floating in it and walks off, back to the cottage.

"Ma'am, Ma'am, please," Bahi pleads, briskly following behind her as she walks. She rapidly shuffles her short legs and stops abruptly, turning to Bahi, who almost runs into her.

"One, *Ma'am* is what you call my mother. And two, not *please*, but *thank you, thank you* for even allowing you to find the cottage. Now be a good boy and go eat with the chickens." Her short speech is followed by another slam of the door.

"What does that even mean?" Bahi yells at the door.

"Well, well, seems like it's going smooth," Ajee says, teasing him.

"Ajee, not now, please."

"Well at least we know where to find some chickens if we get hungry."

Just then the door opens and the nun yells out, "If you touch so much of a feather on those chickens, you'll be asleep so fast that when you wake up you'll be reborn as the feed I throw on the dirt for them. Am I communicating, people?" They are both silent, taken aback. "Am I communicating?"

"Yes, Ma'am," Bahi concurs.

"Ma'am this!" she says as she slams the door again. Bahi smacks himself in the head.

"We are not off to a good start, Bahi."

"No, we are not."

"Wait a minute. How could she understand what I said? Can I talk to all humans now?" Ajee asks in wonder.

"I have no clue," Bahi says, not caring about her understanding Ajee, but more concerned with how perturbed she was.

"Say, Bahi, how are you able to communicate with me? I've been meaning to ask you."

Bahi gives a brief explanation to a curious Ajee before walking off in frustration to the yard. Pacing with the chickens Bahi can't help but notice the nice, calm energy that surrounds the house. The sun beats down on him, and his dry, cracked lips beg for water. Going over to the fowls' water, he kneels down, looking into the rectangular, long reservoir. He brushes off small, white feathers that float atop. One chicken looks at him curiously as he scoops some water into his hands and drinks. Ajee comes over, scattering the chickens as they fearfully retreat to the small barn at the back of the yard. Lapping up water, he lifts his head to look at Bahi, a small white feather sticking to his mouth.

"Oh jeez, get that off before we end up as chicken feed," Bahi says quickly swiping the feather from his mouth. Spending the whole day in the yard, Bahi is now starving and decides he is going to fast until he can see Maha Bharat.

As night falls, they cuddle up among some hay. After a sleepless night and no food, Bahi falls fast asleep. In his sleep, he dreams he is knocking on the door again, and that again the nun comes out. Her pudgy bald head wears a sour puss, "Who do you think you are, coming here and thinking the great Maha Bharat will just see you? The Dalai Lama himself is on a waiting list. Go on. Go back from where you came. You have no business here." Bahi tries hard, but can't speak as the house sinks into a deep hole that caves in all around him, and suddenly he wakes up as dawn is again upon him. Curiously they are on the front stoop again. Bahi has no idea how they got there.

"Morning, buddy. Nightmare? You were yelling a bit there."

"Yeah, I mean no, I mean I don't know, I think we should leave."

Just then the nun opens the door and places a tray with food on the ground. "Eat up," she says before closing the door.

They rush over and feast on the steaming noodles, tofu, and vegetables. Bahi didn't realize how hungry he was. He can feel the warmth of food slide down his throat and nestle comfortably in his empty stomach. After the meal they sit in the shade up against the front of the house.

"Do you wanna split?" Ajee asks.

"I don't know, I mean, maybe I can find Shambhala on my own. What if he can't help me to find it. If his speech is all cryptic like that nun's, then I'm really in trouble," Bahi laughs.

"I'll do whatever you want to do."

The door opens again and the nun steps out, "Still here, huh?"

"Yes, I have nowhere else to go," Bahi implores.

"Nonsense. Look around you. This world is big. Just pick a direction and go."

"Please Ma . . . ," Bahi implores, stopping himself from saying *Ma'am*, "please, I beg of you, only five minutes."

"Maha Bharat agrees to see you, but on one condition."

"Sure, anything, what?"

"Tonight you sleep in the barn, and first you and I talk, and if it's deemed beneficial he will see you."

"Sounds good to me," Bahi says lightening up for the first time in days.

"Oh, and another thing: the mutt's gotta go," she says looking over at Ajee.

"But he is my friend, I can't"

"Then you can't, and I'll bid you a good day," she turns to walk back into the house.

"No, no, it's fine. I was just leaving anyway. Yeah, full moon party and all. You know us wolves."

"It's only a half moon," Bahi points out.

"Yeah well, wow half moon already, we start preparing early, usually at the new moon, so I better get going," Ajee says loudly as the nun stands unflattered by his lies.

"Listen, Bahi, this is why you are here. It's not about me. When you're done, whenever it is, two hours or two weeks, just whistle and I'll come back," Ajee whispers.

"You promise?"

"A wolf always keeps his word, well except that one time, but she was a little kookoo. And, oh, forget that, a wolf always keeps his word," Ajee says puffing his chest up proudly.

Bahi bends down and hugs Ajee goodbye. "Thank you, friend," Bahi says softly in his ear, "how can I ever repay you?"

"By staying here and finding the way to Shambhala. Now, can you whistle? Let me hear it!" Bahi lets out a loud whistle. "That a boy!" Ajee says as he walks off. "All right, Jack. See ya on the other side."

"Be safe, Wolf. Thank you!" And with that Ajee runs off into the hillside, out of sight.

"Now you wait in the barn and I'll come out in a while to talk."

"Yes Ma'am, oh I'm sorry, I mean yes, what's your name?"

"Robina, Venerable Robina," she says.

"Yes, Venerable Robina, I'm Bahi."

"Or is it Jack?"

"Jack, Bahi, Paul, I really don't know."

"You're not on drugs are you?" she asks skeptically.

"No, no, ha ha definitely not, although if I told you how I got here you would bet otherwise."

"OK, Bahi, off with ya, I'll see you in an hour." Robina closes the door softer than she had before.

Making sure she is totally in and can't see him, he jumps up in silent celebration and with a smile makes his way to the barn. Opening the small, natural-wood-colored, barn door, two goats look up from their rest in a bed of hay. The rest of the barn is empty and clean except for hay that lines the floors and the loft that is led up by a makeshift ladder reminiscent of the manger scene, "Where's baby Jesus?" he asks out loud, humoring himself as he looks around.

"He's here," Robina says startling him to turn around.

"That was the quickest hour I ever experienced."

"OK, let's not be a wise ass, now sit down and tell me what you want with Maha Bharat."

"Oh man, where do I start?"

"You start with why you're here. Life's too short for these mamby pamby games."

"So then why make me wait for days?" Bahi asks.

"Let's get one thing straight. You made yourself wait, the path you have chosen was created by your actions, and your actions alone. We can never post blame for anything on anyone else. You are the boss. If you don't like your life, change it by changing the causes that create your conditions. It's that simple. You want different conditions, then look at the causes that create them and adjust. The problem is we are always doing the same thing and wishing for different results. This is the definition of insanity, actually."

"Yes, I understand, but you made me wait. If it were up to me I would have had this talk the other day," Bahi rebuts.

"Oh, here we go again. Do I need to spell it out? You create exactly the situation you are in. You know what made the difference between me sleeping in a warm house the past two nights and you out in the cold?" Bahi thinks as he examines Robina's distinctive face. "The past causes we created to reach those conditions and to blame others is not only immature and childish but illogical," she says staring him in the eyes.

"So, it was a punishment for my past actions?" Bahi asks.

"Not a punishment. It's like if you were walking along and decided to throw a rock straight up into the air, a punishment would be if someone grabbed that rock and chucked it back at your head. What is happening here is that the rock, logically, must come back down, and when it hits you on the head you're all surprised: 'Where did that rock come from?' Your ignorance forgot that you threw it up there. But let us not get into a lesson on karma or we'll be here all night. So to the point, Bahi, what is it you want to ask?"

"How do I find Shambhala?" Bahi quickly belts out.

"Wow, going straight for the gusto! And what makes you think that, one, Maha Bharat even knows? And two, if he does know, why would he tell you this? And three, how do you even know this place exists outside of the fairy tales and village folklore? You've been hanging out with the goats, haven't you?"

"Well actually . . ."

"Yeah yeah," Robina cuts him off.

They sit in silence as she stares at him almost sizing him up, "and why would you even want to go to Shambhala, what's your motive, what's the intention?"

"The motive, the intention, is to find answers to this riddle of suffering so I can help others find answers."

Robina is silent again for a moment before speaking. "And say he did know a way there but that it was so risky that you would have about a ninety-percent chance of death, then what would you say?"

"I would say there is a ten percent chance of making it and that I am willing to forego the ninety-percent risk. We're all gonna die, right? Might as well risk it to help others. I mean someone has to, right? Have you been in that jungle lately?"

Robina smiles. "And what if I was to tell you that if you reached

Shambhala with this intention to help liberate others you would have to go back to this so-called jungle of suffering, fear, and delusional ignorance in order to help. And what's more, you won't want to leave the peace of this place. And if you do, most won't even believe you found such a place. Some may even try to kill you."

"And some would believe, and thus the answers I find even to help a few would be more important than just myself alone staying there. I would know the path, the map, and would have to return to lead others there."

"And would you forego your entrance into Shambhala in order to let another in?"

Bahi thinks honestly, searching his heart, finding a resounding "yes."

"Yes! Yes, I would."

Again silence fills the barn. Struggling to her feet, she motions to the door. "Come with me."

"Am I going to meet him now?"

"Just come with me, will you?"

Walking out into the sunlight and rounding the corner of the yard, she enters the cottage. "Take off your shoes and be silent," she says looking back sternly into Bahi's eyes before he steps in. He quickly flops his shoes off outside, and as soon as he crosses the threshold, a feeling of joy overcomes him. The smell of sandalwood permeates the small, dark cottage. It is dimly lit by streams of rich, golden sunlight upon the walls that bask an image in shadow, which Bahi can barely make out in the far corner of the cottage. He squints to see what seems to be someone in a meditative pose, whom he only assumes is Maha Bharat. His uncertainty turns back to Robina, who whispers, "Go and bow to him."

Walking over, he still strains to make out Maha Bharat. Even at such close proximity, it's as if Bahi has a shadowy film on his eyes that blocks the image out no matter which angle he looks, a peculiar situation indeed. He gets on his knees with great reverence in his heart and bows before standing to his feet with hands in prayer position and head lowered. Raising his eyes up softly to look, he notices the sun has slightly shifted, exposing the image of a gold statue of the Buddha. Bahi turns back to Robina to find a short, frail Indian man where Robina stood. Confusion washes over Bahi's face.

"What did you expect?" the Indian man asks.

"Um, expect? I . . .I don't know. Are you the Great Maha Bharat?"

"What do you see?" the short Indian man asks with a soft smile.

"I see the Great Maha Bharat."

"Then you are correct. Be careful what your mind perceives. Just a minute ago you thought I was a short, stubby nun from Australia, I ask you to search yourself and tell me what you feel."

"I feel relieved to be in your presence," Bahi says with sincerity.

"And what of the Buddha?" Maha Bharat asks, turning his attention to the statue. Bahi turns to look, and to his amazement the statue of the Buddha is now the Hindu god Shiva.

"But I . . ."

"This is what I mean. Be careful what you want to believe, because it may become real. Now sit," Maha Bharat signals toward the statue, which is again the Buddha, but this time the statue stands in teaching mode, the Buddha's right hand raised. Bahi laughs in wonder.

"Does this amuse you?" Maha Bharat asks sternly.

"No, sir."

"Why not? Let us not lie to ourselves. What do you feel?"

"I feel laughter," Bahi says, noticing a giddy rush welling up from his gut.

"Then feel laughter. Don't lie to yourself. Listen to your heart. Bring up your truth from there. Stop worrying about how you are supposed to be. Stop looking at others for the answers to how you are feeling inside. Just feel and be. Laugh when you laugh, cry when you are sad. Let us not lie to ourselves."

"Its just in the presence of the Great Maha Bharat, I. . ."

"It's Bharat. *Maha* means *great*, you're being redundant," Bharat says as a matter of fact.

"OK, sorry sir. Bharat, Maha Bharat, I am Bahi."

"Yes yes I know. Tell me, Bahi: Why is it that you choose the wrong choices time and again?"

"Do I?" Bahi asks sincerely.

"Most do. Feel it in your heart. Stop letting your head be your master. It will almost always misguide you. It's concerned with what others think about it, what's in the best interest of the self and the ego. The brain's concern is survival in the most illogical terms. So tell me why you feel you make the wrong choices?"

"Well I think that . . ."

"I said feel it, with your heart, not your head, no thinking," Bharat interjects harshly.

Bahi closes his eyes and notices the voices screaming from his brain trying to give answers in a frenzy of survival. He tries to tap into the feeling, "I feel . . ."

"Yes, go on."

"I don't know," he says opening his eyes.

"Stop running away from it. Stay with it. Feel it. Why do you want to make the wrong decisions? And by this I mean the ones that are creating undesirable results in your life, time and again? Answer the question, Bahi. Why do you feel you want to make the wrong decisions?" Bharat says abruptly, not letting Bahi off the hook for even a second.

"Because they feel comfortable. The right path is scary and unknown," Bahi feels tears welling up in eyes.

"Very good," Bharat says, softening his tone. "Tea?" he asks, sliding a tiny porcelain cup of green tea toward him on the small, knee-high pine table they sit on either side of.

"Sure," Bahi says, a bit shaken up from this very abrasive introduction. Looking back toward the Buddha statue Bahi sees that it is now again in a meditative pose. "How do you do that?"

"Do what?"

"The statue?"

"You mean Buddha?" Bharat says. He places a cup of tea in front of the statue.

"Yes, the Buddha statue," Bahi says alluding to the movement and change of its position and structure.

"You see a Buddha statue. I see Buddha, and that makes all the difference. Now finish your tea and off to the barn with you. Dawn comes early around here, and you have much to work on if you wish to reach Shambhala."

"So you will help me?" Bahi asks in excitement.

"I didn't say that. I said you have much to work on if you wish to reach

Shambhala, and it's obvious listening is a big part of that. So, off to bed," Bharat orders as his blue eyes sit calmly in his dark, golden skin, noticeably old yet uncannily full of youth.

"Bed, but it can't be even four o'clock," Bahi argues.

"I tell you something once and my job is done. You choose to react to it how you wish. I have no time for your silly redundancies." Bharat closes his eyes. He sits in the lotus position, each foot atop the opposite thigh.

"So what time do we get started tomorrow?" Bahi asks. He stands up, getting no response from the deeply meditative Maha Bharat. "OK, then, it's off to the barn with me then," he says as he quietly exits the cottage, wondering if Venerable Robina was even real or if he just projected her.

Bahi makes his way to the barn and wonders at the strange encounters he has had here at the cottage, inwardly hoping he is making the right decision by staying. He opens the barn door. A plate of noodles and sprouts lie on the floor, freshly cooked. He sits silently and eats, noticing the absence of any animals in the barn. After finishing his warm meal he lies back on the floor, staring at the ceiling. Large, thick pieces of pine stabilize the barn as he ponders, *Why do I want to make the wrong choices, was coming here the right choice?* Lying on the floor, he feels how Shambhala seems to be the only thing that is right, and if he is making the wrong choices, how will he ever reach it? Slowly his eyes begin to close. Noticing how each night seems to get colder and colder, he wishes Ajee were there to keep him warm. Stretching up, his arm brushes a wool blanket. *How did I not see that?* he thinks as he unfolds it and wraps it around himself. The brown woolen blanket warms him as he lays his head on his shawl that he has fashioned into a pillow. "What an amazing journey," he reflects as he closes his eyes, which even at this early hour, are heavy with the weariness of a long travel. A smile washes over his face as he feels Maha Bharat may actually be able to help him on his way. He drifts into a deep sleep.

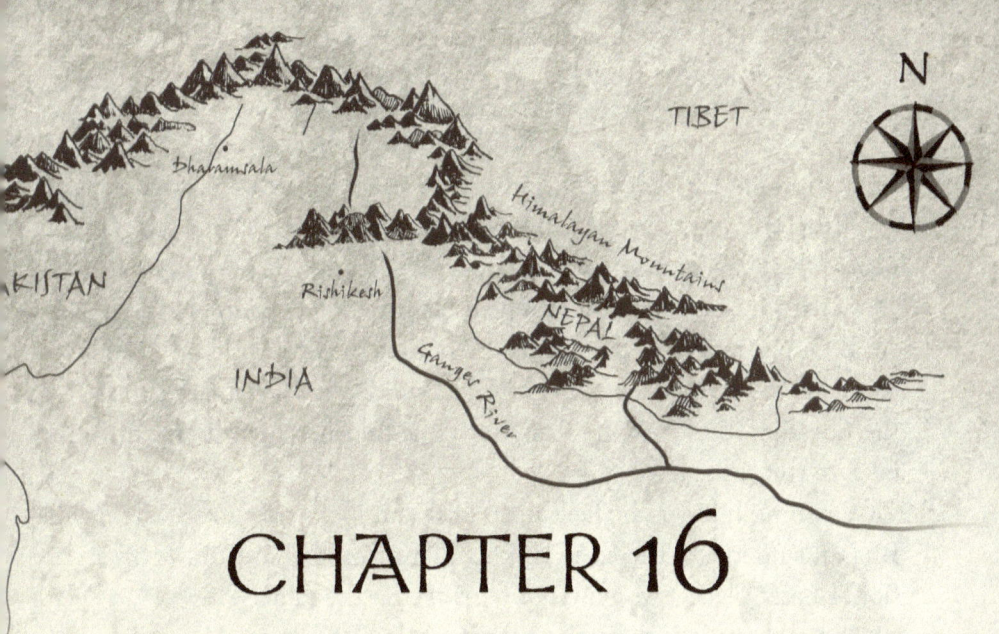

CHAPTER 16

"WAKE UP!"

An urgent whisper alerts Bahi to open his eyes in the cold darkness. He sits up and notices a flame flickering on the other side of the barn. Wrapping the wool blanket snugly around himself, he walks over to the white candle, which occupies a silver holder. He looks in confusion around the barn for whomever may have left it. As he picks up the candle, the barn door cracks slightly open, almost inviting him out. His heart beats faster.

He nears the door. Cautiously opening it, he peeks out into the pre-dawn yard. A stream of smoke billows out of the cottage chimney. A candle flickers in the window. It seems to call out to Bahi as he walks toward the front door. The sweet smell of incense guides him into the warm cottage, where he finds Bharat in meditation, exactly where he had left him the day before. The only indications that he has moved are the water bowls and lit incense that sit upon the altar in front of the beautiful, large golden Buddha. The statue evokes peace from within Bahi as he gazes upon it. Bahi sits cross-legged, staring at it. Closing his eyes, he breathes calmly, becoming aware of each sensation as his mind goes deeper and deeper, almost as if he is being guided. Bahi drops down into a subtle state of meditation with the ease of a seasoned master. The world falls away, his body ceases to exist, and a space of unexplained clarity opens up.

Then, the question from the night before arises: *Why do you want to make the wrong choices?* Suddenly fear wells up, and he pushes it away. "Stay with it," he hears Bharat say in his mind, "feel it, accept it."

Bahi allows the uncomfortable emotion to consume him. "Where is this fear?" he hears deep in his psyche. Bahi looks for it, unable to answer the question. Suddenly he feels his leg is asleep, which draws his mind back to the cottage.

Opening his eyes, he feels deep bliss and looks over to see that Maha Bharat is no longer there. A clanking plate, from behind, draws his attention. Bharat places two bowls of porridge on the table.

"So, you made it through another night?" Bharat says.

"Amazing, huh?" Bahi says, somewhat sarcastically.

"More amazing than you give credit to. You know how many people will not wake up today?"

Bahi thinks about this as through the window he watches the golden sunrise advance across the valley. "Yeah, guess you're right," Bahi says with a soft nod. He sits bundled in his blanket, knees huddled to his chest.

"Fools we are to think we'll live forever. Every moment may be our last. So it is imperative to practice upon the right path."

Bahi looks up, eyes wide. "In my meditation, I felt the great fear of not wanting to make the right choice."

"And?" Bharat asks.

"And, uh, and I guess this is why we opt for the wrong choices. They are easier."

"Seemingly. So to the ignorant mind, these choices in fact lead to more fear, more uncertainty, more pain and suffering. So we want to make the right choices on a level that we don't want to suffer and want to be happy, yet we are constantly pushing away our happiness and chasing suffering."

"Why?"

Bharat laughs inwardly under his breath. "Because of that fear, for starters, a fear that does not even exist, a lie we create that keeps us stuck."

"But surely it exists, I felt it," Bahi argues.

"It's like a brilliant painter who paints a scary monster. He is so skilled that it looks lifelike. This painting stands ten feet tall. Then one night, years later, he has forgotten that he has painted it and roams into the room where it stands. He shrieks with fear. It is like this for us too. We create all of it. Now eat your porridge."

"Oh, thank you," Bahi says, standing up to make his way to the small table on the floor where he sits across from Bharat.

Thick, steamy vapors pour from their bowls, creating a thick mist as Bahi watches Bharat praying over his food. Bahi closes his eyes and gives thanks for the hot meal and warm, cozy cottage to enjoy it in. Looking up, Bahi smiles at Bharat, whose eyes smile back.

"So, why do we do it?" Bahi asks.

"Do what?"

"Why do we create these monsters that impede our path?"

"You're asking me? You're one of the most elaborate artists I've met. Why not ask yourself?"

"I thought a lot about what you said last night," Bahi says feeling Bharat's last comment was condescending.

"That's the problem isn't it? We think ourselves to death. We pride ourselves in having an intellectual mind, which in one respect is great, but then it stops there. We've forgotten how to feel. So much weight in our contemporary societies is placed on our intellectual minds, which we believe make us civilized, when in fact it makes us more primordial. All this intellectual knowledge is useless without wisdom. Many fall back one hundred percent on this intellect and almost totally forget how to feel, even drowning their intellects in poisons of body and mind through substance and thought. I've even seen these systems these days that guide us to our destination, navigation systems, so we don't have to follow our gut or heart. In fact, in this case we don't even have to think."

"Sure, people feel. Isn't that the problem? We feel the fear that paralyzes us?"

"We create this false feeling with our minds. Our brains think and overthink. What happened to that fear when you allowed yourself to just feel it, just letting it in and accepting it?"

"At first I tried to find where it was. I thought I felt it in my stomach, but when I placed my mind there and let it be, it dissipated and went away."

"Right, so then you used your intellectual mind to look for it in conjunction with your feelings, and dismantled it. If only the world could do this! Do you think if heads of power sat and took their intellectual plans to destroy the Earth and kill others in war, and took the time to feel it, that the right choice, from their hearts, would allow them to kill another living person? We have no respect for others. We have no respect for our Earth. And this is because we have no respect for ourselves. We can't even feel. Our thinking takes over. And this is what we believe it is to feel the right answer. It's the brain that got us into this mess of wrong choices to begin with. The brain creates delusions of fear, anxiety, anger, hate, and so forth out of a fight-or-flight response. We blindly follow this, allowing it to be our master. Yet if we use the heart to feel what's right, the world would be a completely different place. So feel it, Bahi. Break free from the weakness of the world's fears and angers. Develop this, and you will be a true warrior who walks the right path. Shambhala will be easy to find. Trust your feeling, and you will know the truth. The warrior of our modern age works out of fear, killing to protect, ignorantly thinking he or she is making the right choices, but that warrior is blindly following the orders of someone who is following the fear-based orders of the brain. The warrior who leads with his heart is the true warrior. The other warriors are no match for the truth. Fear is weakness. Truth is strength, and truth resides in our hearts."

"This sounds like a lot of work," Bahi says, stirring his porridge, still too hot to eat.

"Work? We work so hard developing fears that impede us from the happiness we seek," Bharat says as Bahi looks down into his bowl, regretting his last sentence.

Silently they sit eating the porridge, enjoying every bite, and when they are finished Bharat slowly stands up in front of Bahi. "After you finish washing the dishes, meet me outside," Bharat says, gradually making his way toward the door to exit the cottage. Bahi looks up at the large, iron pot Bharat used to make the porridge. He gathers the two bowls and spoons and walks over to the counter. He places them next to two shallow sinks, one filled with cloudy water, which he assumes is soap, and another steaming clear for rinsing. He happily washes the pot and bowls, rinsing them thoroughly in the hot water. Then he dries his hands, on a small, red towel that hangs on the wall of the rustic, wood-paneled kitchen, and makes his way outside to meet Bharat.

Bahi steps out onto the porch, approaching Bharat, who stands facing the rising sun. He feels the warmth and comfort beaming upon him. The silence of the moment engulfs his being as he stands next to a still Bharat, whose light-wool gray shirt humbly hangs down onto his black cotton pants, ending at his small bare feet that dig into the ground, unifying with the thawed earth. "When I was a young man I lived in a small village a long way south of here. There was a widow who lived alone close to where my family lived. One day as the sun was setting in the sky I was on my way home from meditation in the jungle and I saw this woman searching for something on the dirt road. And so I asked her what she was looking for. She was an old woman, her eyes were not as they had been when she was young, so I decided to help her out. 'What are you searching for?' I asked. She became frustrated and told me that the question was irrelevant. I told her if I knew what she was looking for I could help her to find it. My eyes were young. In a huff, and on her hands and knees in the dry dirt, she looked up at me and said, 'I am searching for my needle. I lost it, OK?' She was very frustrated."

Bahi listens intently to the story.

"I looked up at the wide dirt road and before searching I asked, 'Do you remember where exactly you lost it, the exact place you may have dropped it?' To this she looked back up at me and said, 'Again with the silly questions, how will this help me in my search?' I laughed and told her if she knew where she may have lost it, it would save us the time of searching the wide and long road. 'OK, if you must know, I lost it in my house.' I laughed again and thought she must be mad, 'If you lost it in your house, then why are you looking out here on the dirt road?' Again she looked up at me and with a furrowed brow she said, 'Because there is no light inside.' Because there is no light inside she said." Bharat looks off into the sun.

"So, did she ever find the needle?" Bahi asks, laughing.

"She never found the needle, Bahi. Few do find the needle."

"She could have just bought another needle," Bahi adds.

"Or she could have gone inside and sat there until her eyes adjusted to the dim inner light. Then she would have found what she was seeking. You see, we are all like this, and the old woman was right. There is no light inside, and so we go on searching outside because it seems clearer and brighter. And so the seeker is inside, but the light is outside, and so the seeker moves searching outside for something, yet the seeker never finds it because what he seeks is inside the whole time. We spend our whole lives outside in the sun and never go inside to get to know the seeker. And because we do not know the seeker, the right direction toward what we seek is impossible. It is important to know what we are searching for before we go inside, or else you will go stumbling around in the dark. If, perhaps, we were to find this seeker who is inside, the question of 'who am I' that you have been asking before you came here, then you can begin to find what you seek."

"I have been searching for this answer, Bharat. You are very wise."

"You have been out on the dirt road searching for your needle because you are afraid of the darkness inside. But if you move into the dark, you will find it is very dark because you have been out in the bright sunlight your entire life. As you sit patiently inside, your eyes will adjust, and you will notice it is not totally dark. There is a subtle light, a soft light, and with time you can see inside and will come to appreciate the soft inner light of peace. Only then will you find your answers."

"Like meditation," Bahi says.

"So you want to know how to reach Shambhala?" Bharat asks, squinting his deep blue eyes towards Bahi.

"I do. I have been told it is there, where I will be able to answer that question of who I am truly. I search for a way to help all those who suffer on this Earth, as well as the Earth. I have come to find we are creating great suffering for the Earth as well."

"Mmmm," Bharat confirms, looking deeply at the Earth as he bends over to pick up a stick. He draws an X in the dirt in front of him, then a circle next to it. Looking up at Bahi, he smiles in silence. Bharat is much shorter than Bahi, yet seems to tower over him with the power and energy he humbly omits. Pointing with the stick at the circle, he says, "Here is Shambhala." Gracefully he moves the stick toward the X, he says, "Here is where you don't want to go. It represents what you seem to always be getting, the result you wanted to avoid, but seem to always be coming to." Bahi nods quietly. "So I ask you, why don't you want to reach Shambhala? Why do you want to go to the *X*?"

"I don't. I want to go to the circle."

"Your brain says that, but feel it. Why do you want to make the wrong choices and end up here?" Bharat asks pointing to the *X*. "Just feel it, don't think, stop looking out on the sunny dirt road."

Bahi allows himself to feel it, going inward to his heart. *Why do I want to make the wrong choices?* he thinks.

"What do you feel?" Bharat asks.

"I feel scared. I don't know what I will find at Shambhala. And what if I never find it? What if it is a fairy tale, and the results of not finding it almost feel more comfortable?"

"Go on, go deeper, feel it. Allow your eyes to adjust inside the dark house."

Bahi feels a sense of meditation, as if Bharat is evoking this in him, "I feel I don't deserve it. I'm not worthy of going there." tears well up in Bahi's eyes.

"Feel it Bahi, the fears, the unworthiness, accept them, allow yourself to just feel them."

Bahi goes very deep inside, feeling the discomfort of his inner demons of fear. Slowly he opens his eyes to look at Bharat.

"Pawo," Bharat says.

"Pawo?" Bahi asks, readjusting his eyes to the bright sunlight.

"It means one who is brave, the warrior. The warrior masters himself in order to help others. Only when you can feel your enemies inside and know them, can you conquer them. A true warrior does not escape these, does not run away. He stands and fights the inward battle. The Pawo comes to realize, like the painter who paints the monster, that these inner demons or enemies are nothing but his own creations. Yet if we spend our lives running scared of these, we breathe life into them and allow them to dictate our lives. The end result is that we cannot help anyone, because we can not even help ourselves," Bharat shakes his head.

"Pawo," Bahi says under his breath.

"The path toward Shambhala can be traveled only by a true warrior, a Pawo, for these inner demons will do all they can to impede you from getting there. Again when I say *warrior*, I mean not the ones who make war on others. That is anger and aggression, and that's how we got into this mess in the first place. Those are the warriors who allow the inner enemies to run their lives. It means to be brave and not be afraid of yourself. This warrior I talk about is selfless. When we are afraid of ourselves and the seeming problems of the world, we become very selfish. And so we build our little security nests and choose the *X* because it feels safe. We stay outside searching because we fear the darkness inside. Ignorantly, like children, we create our own suffering. So, Bahi, do you wish to be a Pawo or a fearful child?"

"A Pawo," Bahi instantly answers.

"Feel it. Be sure. Why do you want this?"

"Because I want the truth."

"But why?"

Bahi thinks of all the suffering he has encountered along his journey, the homeless woman, Kamini, the spider, and so on. The thought of the endless suffering in the world ignites great compassion, giving him a sense of strength. "I want to help others. I want to lead them to liberation from the suffering they're creating for themselves and others, and I know that in order to do this I need to find Shambhala, where I will find these answers. I will be able to find the answers there, won't I?" he asks, exposing his misgivings.

"Perhaps, Bahi, perhaps. More importantly, would you be willing to sacrifice your own happiness, your own opportunity for liberation in Shambhala in order for someone else to get there?"

"I would," he says quickly from his heart, as Ajee pops into his mind.

"I know you would, and this is why I will teach you the way of the Pawo. Tonight I will show you who you thought you were, and then we can begin to look at who you truly are."

"Thank you, Maha Bharat, thank you," Bahi says, finally feeling assurance for the first time that he may actually reach Shambhala. "So now what?"

"Now I meditate, and when the sun reaches a pinkish hue, come to the cottage."

"What should I do in the meantime?" Bahi asks, realizing he will have the entire day.

"Meditate, think about and meditate on what we just went over. Be firm in your resolve to walk the path of the warrior, for once you step on this path, completion is the only option, no matter how many lifetimes it takes you." Saying this, Bharat slowly walks off to the cottage.

Bahi stands in the sun for hours contemplating the conversation, coming to a strong resolve to walk the path of the warrior, to lead others to liberation by finding Shambhala and finding the answers he seeks. The day has seemed to go by very quickly, and before he knows it the sun has dropped down, creating a beautiful scene of pinkish orange hues that softly lay upon the valley's horizon.

Making his way to the cottage, he can smell the spicy, sweet fragrance of food being prepared. And having taken only a bowl of porridge early in the morning, his stomach rumbles with excitement and anticipation of a meal. His mouth waters as he opens the cottage door. Steam from the meal, which is prepared and setting on the table, pulls him into the cottage as he seemingly floats in ecstasy toward it.

"Sit," Bharat directs, wiping his hands on the red towel.

Bahi sits, taking in the feast of noodles and vegetables. "I am so grateful for all you are doing for me," he expresses.

"You did all of this. It's your karma, your actions that allow you to receive my teachings and meals, so thank yourself." Saying this, he places his hands in prayer. "Let us be thankful to all the kindness of sentient beings who made it possible for this meal to be on this table, to the kind and selfless Earth as well," Bahi closes his eyes as gratitude wells up in his mind, "and to repay this kindness we enjoy and savor this meal," Bharat says picking up his fork.

Bahi smiles as he takes a sip of water from the wooden cup before him. Mixing the noodles around on the white plate, he remembers the Baba and the wise teachings of how all of this is dependant upon causes and conditions, like Bharat said, 'to bring this to his plate.'

After dinner Bahi graciously accepts his task of cleaning the dishes, and when he finishes up, he comes over to the small area in front of the Buddha statue. Bharat prostrates three times before sitting, and Bahi does the same.

"We prostrate not because the Buddha needs us to bow down to him. We offer food and drink and incense and so forth not because the Buddha needs things. We do this for ourselves. Prostration teaches us respect and reverence. When we are bowing, we are bowing to ourselves, the God, Buddha, the source, whatever you may call it, which is in all things and living beings. We are recognizing this every time we bow—unity, interconnection. As we offer we practice giving, selflessness. These things we do for our psychological mind, to develop habits that empower us to help others and recognize that we are not separate from anything," Bharat says, eyes fixed upon the statue that sits with strength amongst the soft smoke of incense that dances around it's body. He looks over at Bahi, who sits to the right of him. "So to realize who you are, first you must look at who you are not." Saying this, he snaps his fingers, sending Bahi into a deep nod of hypnosis. "Search yourself, Bahi. Remember who you were, how you got here."

Bahi's mind brings him to the log where he hit his head. It's as though he is actually there. He remembers Bandar and all his kindness and help.

"What happened before this?"

"I don't know. I don't remember," he mumbles in a hypnotic state, head hanging low.

"Yes, you do. Feel it, Bahi. Who were you? How did you get to that log?"

Bahi goes deeply into the dark abyss of his mind, where he attempts to look around, but sees nothing, when suddenly he is on a busy city street making a phone call as a taxi nearly hits him. He feels very busy as he pans out and sees himself, "Paul!" He exclaims.

"Very good," Bharat says, "Who was Paul?"

"Paul was me," Bahi sits, as the memories flood in. He remembers his busy life, the family he now misses, and all the hardships and joys. Opening his eyes, he says, "I remember," still calm from the meditative state.

"Very good, this Paul character, is this you?"

"It was me."

"So are you now Bahi?"

"I, I don't know, I'm not Paul anymore, so yes, I am Bahi."

"And one day will you be someone else?"

"I don't know."

"Bahi, Paul, whatever you call yourself, you need to realize you are constantly changing and that the true nature of who you are is the answer you seek at Shambhala."

"Yes, so who is that?" Bahi asks.

"This you need to answer for yourself. My job is to give you the tools necessary to reach Shambhala, but it's up to you to get there. It's up to you to discern if there even is such a place."

"What do you mean? It exists, doesn't it?"

"It exists just as much as Paul or Bahi does," Bharat answers. "Do you still wish to know who you are?"

"Yes, now more than ever," Bahi pleads.

"Bahi, remember as a warrior your obligation, your mission, is to help others. Everything you do is for the benefit of all sentient beings and the Earth. Keep this resolve strong and all you seek will be found. So rise now, Pawo, for the journey is long and our time on this Earth is as brief as this candle. Make no haste on your quest."

"But I still don't know where to go," Bahi says nervously.

"In the morning you will leave. I will give you a direction, but it is up to you to discern the right path. You are the boss. Trust your feelings. Go into the dark house and allow the soft light to illuminate what you seek, and you will not fail."

"I'm not ready."

"You were ready when you were born. Your whole life has been leading up to this moment, Bahi. Trust in that order, surrender to the integrity of order."

"What if I fail?"

"What if you succeed?" Bharat asks as he closes his eyes in meditation.

Bahi sits, nervous. His hopes of having all the answers laid out for him are dispelled. Closing his eyes slightly, he goes within. In his meditation he feels a sense of power, and remembering his life in New York, feels an urgency to press on toward Shambhala so he can quickly return and help others.

That night, Bahi lies awake in the barn, reflecting on what Bharat has taught him. Remembering his life is like coming out of a movie feeling the emotion of it all, but still there is a sense of disconnect. He allows the fears and doubts to arise and meditates dissecting them, logically examining the lies he has been telling himself in the form of fantastic fear. The inner demons begin to lose power as they struggle to hold on. Slowly he feels more empowered, more confident, and a clarity of mind that gives way to peace settles him into a deep night's rest.

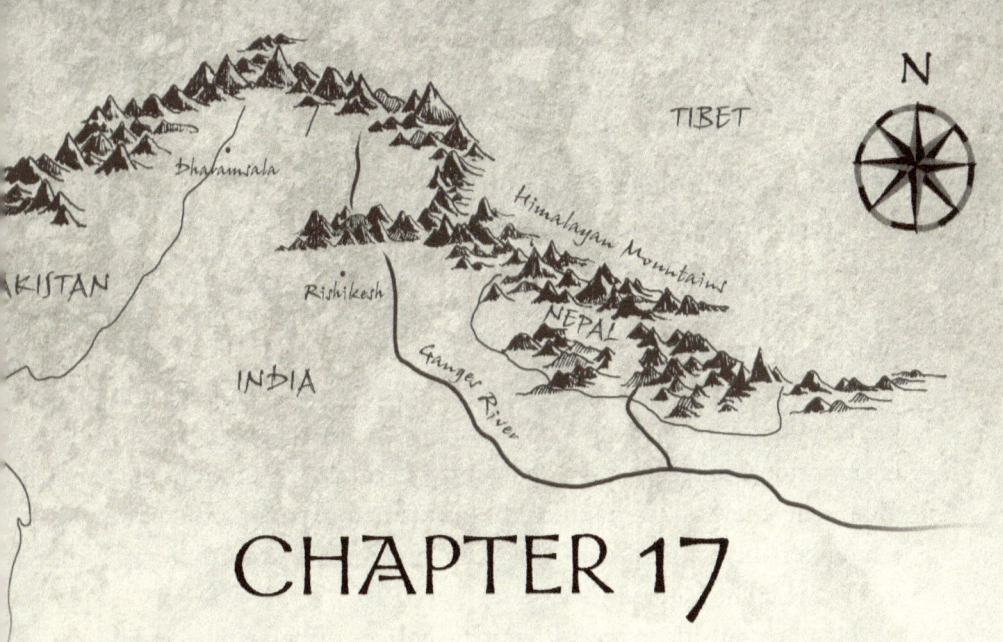

CHAPTER 17

AGAIN BAHI AWAKES to a flickering candle, which dances to a warm orange glow on the wall of the barn. Rubbing his eyes, he feels his beard, which has seemed to grow thicker overnight. Rising up, he makes his way over to the candle, and picking it up he walks out of the barn. He feels he has done this a thousand times before. The weather has seemed to grow starkly colder than the day before as he bundles tightly in his blanket. Making his way to the cottage, he thinks of how these past few days have felt like months. He feels more confident, stronger, and excited to get along on his journey. Coming into the cottage, he sits down across from Bharat, who smiles, head tilted. "You are ready?"

"I think so. I feel very diffcrent from when I came here a couple of days ago."

Bharat laughs, "How long do you suppose you have been here, Pawo?"

Bahi thinks, noticing the darkness outside, where the sun is usually already on the rise. "I came three days ago."

"It has been three months," Bharat says.

"Three months?" Bahi begins to consider that he has been there for three months. His beard is fuller, even his clothes are worn out more. "But how? I don't understand."

"Time is not to be understood. The fabrication of such a convention is

illogical in itself. You need not worry about these details. What is important is that you feel ready to leave."

Bahi searches himself and confidently utters, "I do."

"Let us eat," Bharat says, coming into prayer before they silently eat
their porridge.

After breakfast Bahi washes up the dishes, still in wonder of how he
has been there for such a period of time. It makes sense when he ponders
his emotional and physical state, but his mind can't fathom it. He thinks
of how he knew only a fragment of his life before coming there, and now
remembers his entire life in New York, and feels even further away from
it than when he had amnesia.

Heading outside to meet Bharat, he notices a small satchel in his hand,
which he hands to Bahi, "Here are some provisions for your journey."

Opening the satchel, he finds two small loaves of bread, a bunch of
apples, some nuts, and a book of matches that sit on top of a beautiful
shawl, which he pulls out. "Beautiful, thank you!"

"This is a special shawl made from the wool of yak. It is highly blessed
and will protect you from the coldest of conditions."

"How can I ever repay you for all the kindness you have given me?"
Bahi asks sincerely.

"By giving it away to others when the time presents itself."

Bahi feels near tears as he begins to draw closer to Maha Bharat for
a hug. "All right," Bharat says, squashing the moment and impeding the
hug. "Let's not get ahead of ourselves. You still have a long journey ahead
of you. Come."

Bharat begins to walk northward, picking up a small canteen that sits
on his stoop. They walk a short distance to a still pond framed by ice at its
edges. Bahi looks at the striking reflection of trees in the quiet pond. It is
like a painting of the sky and pine trees that surround it. Birds fly through
the sky in the painting as they watch in reverence of such beauty.

"This is like your mind. There is Shambhala," Bharat says, pointing
to the images cast upon the pond. "Stay with the stillness of this pond,
and Shambhala will be clear to you." Picking up a rock, he lunges it in
the air. It comes splashing down in disturbance of the image as ripples
echo toward the icy edges. "That rock is like the agitations of your mind,

the fears, the grasping outward, the frustrations of searching for a needle outside when all the while it is in the house. These agitate our mind and obscure our view. The inner silence will reveal its beauty, its truth." Just then the pond becomes still again and the images clear. "Be gentle with yourself and know that the agitation will pass if you don't keep throwing more rocks. Be patient, Pawo." Bharat dips the canteen into the water, breaking through some thin ice that has begun to form at the water's edge as the cold mountain air ushers in the late fall winds, he fills it up. Sealing it off, he hands the chilled, brown, leathery canteen to Bahi, who slings its thin white rope strap over his shoulder. Bharat walks off again as Bahi follows.

They come to a narrow dirt path, Bahi turns back to see the cottage in the distance. "Will I ever see you again?" he asks.

"I am certain of it," Bharat says.

"How will I know where to go?"

"Trust your heart, my son, you know the way."

They stand in silence for a moment before Bharat turns away and begins to walk toward the cottage.

"But which way do I walk?" Bahi yells out.

"Go North my boy!" Bharat yells back as he breaks out in an almost hysterical laughter.

Bahi looks out upon the trail, squinting to see what lies ahead. As the laughter fades, he turns to see Bharat, who is gone from sight. He looks off further and realizes he can't see the cottage. Running back almost frantically toward the cottage, he finds an empty space, as if there never were a cottage. Catching his breath he laughs.

" Go North," he says outloud to himself as he turns with a smile. "Go North, my boy," he says mockingly as he walks, fixing the satchel to his back. *Why is it my relationships seem to keep ending like this?* he thinks, remembering a similar situation with the disappearing Baba.

As he steps onto the path, the silence of the morning exasperates his every step as he crunches rock and dirt underfoot. He thinks of Ajee and begins to whistle loudly as he looks around. After a few moments of whistling he walks more. *Perhaps it's been too long,* he sadly thinks as he whistles again, coming to a small hill that shades the trail.

"Well, it's about time!" a voice says from a small hill above him.

"Wolf!" he says excitedly, standing as Ajee leaps down tackling him to the ground and licking his face, playfully laughing as they embrace each other.

Coming back to his feet and brushing off his clothes, he smiles. "What's new?" Bahi asks.

"I should be asking you that question. I thought I'd never see you again. For a few weeks I would sit atop that hill awaiting your whistle, but then I gave up, and now here you are. So how was it?"

"Amazing!"

"You look different, in a good way. You seem stronger," Ajee says, sensing a noticeable difference in Bahi's energy.

Bahi smiles. "Come Wolf, we have a long journey ahead of us. Are you still up to it?"

"Well, let's see, I did have plans to wait on a hill for my friend. Oh wait, here you are, haha, of course Bahi, lead the way!"

Together again, they go off northward. The day seems to stay cool in spite of the shining sun.

"So tell me," Ajee says as the cold morning air outlines his breath with fog, "did he tell you where to find Shambhala?"

Bahi stops walking, and looking North toward the massive, snow-lined mountains that sit among the rich blue sky, he says, "He taught me how to find it," he says feeling an assurance that he would.

"So, no map, or directions?"

"Oh there's a map, Wolf, and it lies right here," Bahi points to his chest and smiles.

Ajee looks in silent confidence that Bahi knows the way. And looking toward the mountains, Ajee takes a deep inhale, exhaling a thick, warm breath that swirls out into the crisp, dense air.

"Those mountains are not to be taken lightly, my friend. There is much one must be aware of, believe me. I grew up there."

"Well then, how fortunate I am to have you on this journey with me," Bahi says, beginning to walk toward the mountains ahead as Ajee follows.

As the sun rises directly above them, the air turns to an afternoon cool from the cold of morning, and their breath is no longer visible. After walking several hours they sit to enjoy some bread and apples from the satchel. They enjoy each other's company once again. Finishing up their lunch, they keep on toward the mountains, which seem to be moving away from them with every step.

"These mountains seem closer than they are. We've walked so much, and still they seem the same distance as this morning," Bahi says.

"We'll get there. Probably by nightfall we'll be at the foothills," Ajee assures as they walk the vast, open field.

The ground is dry, and trees that once secured the field in the shelter of leaves now stand barren, like a collection of sticks sporadically strewn about. Frosted rocks line the bed of what was once a river as they pass by. They notice the smell of fire from a nearby village. The scent settles into their senses as they quietly walk on, allowing only the sounds of the ground below their feet to be heard. Ajee runs along, often hanging his head low to smell the ground as Bahi takes in the immense beauty of the Himalaya Mountains, almost dreamlike, inviting serenity with a single glance. The days are shorter now, and the sun begins to dip behind the western hills.

"Maybe we should set up camp and continue in the morning," Bahi suggests.

Ajee looks around the open, vast field, "I agree."

Placing his satchel on the ground, Bahi gathers some rocks to create a large circle, fashioning a fire pit. Ajee gathers pieces of dried, dead wood and sticks. Completing the fire pit, Bahi joins him, gathering a large bundle of wood that is sure to keep them warm all night. Each piece of wood is strategically placed. Bahi uses dried leaves to catch the heat from his matches. A small flame slowly engulfs a few slim sticks, which surrounds larger pieces in flames. Ajee had run off, as he often did, at the onset of the fire.

Flames are reflected in Bahi's eyes as he sits and watches the fire grow. Glancing off at the mountains that are now large shadows of mystery upon the darkening sky, Ajee walks up behind Bahi, dropping a rabbit at his feet.

"Again?" Bahi asks, feeling bad for the little brown rabbit that lies mangled and lifeless.

"If you don't want to end up like that rabbit, I suggest you eat and keep your energy high."

Bahi nods in agreement and proceeds to cook the rabbit, which he pierces through with a stick, remembering how he cooked it the last time.

"Do you eat anything but rabbit?" Bahi asks rhetorically.

"Of course I do. But these buggers are easy to catch in a jiffy. Maybe tomorrow we can have a goat. I saw a heard off by the mountain," Ajee says as his eyes widen pulling a smile across his face.

"Rabbit is fine," Bahi says, trying to picture how he would even begin to cook a goat, and remembering the old goat, who was so good to him.

As the night settles in, they eat the rabbit, along with some bread, washing it all down with water from the canteen. The fire blazes strongly as thick white smoke clouds up toward the stars. Bahi takes out the shawl that was given to him by Bharat and appreciates the intricate design of a colorful tree of dark blues—rich reds and saturated yellows—that intertwine to create a swirling tree with birds laid upon the soft canvas of a light gray. Laying his old shawl on the ground for bedding, he wraps himself with Bharat's shawl, warming him instantly. *Wow*, he thinks, *this is quite a shawl!* Ajee curls up next to him, and the two watch the flames dance in the pit, enjoying the show as the heat from the fire penetrates their cores, energizing them in a relaxing warmth as they drift off to sleep. Ajee sleeps the night with one eye open, knowing the dangers of being in an open field at night.

CHAPTER 18

MORNING BREAKS AS the red cinders of last night's fire still glow warm. Bahi, pulling his hat snug to his head and wrapping the warm shawl around his body, throws the last pieces of wood on the burning cinders. They quickly catch fire as Ajee stands and stretches, drawing closer to the flame, to sit on his hind legs, warming his back as he looks toward the mountains. Eyes half closed in the bliss of warmth, Bahi tongues his teeth and uses a small stick to scrape them clean, as he has done many times before on this journey. Handing Ajee some bread and an apple, they sit and eat as the fire dwindles.

Finishing up, Bahi closes his eyes and goes inward in mediation. Sitting and breathing, he goes deeper, dropping out of all thought, attuning to the forest around him, feeling the energy of the mountains and connecting his heart to it. After only a short time, he opens his eyes and prepares for the journey ahead as he packs his satchel.

"We can reach the foothills of the mountains by dark and spend the night by the mountain pass. Let us be weary of hungry beasts, like ourselves, that will stop at nothing for a meal. The cold creates desperation in these lands," Ajee warns.

Bahi looks off into the distance. A tinge of fear sparks up as he thinks of how they will know the way once they get up into the mountains. Reflecting on the fear, he allows himself to feel it and thinks, *With or without the fear I am going.* So he opts to go without the fear and allows the fear that is there to act as awareness as he nears territory he knows he will have to be alert in.

"Everyone's gotta eat, Wolf," Bahi says, breaking the silence.

"That's what I'm afraid of," Ajee fires back.

Bahi smiles to relieve the tension and begins to walk along the hard, cold earth, crackling the frost that melts into each step. Again they walk all day, stopping only once to rest and eat some nuts, apples, and bread. The field finally closes in as they come into the foothills of the vast mountains that shadow the valley at the mountains pass. The air is crisp and feels good as it pours deep into their lungs. Bahi notices an incline that wraps up into the vastly covered pine forest. A crystal blue stream runs slowly under a partially iced coating, where Bahi fills his canteen with water. He takes down a large gulp of the freezing water, which strikes with the wrath of a piercing headache. Ajee walks over to see Bahi squinting in pain as he rubs his temples.

"You, uh, all right buddy?"

Bending his head as the pain dissipates, Bahi looks up. "Yeah, ice cream headache."

"What's that?" Ajee asks.

"When you drink cold water too fast and get a pain in your head."

"Ice cream?"

"Ice cream is a dessert we have back home. Maybe one day I'll show you."

"I assume it's a cold dessert, like berry juice that has dripped on snow. Let this be a warning to take these mountains slow, or a headache will be the least of your problems."

Bahi looks up in thought.

"Where is home, Bahi?"

Bahi thinks again for a moment before speaking, "Home was a place very far from here, but this is my home now, planet Earth is my home."

Ajee nods, "Now you're thinking like a true, lone wolf."

"Except I am not alone. In fact, I don't think I would have come this far without you, Ajee. Thanks," Bahi says as he stands up from the stream.

Ajee smiles, bending down at Bahi's feet. "I am at your service, friend."

"Oh, Ajee, It's you I should be bowing to."

"We're a team now," Ajee says as they walk off to a spot secured by a rising hill.

"This seems like a good place for the night," Ajee says, and in agreement they again prepare for the night by building a fire pit and collecting wood.

As the fire once again begins to blaze, Ajee asks, "Goat?"

"I don't know, maybe I'll order the rabbit again tonight," Bahi says realizing the absurdity of his request.

Ajee runs off into the mountains, and again Bahi waits alone. He feels insecure as he waits. He keeps looking up behind as if something is watching him. The time passes, and Ajee has been gone longer than usual, Bahi begins to worry. About an hour passes when Ajee finally arrives back.

"Where were you? I was worried."

"I tried my best, but no animals in sight except the goats, and they were snatched up by a couple of panthers."

"Panthers, huh? Well, looks like bread and apples for dinner then," Bahi says, pulling out the last of the bread and the two last apples.

After they finish, Ajee still feels hungry and lies down feeling the instinctual fear of urgency to find food at daybreak. They curl up, warmed by the fire's glow. Both have trouble falling asleep and engage in conversation long into the night, subconsciously on alert. Finally, deep into the night, as Ajee goes on with a story which ends with a question, he notices no reply from a sleeping Bahi and Ajee too drifts off to sleep, waking often with intuitional alarm for his surroundings.

CHAPTER 19

F EELING A THUMP on the ground next to him, Bahi opens his
eyes to Ajee proudly standing over two large rabbits.

"Breakfast!" Ajee proudly affirms.

Bahi cringes at the sight of death so early in the morning, but his
belly rumbles in the empty canyon of his stomach, prompting him up to
make a small fire to cook the rabbits. Ajee eats his raw. Bahi is tired of
eating rabbit, bread, and apples, but knows he must sustain himself if he
is to make it up into these mountains. Biting into the gamey thigh of the
rabbit, he thinks of how the simple act of eating creates so much suffering. *Soon I will be hungry again*, he thinks. *I will consistently feed my pains
until what?* Then, shifting his focus, he becomes grateful to the rabbit for
giving its life for him, grateful for Ajee bringing it to him. He watches as
Ajee crushes the bones in his teeth. He thinks of all the plants this rabbit
must have eaten to grow so big and how those plants come from other
plants as seeds that ate the nutrients in the soil. *And so it goes*, he thinks,
and he is grateful for it all. *And what if a panther eats me?* The cycle will
go on and on, unending.

"Good rabbit?" Ajee asks, interrupting Bahi's thoughts.

"Very good, thanks," he responds tossing the bones on the fire and
throwing the charred head aside.

"Oh, that's the best part," Ajee says as he cracks the skull in his mouth.

Bahi turns away in disgust and begins to pack up his satchel, after cleaning his hands with water from the canteen and drying them on the fire, which slowly begins to burn out.

Tossing his satchel on his back, he looks over at Ajee. "Shall we?"

"Lead the way," Ajee says feeling comfortably full.

Bahi feels that once they get into the mountain he will know which way to go. They ascend up the pine-lined path that curves around toward an opening leading out toward the edge of the large mountains. Walking across the flat ground that sets between two large mountains, Bahi is in his head as they walk. Ajee can feel the seriousness in his silence. Biting Bahi's shoe in an attempt to lighten the mood, it sends Bahi tripping down as Ajee jumps upon him.

"What are you do…?" Bahi is interrupted by Ajee's large tongue licking his face as he pins him to the ground.

Bahi begins to laugh uncontrollably and grabs hold of Ajee's fur, throwing him aside, but Ajee playfully pins him down again. Bahi is no match for Ajee's strength. The two engage like little children playing.

At the same moment two men round a clump of trees not too far across the field. One man, a tall white Englishman, notices the two tussling on the ground and instructs his Tibetan Sherpa who carries a large sack and rifle on his back to come close.

"Good Lord, that wolf will have him for supper," he says as he draws his rifle from the Sherpa's pack.

Taking aim, he fires a shot that echoes a crackling far off into the mountains. Ajee lets out a loud yelp and shoots off across the field as Bahi quickly springs to his feet, confused. Ajee drops down to the ground, and Bahi notices the two men as he runs over to Ajee, who breathes rapidly, bleeding profusely from his side. "No, no, no!" Bahi yells out as his heart races in the realization that Ajee has been shot. Dropping to his knees, he puts his hands on Ajee, who pants rapidly, staring at Bahi in shock. "Ajee, Ajee, you're gonna be all right!"

Ajee begins to pant more slowly as the two men stand and squint, trying to understand what's going on. Handing the rifle back to the Tibetan Sherpa, the Englishman makes his way slowly over to them, followed by the Sherpa.

"Bahi," Ajee says looking up into Bahi's Panicked eyes, "everything ends," he continues, letting out a final breath, his lifeless eyes still staring as Bahi picks up his head looking to the sky. "No, no, no, Ajee," he sobs, tears streaming down his face as he shakes Ajee. "No, you can't, Ajee, please!"

In scared confusion, Bahi looks back at the two men coming toward him as he rises up in anger and runs full force toward them. Bahi's face is wet with tears as he swiftly draws closer to the assailant. "Well, boy, I must say you were close to dead there." Just then Bahi tackles him to the ground and just as fast, he pops up, pulling the rifle from the Tibetan's pack, taking aim at the Englishman and Tibetan, waving the long, narrow, steel barrel back and forth in a craze. "That was my friend!" he yells, waving the rifle.

"Do say? I am sorry. I was unaware that was your pet. I thought . . ."

"You thought what? I should kill you both!" he yells, overwhelmed with rage.

"That would be just fine," the Englishman says calmly, "but you would have a hard time with an unloaded weapon," he adds, grabbing the barrel of the rifle, pulling it from Bahi's hands, and handing it back to the Sherpa.

Bahi stands in silent confusion. "Why?" he cries out.

"Sorry chap, I thought you were in danger."

Bahi gathers himself, consciously breathing as he stares at the two men in disgust, realizing their misconception.

"Look, come back to the village with us, and I'll give you another pet, whatever you want. We have many," the Englishman offers.

"I don't want a pet; he was my friend," Bahi says under his breath, trying to contain his emotions.

"I am truly sorry. You can see my miscalculation from here. Thought you were in danger. Please come. We'll warm ourselves by the fire, have some homemade rum, eat, and resolve this misunderstanding."

"I can't," Bahi says, looking back at Ajee's lifeless body lying before the massive mountains. "I am heading into the mountain," he says wiping tears from his face.

"The mountains?" the Englishman asks, looking over at the Tibetan Sherpa, who cracks a smile in his weathered face, which is permanently tanned like a piece of rawhide, from a lifetime of wind and sun. "Where are you headed? We are in for quite a storm tomorrow. You might want to know," the Englishman looks up at the sky, trying not to laugh at Bahi, whom he thinks is a bit on the kooky side.

"I'm headed to Shambhala."

"Shambhala?" the Englishman lets out a deep belly laugh. "No, come on, really."

"Really, I'm headed there now."

"Oh yes, and we just came from the kingdom of heaven, Jesus says, 'hi'," he says as he lets out another laugh. "Boy, Shambhala is a fairy tale told by the Tibetans. Surely you know this?"

Bahi cringes the anger that mixes with fear that he may be right.

"Come, you can stay at my place in the village and wait out the storm."

Bahi nods his head "no" and turns toward Ajee. Walking over, he drops to his knees as a silent cry overcomes him. The Englishman, now thinking Bahi is insane, comes over with a small sack. Patting Bahi on the back, he looks up at the Englishman silently.

"Here is some food for your journey and a small bottle of rum. Are you sure you know what you are doing? These mountains are no place for the solo traveler."

Bahi takes the food wrapped in white cloth. "So will you come back with us? We can provide you with better provisions for your quest."

Bahi remembers the words of Maha Bharat telling him not to make haste. "I must keep moving."

"The village is only a few hours from here. Are you certain?"

"I am certain," Bahi says with a strong determination.

"OK, boy. Well then, we must move on as to reach the village by nightfall. Good luck. And if you change your mind, just walk southeast, we'll be there. I am terribly sorry for this," the Englishman says as he casts a shadow, looking down at Ajee before walking away.

Bahi's mind races, he thinks perhaps he should go back to the village as he looks back at the men who walk off. A cold wind blows. Pushing his hair in front of his eyes and turning back toward the mountains, into the wind, his hair is pushed back and he feels the right choice is to keep going. Filled with fear and confusion, he weeps over the body of Ajee, whose blood soaks into the ground. Bahi stands up and walks over to his hat, which fell off when they were play fighting. He can feel the cold wind behind his ears shooting into his head. Putting on his hat, he paces back and forth, talking to himself, "I gotta move," he mumbles as he walks back to Ajee's body. Bahi's shadow streaks across Ajee as he stares down on him. "Where are you now, friend?" he whispers.

Contemplating what to do with the body, he realizes the best thing to do is to leave it there. The ground is too cold for burial, and by the time he gathers wood to burn it he would waste valuable time he needs to get into the mountains before dark.

"Go back to where you came Ajee, everything ends," he says before saying a prayer over his still body, a prayer for protection, a prayer for serenity, and a prayer for gratitude. "I'll see you soon," he says, choked up he walks away. Ajee's fur blows in the cold mountain air as Bahi walks toward the opening that leads up the mountain.

CHAPTER 20

AFTER WALKING FOR about an hour, he stops. Staring off into the cold shadow of the mountain forest, he feels empty, tired, and alone. "I have no idea where I am going," he thinks as he stares at the sun that sits in the western sky. He continues North, and as the path becomes narrower, he has to climb up using his hands in several spots. Coming to a precipice, he looks out, noticing the forest below is far down. There is no way he can climb down there. Looking around, he realizes he can circumvent the gap by walking around the perimeter of a narrow rock ledge to get back around heading North again. Feeling drained, he decides to gather some firewood and set up camp here. *This is probably the safest place for the night,* he thinks, not knowing how far the rocky perimeter will travel until he can go North again. He doesn't want to get caught there at nightfall.

After lighting a huge fire, he only has two matches left. *I must make it to Shambhala soon,* he thinks, untying the cloth of food from the Englishman. Bahi thinks he may be going a little crazy as he reflects on his logic of not following the men back for provisions. He takes out a piece of chicken and some bread, then makes a sandwich and slowly eats it. His stomach feels ill from all the emotions running through his body. Placing the small, clear glass bottle of rum in front of him, he stares at it as he eats. After finishing the sandwich, he unscrews the silver top, and taking a large chug, the warm sensation runs down his throat, heating his belly and soothing his aching mind. He sits and thinks about Ajee and how he misses him so much already. He thinks about his family and remembers laughing with them and begins to form tears as he takes another shot of the rum. The strong liquor doubly affects him. It kills much of his pain on the one hand, making him more sentimental on the other.

He looks wearily at the final portion of clear brown liquor and raises it up. "To Ajee," he says as he tips back the glass, gulping down a sizeable shot, squeezing out every last drop of the small bottle. Standing up, he stares at the fire, his right hand dropped to his side, holding the empty bottle. *What is it all for?* he wonders. *What if Shambhala is a fairy tale?* he worries. He thinks of Kamini and Bandar, then remembers Eva. *Maybe I should have listened to her.* He wishes he were cuddled in her bed with the sweet smell of her hair in his face and the warm touch of her body secured to his. Suddenly he drops the bottle. He sits down, taking a deep breath, wrapping both shawls around his body. He hears a voice in the wind that whisks by his ears. "North," he swears he hears as the fire blazes higher. Lying alongside the fire, feeling the security of liquid courage, he closes his eyes in exhaustion and falls fast asleep on the ground, bundled up in the shawls.

A loud crackling in the trees above him springs him awake. He quickly grabs a stick that practically freezes to his hands. Confused about where he is at first, he gains his wits and looks around, but can't see or hear anything. His heart pounds in his chest as he throws a few more pieces of wood on the fire, creating more light. He hears the noise again far into the woods. Using the stick to stir the fire, he burns the end, making it red hot in preparation for any predators. Sitting in front of the fire, he stays awake, unable to sleep from fear that pumps through his veins. He sits for hours, feeding the fire until daybreak. The silence of morning eases his nerves. Standing up, he feels woozy from the exhaustion of not sleeping. Small patches of snow randomly dot the forest floor, covering brown leaves fallen from the slumbering, bare trees that live amongst the strong pines that dominate the area. He looks over at the empty rum bottle that lies next to the jagged-rock fire pit smoking out its last breath, Ajee's words echo in his mind: "Nothing lasts forever."

The air is a damp cold that seeps into his bones and pounds in his head. Tired both physically and emotionally, he secures the yak shawl tightly to his body, noticing the uncanny warming effect it has. *This would warm me if I were naked in an ice storm*, he thinks, trying to stay positive in an otherwise gloomy situation. He walks to the edge of the precipice, then looks off at the vast trees below that melt together in a sea of pine needles. Mind clouded, he sits at the edge, taking a deep breath as he closes his eyes slightly to meditate. He consciously relaxes his body and mind, then allows his mind to abide in the silence. Taking his attention from the busy thoughts that dominate his head, he brings it down into his heart. The damp wind presses itself against his face as he breathes out busy thoughts of his mind. His eyes are heavy from the burden of loss and no sleep, and his brain feels tight and tired, but finally he relaxes them and finds a small space of peace in which he abides for a few minutes, going deeper with every passing moment. Slowly he opens his eyes and gazes around at the forest before him.

He is drawn to the rock ledge that he believes will bring him back onto the northward trail. He realizes that to get to the ledge, which twists back to the North, he will have to walk back down, around and up the side of the mountain. So he acts quickly. He stands up and laughs at what the Englishman must have thought of this wild white man set to find Shambhala. *I must be insane*, he thinks with a laugh. The winter storm warnings of the Englishman play over in his mind as he gathers his things to begin the journey once again northward. The sky is dark gray, making his already sullen mood even darker. Walking down the path, he smells the pine trees. The forest is silent. A bird hops around in search of a morsel. The wind grows stronger as he walks. His stomach rumbles. He feels like the bird, alone without any food, in the solitude of the snowy mountain forest. All the food is gone even the few nuts he ate after his meditation, which seemed to only make him more hungry. He begins to think more and more that his decision not to go back to the Englishman's camp was a bad decision. He contemplates turning back, as he realizes he is foolishly unprepared for the vast mountains ahead of him. He does not know how to catch a rabbit. There are no fruit-bearing trees. His only hope is to find Shambhala or starve to death. Focusing on the task ahead, he diverts his mind from the hunger, which passes in waves.

Finally, he reaches the bottom of the slope, where he will begin his ascent up the rock ledge that wraps around to where, he hopes, will take him back onto the northern path. Standing at the almost vertical slope, he realizes he will have to climb the rock face in order to get to the flat edge above. He Grabs a jutting rock, then lifts himself to secure his foot in a divot a few feet up and continues on. About half way up he realizes this is higher than it had looked from below. Making the mistake of looking down, he feels his stomach buckle and mind spin. Staring the rock face directly in front, he breathes and calms himself before reaching for another rock, which crumbles in his hand. He thinks this is a bad idea. He contemplates going back down. *Maybe I should just go back to the village and get some food.* Thoughts of self-defeat begin to seep in, but he finds another stable rock to grab and ascends a few feet higher. Arms tired, he hangs on, trembling. Up further, still only a few feet from the top, yet far from the bottom, he knows that if he falls it would mean much harm or even death. Sweat beads his forehead and lines his body, mixing with the cool air. Desperately grabbing the edge of the ridge above, he struggles to pull up. Butterflies in his stomach propel his left leg atop the ledge. Now awkwardly hanging in limbo he tosses the satchel upon the ledge, takes a deep breath, and uses all his might to bring his body up, scraping his legs and arms on the cold, wet rock, which cuts through his skin. His mind does not worry about tearing flesh because the fear of falling trumps. He pulls and pulls, getting half of his body to the top, scraping his head as his hat falls off. It slowly floats to the ground far below as he finally lifts his sweating body secure to the flat top of the ledge, where he lies, gasping, on his back. His face is beet red, his heart hammers his chest, trying to escape this madman. He begins to laugh, psychotically grabbing his head as he looks over the ledge at his hat, before standing up. The wind blows thick across the flat ledge, acting as a corridor, streaming wind along the jagged rock wall that shoots up the mountain, offering only a narrow space where Bahi now stands, looking back at where he was earlier. He can see the barren fire pit still smoking from the embers, which are subdued by the now light snow that has begun to fall. Wet flakes sweep through, smacking his face like raindrops as he walks around the corner of the ridge, realizing he has a far walk along this rocky ledge before he makes his way to any open area in the mountain. The air suddenly grows colder and the snow thicker, hitting his face like ice pellets as the wintery air permeates his bones, prompting him to take the yak shawl from his bag and wrap it around his head and body. Instantly he feels warm from this almost magical shawl, which gives him the will to press on. The winds are against him as he works to both stay on the ledge and keep moving forward. The snow blows thicker with every step, and what he thought would have taken him an hour at most has turned into two. Traversing the narrow ridge, he feels a sudden gust of wind punch him in the chest as he grabs a piece of rock on the wall, losing his grasp of his shawl, which blows off down the cliff. "No! Damn it!"

He watches as the shawl flutters down, dancing in the windblown snow like a large, free-falling butterfly. Taking the former shawl from his bag, he wraps it around himself, barely shielding himself from the cold. It's not as warm as the other shawl, but better than nothing. He keeps moving as the snow pours thickly down like white rain that is both beautiful and terrifying. Bahi walks on, tired and hungry, confused and angry, his face red from the frost that numbs his cheeks and burns his eyes. Finally he comes to a turn, and hoping this will lead to a secure opening, he walks faster. His leg begins to ache from the dampness as he nears the turn and rounds the bend only to find that the ledge stops at a rock wall.

"Dead end!" he yells out loud. "Dead end!" he screams at the rock wall as he falls to sit at its base, which shields him from winds that blow from the other direction.

Laughing almost uncontrollably, putting his face in his hands, he realizes he must go back down and seek some shelter from this storm. *Perhaps I can make it back to the village and regroup*, he thinks.

He stands up and walks back, forced to hold onto the rock wall that lines the ledge, as the winds have now accelerated. He walks slowly. He fears it will be dark by the time he reaches the bottom again and that he won't be able to climb back down in this storm. His body is freezing and his mind reverts to a primordial survival mode, focusing on getting out of there like a hungry leopard in search of food for it's young in the depths of winter.

A rush of energy washes over him, clearing his mind, allowing him to keep on. A few hours pass, and he reaches the spot where he had climbed up. His stomach is now a burning pit of hunger. His eyes are dilated from the white world that has suddenly taken over, covering the mountain in a few feet of snow. Looking at the rock face, he realizes it will be almost impossible to get down. *But what choice do I have?*

He tosses his bag down as he searches out through the falling snow. *The Englishman has formed a rescue group to come find me. Is that them?* He realizes that the human-like shapes he sees are only small pines disguised by the snow. Quickly shaking the fantasy from his mind, he takes a deep breath and begins to hang off the cliff to descend. One foot and hand grasp the jagged rocks. Then another, Then another—lowering him slowly. Making it halfway down, fear just doesn't make sense to him anymore, adrenaline pumps through his veins, and he focuses on each next step down. Securing with his right foot, he releases his right hand as his foot slips.

Falling, he almost faints, then smacks into snow-covered rocks at the base of the cliff. A white haze washes over him as he passes out. Coming to, he sits and manages to drag his body up against the rock face. Bleeding from his head, feeling a familiar throbbing pain in his leg and arm, he tries to stand up and shrieks in pain. Now sitting, nausea rips through him like a storm, leaving him faint. The snows blow hard as he sits, defeated, staring out into the white forest, an odd feeling of numb serenity washing over him as he wonders where that little bird is. He surrenders to the mountainous forest, surrenders to the storm, surrenders all of his ambitions. He turns his head to the side, vomiting the little food he still has in is stomach from the night before. He tries once again to stand, but the pain in his leg and arm is excruciating. He knows they must be broken, and he refuses to look at his leg, which lies mangled and twisted. His breath is short and weak and his mind begins to shift, disconnecting from the pain, drifting off like the snow that covers his limp body.

Opening his eyes in an attempt to rally himself, he remembers his family. Tears freeze to his cheeks. He remembers Eva and the warmth of her body. He remembers all his friends on his journey as tears stream down past the pain, washing over his face. With a look of bliss and surrender, his eyes begin to shut. *Strange how the cold freeze of death seems to warm a man in his final hour, slowing the heart, glazing the eyes, drifting the mind back to where this all began. Where did I go wrong?*

Head nodding, he drifts away, body frozen in time. Darkness permeates his world. The wind howls and whistles in his ears until finally all is silent, all is lost, all is gone and he opens his eyes in a green, familiar meadow of dreamlike warmth. Trees grow oranges and apples lush in all directions. He notices a figure coming toward him. Crystal-blue eyes glow in her pure white skin, raising him to his feet as she gazes, drawing him into her arms. Swimming in the peace of her eyes, he takes her in as she smiles. Warmth fills his entire being. Picking an apple from a tree above, she says, adoringly, "Do you wish to stay here with me forever?" The words come out without her moving her lips.

A resounding, "yes!" echoes from Bahi's mind, in relief as she presses her supple lips against his. Feeling her warm body, he wishes to stay there forever. Opening his eyes as they kiss, he notices the sky growing dark behind her as the trees rapidly begin to decay. The fruit grows rancid and brown and drops from the trees, which begin to whither and die. He notices her face begins to age, and as he pushes her away she laughs like a witch. He shrieks in terror, watching her jaw dry up and fall off as her eyes sink into her head and skin rots off, almost instantly turning to dust, leaving a laughing skeleton amongst the dead trees that fall to the ground and begin to suck into a whirling black abyss in the middle of the meadow, sucking in the dust from her bones, which blows away. The rivers freeze over and the air grows colder. He tries to move, but is frozen in this void and drops to the solid ice, which now engulfs the world. Shaking uncontrollably, freezing and curled up, he feels the void of black seep in darker. He can't see anything. The ice has immobilized him in a shadowy emptiness. All comes to a halt in the darkness.

A small pocket of light twinkles, emanating from the black void all around him, beaming down upon his frozen body, warming him as he begins to thaw. The light's a familiar glow. His eyes are frozen and fixated on the light as it begins to expand, thawing out the entire earth around him. He recollects the familiar light, which he realizes has always been there. Sprouting grass rises out of the now defrosted dirt as Bahi stands up, feeling a sense of refreshment. Sprouts of vegetation pop out in front of him, growing up a pea pod, which shoots out, dropping a fetus to the grass which rapidly grows into a small girl, morphing into a woman, who stands as the Goddess taking Bahi's hand as they glide through this fantastic world. He notices they are aging with every second. Looking at his hands, he sees that they begin to wrinkle and dry, and soon are very old, as the earth around them grows and withers in cycles of rapid succession. As they begin to whither away, Bahi is not frightened. His fear is non-existent as they decay and drop to the ground. Skin and bones become the dirt below, and all that is present is consciousness of the moment, which observes his body seeping into the ground and breaking down into nutrients that are absorbed by a seed, which breaks the Earth and grows up tall to the light in the sky. Bahi's consciousness pervades all things in flux around him, an omnipresence of indescribable bliss. The plant continues its growth and bears berries, which are eaten by small, majestic birds. He realizes he is all of this, all of this is he, and in that moment he realizes that all the suffering he experienced came from his isolated view of himself existing independent from the tree, independent of the world, independent from Shambhala. Suddenly a cocoon grows on the side of the tree, and he sprouts out a beautiful butterfly, he is Kamini as he floats gracefully across the meadow and sees the body of Ajee, which is being eaten by small animals as it decays into the ground, sprouting out a tree and growing flowers, which Bahi settles upon in his butterfly body, enjoying the nectars that flow out. A fetus again grows from a pod in the tree, which drops down and grows into a man, which is Bahi, Paul, Pawo, Ajee. Ajee smiles at Bahi, who floats around. *I am that which is! The sun shines down love and joy, pours out across the world, excluding nothing. Nothing is separate, everything ends, and death just places all in a different part of the whole we exist upon, constantly changing, constantly in flux, formless. All is impermanent and in perfect rapture.*

He flies off, watching the world in rapid change. *We all need each other, that's what makes it work, we all are each other*, he thinks, as the light wind decays his butterfly body, blowing in fragments as the light shines bright. "Everything returns to the light from which it always was," he hears as light pervades—bright, white pulsating luminosity, which glows in and out and is all that can be seen in a blinding burst before turning to a soft darkness, peacefully encompassing his mind.

Paul opens his eyes to see the deep blue sky above fixated on a puffy white cloud that floats along the sky. Sitting up, the lush land of beauty he sits in is not as dreamlike as where he just was with the Goddess. A waterfall streams down behind him, and he feels a sense of recognition in where he is. Looking down, he has no cuts, and his leg and arm are fine as he stands, wearing only blue boxer shorts. *I am back in Rishikesh,* he thinks as he feels the beard on his face still thick as he smiles, and looks around the forest, reveling in the bliss of peace that pervades him in the moment, realizing his revelations. *All is impermanent and in perfect order.* The words play in his being.

A rustle in the trees above brings his attention to some monkeys going about their business. One monkey drops down, eye level on a branch, staring at Paul.

"Bandar!" he yells out, excited as he runs toward the monkey, who screeches and shows his teeth before climbing further up the tree. "Bandar, it's me, Bahi!" he says, thinking the monkey may not recognize him with the beard.

The monkey lets out a rant of hoots and haas as he shakes the tree before springing along, out of sight. Walking off in wonderment, *Did I dream all of this?* he thinks as he sits by the waterfall. Feeling a sense of deep unity with all that is, he remembers the world outside of the jungle. "It's time for me to go," he says in a whisper as he smiles at the waterfall.

THE END

EPILOGUE

THE LIGHTS SLOWLY come up on the platformed stage-like perch of a New York City class center. Paul sits cleanly shaven and clothed. He is in mid-sentence, a sentence directed to a gathering of students: "And because we have this wrong view, this mistaken view that we are limited, fixed, unchanging, existing independent of everything else, we feel isolated and imbalanced, so we crave anything that will relieve this suffering. We grasp at people who we think will make us happy, things, places, jobs, anything that will dull the pain of our isolated view of ourselves. This is an utter lie we engage in every day, that somehow there is peace and light. But it's not us. And therefore we must reach for it all day long. And finally these things we reach for do not keep us happy. So we grasp at more and more, like children in a candy store feeding their faces with chocolate, thinking the next piece will surely be the one to bring lasting happiness, final contentment. But instead they get sick to their stomachs. We are slaves to this independent self, which is insatiable because 'an independent self, separate from everything,' is a wrong view. So we will never be satisfied because we are seeing it all wrong. So we attach ourselves to people and things that make us happy and push away and get angry at things and people who cause us suffering. If only we relate to things how they really are, we realize everything is constantly changing, existing only because of others. And in this way we learn to respect this body, this Earth, and we realize we are all the light, and nothing is separate from that. Everything exists in dependence on all else. This is logic. Check up on this yourself. Don't take my word on it. So we need to relate to the world as it is. We all need each other, and that's how it works. We need to respect the Earth, our mothers, our friends, and our enemies, because none is separate from anyone or anything else. And our deluded view that we exist independent of the Earth or other people is a misconception of reality, a fantasy we have conjured up.

In this way, we can just relax and enjoy each moment, each person, each thing knowing we don't have to grasp at them or push them away, because they will soon end, and change and flow back into that unending flux, which is all. You can think of it like this: Without the sun nothing here would be alive. A plant grows. We eat the plant, creating our muscles, or we eat animals who eat plants. And so the sun just moves through everyone and everything. The energy it creates enables us to create, build things, come to this lecture, and so on. There is a an untapped resource of this all-pervading light, and the sun is part of this as well, because one day it, too, will burn out, but it will not end. It is endless, beginningless.

A silence washes over the crowd as Paul looks out in thought. Taking a sip of water from his glass, which sets beside him, he notices a familiar face in the crowd. It's Eva. She smiles at him. Returning the smile, he focuses again, placing down the glass.

"I would like to share a story with you for a moment. There was once a modest farmer who lived by the shores of India. Having lost his beloved wife, and fed up with the world of his village, he would walk down by the shore every day and stare off to the land far in the distance. He was told of this land. Shambhala, they called it, a place of peace and serenity, a place where men were so wise and enlightened that all of his suffering would be eradicated once he stepped foot there. Every day at dusk he would walk down from the foothills of the mountains and stand at the shore, yearning to go to Shambhala, until one day a boat pulled up to the shore with a sign that read, *Shambhala*. So the man got all excited and hopped on the boat. The captain looked down at him and said, 'This is a one-way trip. Are you sure you want to go?' Ecstatic, he yelled, 'Yes!' And so off they went, thrashing along the sea. And suddenly he missed his children back in the village and began to worry for them. This worry passed, and after sometime he realized what he thought would be a short trip had become a very long and arduous journey. On and on they rode, week after week, month after month, and soon he became complacent with the simple tasks of living on a boat, until one day the boat scraped ashore. Finally they were there. Excited, he leapt out of the boat and ran out to the island of Shambhala. And as he calmed himself, he thought, 'I wonder what India looks like from here?' Looking out he realized, there is no India, there is no Shambhala, there's no boat, no farmer. He was always in Shambhala. Realizing this he surrendered, knowing that giving selflessly and enjoying every second is all he can do, all he wishes to do, and all he need do. For the divine light and bliss of Shambhala is within us all, within each and every thing. So we abide in this, enjoy without thinking, let go our fantasy of separation, and thus respecting ourselves we respect others. Because all we are is others. So to change the world around us we change ourselves, because we are the world around us. So we extend ourselves out to the world, destroying the lie that we need to fend for ourselves. We can easily tap into the joy and blissful light, which pervades everything, and then we will know Shambhala. Thank you."

The lights go up as the crowd bursts out clapping, Paul smiles on the stage of life that he knows excludes no one.

ABOUT THE AUTHOR

BRIAN E. MILLER is a writer and teacher born and raised on Long Island, New York. Growing up, Brian was always crafting stories, whether written or verbal, exhibiting a passion for storytelling from a very early age. Today his stories invite the reader to view their own lives through the lens of his unique and interesting characters along their journeys. Inspired by the magical places and people Brian has encountered along his own worldwide journeys, he creates stories that are not only fun and engaging but often reflect an underlying truth of humanity. Drawing on the mythology and heroes journey that we all walk in our lives, his teachings and writings entice us to delve deeply into the often dark recesses of the mind, discovering truths that can lead us to a more balanced, harmonious and purposeful life.

After a career working in production for commercial television in New York, Brian's dreams and ambitions of writing and teaching prompted him to leave it all behind in the midst of the worst recession he had ever known. A leap of faith took him on a journey to India, where he had visited a year prior working on a documentary film and recognizing a deep connection with both the people and the land, he knew he would return. This next trip, however, was taken alone, to travel, write and deepen his studies and practices of Buddhist Psychology and Yoga, both of which he had been a student and practitioner of for many years.

Brian followed his heart along a fantastic journey with which he still travels today. His current novel, "Shambhala" was inspired by the magical places and people he had encountered along his often arduous and life-transforming trip to India and South East Asia. Brian is always writing, recently finishing the rough draft of his second novel, with several more already underway toward completion.

www.ingramcontent.com/pod-product-compliance
Lightning Source LLC
Chambersburg PA
CBHW020605250626
47154CB00004B/1376